Buckley, Fiona.
Queen without a crown /
2011
SONOMA COUNTY LIBRARY
OFFICIAL DISCARD
37565020378013
heal

QUEEN WITHOUT A CROWN

The Ursula Blanchard Mysteries from Fiona Buckley

THE ROBSART MYSTERY
THE DOUBLET AFFAIR
QUEEN'S RANSOM
TO RUIN A QUEEN
QUEEN OF AMBITION
A PAWN FOR THE QUEEN
THE FUGITIVE QUEEN
THE SIREN QUEEN

QUEEN WITHOUT A CROWN

Fiona Buckley

This first world edition published 2011
in Great Britain and the USA by
Crème de la Crime, an imprint of
SEVERN HOUSE PUBLISHERS LTD of
9–15 High Street, Sutton, Surrey, England, SM1 1DF.
Trade paperback edition first published
in Great Britain and the USA 2012.

Copyright © 2011 by Fiona Buckley.

All rights reserved.
The moral right of the author has been asserted.

British Library Cataloguing in Publication Data

Buckley, Fiona.
Queen without a crown.
1. Blanchard, Ursula (Fictitious character) – Fiction.
2. Women spies – Fiction. 3. Elizabeth I, Queen of England,
1533–1603 – Fiction. 4. Mary, Queen of Scots, 1542–1587 –
Fiction. 5. Great Britain – History – Elizabeth,
1558–1603 – Fiction. 6. Great Britain – Court and
courtiers – History – 16th century – Fiction. 7. Treason –
Fiction. 8. Detective and mystery stories.
I. Title
823.9'14-dc22

ISBN-13: 978-1-78029-014-0 (cased)
ISBN-13: 978-1-78029-514-5 (trade paper)

Except where actual historical events and characters are being
described for the storyline of this novel, all situations in this
publication are fictitious and any resemblance to living persons
is purely coincidental.

All Severn House titles are printed on acid-free paper.

Severn House Publishers support The Forest Stewardship Council [FSC],
the leading international forest certification organisation. All our titles that
are printed on Greenpeace-approved FSC-certified paper carry the FSC logo.

Typeset by Palimpsest Book Production Ltd.,
Falkirk, Stirlingshire, Scotland.
Printed and bound in Great Britain by
MPG Books Ltd., Bodmin, Cornwall.

For Annabel and Geoffrey

ACKNOWLEDGEMENTS

The theory that some artists in the fifteenth and sixteenth centuries may have used a form of the camera obscura to help them with their work has been put forward by the artist David Hockney, whose book *Secret Knowledge* has been most useful to me in writing *Queen Without a Crown*.

ONE

Walking in the Rain

The messenger who came thundering over the bridge to Windsor Castle on that damp November morning in 1569 brought grave news to Queen Elizabeth and a very curious message to one of her Ladies of the Bedchamber, namely myself, Ursula Stannard. He brought me a riddle to solve and also, possibly, the answer to a prayer. If only I could close my hand upon it.

I was a woman in my thirties and I had led an unusual life, for I had for a long time been not only one of the queen's ladies, but also, now and then, an agent undertaking secret missions for her and for her secretary of state, Sir William Cecil. In the course of all this I had acquired some unconventional skills such as picking locks and breaking ciphers. I was accustomed to searching out plots and traitors, taking on false identities, reading other people's letters and listening at doors. I wore divided over-kirtles with hidden pouches sewn inside them so that I could carry lockpicks and a dagger about with me.

I had, however, never learned how to travel into the past, and the best way to grasp the golden prize now dangling before me, which would turn sadness to joy if only I could but win it, would be to turn back time for twenty-three years. It was something of a challenge, to put it mildly.

In an attempt to take a cheerful view of the situation, I reminded myself that although there was serious trouble in the north of England, the queen did not want me to be involved in it. I was not, for once, being ordered to journey into peril on some secret mission. The strange new assignment I was being offered would at least not lead me into danger.

Unfortunately, my mortal ears couldn't hear Fate laughing.

* * *

That morning began in the most ordinary fashion. It was drizzling, but Elizabeth didn't mind walking in the rain and often did so, her ladies and courtiers, perforce, walking with her. One of her gentlemen would always be at her side, while everyone else followed behind, the ladies lifting their skirt hems clear of the puddles, wishing their shoes were stouter and occasionally sneezing. If Elizabeth acknowledged the sneezes at all, it was usually with a sharp glance over her shoulder and a curt command to stop that noise.

At least, this time, she was keeping to the castle terrace, where we had paving stones underfoot instead of wet grass. Christopher Hatton, one of her most devoted friends, was beside her this time, and the hooded fur cloak that protected the royal head of hair and the queenly array of white brocade and pearls had been a gift from him. I wished my cloak were as good.

We all had cloaks of course, for the drizzle was penetrating. It drifted in chilly clouds over the Thames and the open heath below the castle. I said to my husband Hugh, who was with us, that it was wonderful how weather could alter distance. Amid the sloping open land below us stood a lonely cottage. On clear days it looked as though one good throw would toss a stone into its garden. Today, we could barely see its outline and it seemed distant and unreal.

We were both low in spirit. We would rather have been at home in one of our two houses, Hawkswood on the Surrey border or Withysham in Sussex. We hadn't welcomed Elizabeth's summons to Windsor.

It was a safety measure, for the castle was well defended and the rebellion in the north was gathering strength. No one knew how serious the danger was or how far south it would reach, but Elizabeth's person had to be safeguarded and so, she insisted, did mine. 'You would make a useful hostage, if the rebels once got hold of you, Ursula,' she told me.

I had no legal status, for although my father had had a formidable list of wives, my mother was never among them. But blood ties are blood ties and people are vulnerable through their kinfolk. Queen Elizabeth and I were half-sisters. My mother, while serving Queen Anne Boleyn at court, had been seduced by King Henry the Eighth. The facts of my parentage were not widely known, but enough people were aware of them to turn me into a target for conspirators.

I knew I should be grateful to her for taking such care of me and mine. My husband, my fourteen-year-old daughter Meg, and the principal members of our household were in Windsor with us. They included my daughter's tutor Dr Lambert, my gentlewoman Sybil Jester, our good servants Fran and Roger Brockley and an aged and exasperating hanger-on of mine, Gladys Morgan, for whom I had a reluctant responsibility. We were together and well housed, but it fretted me to be cut off from home.

At home, after all, I was the mistress of the house. At Windsor, I was a Lady of the Bedchamber, a promotion from my former place at court as a Lady of the Presence Chamber, but with drawbacks. Attending on the queen in private as I did now, I was more than ever subject to her wishes, her whims (and occasionally her tempers) as well as being compelled to walk in the rain whether I liked it or not – and I didn't.

And that wasn't all. Of our two homes, the one we longed for most was Hugh's property of Hawkswood, a grey stone manor-house set in a peaceful valley, looking south towards Sussex, with a vista of low wooded hills. It possessed a small ornamental lake, a charming knot garden and a rose garden which was Hugh's especial pride. I sometimes thought that his roses occupied the place in his heart which his children would have filled, had he ever had them.

Beyond the gardens and the lake there were cattle meadows, cornfields, and a small beech wood. It was a good property, serene and productive, and Hugh had been born there. He loved it, and gradually I had come to love it too.

And now we were in danger of losing it. While it was still ours, we wanted to be there. We walked side by side in the rain, trying to talk of other things but quite unable to concentrate on them.

Abruptly, I said: 'Hugh, once again, why not sell Withysham instead? I don't feel about it as you feel about Hawkswood. I wasn't bred there; it isn't my family home. Why won't you let me do this?'

'Because the queen gave it to you for services rendered, and they were dangerous services. You earned Withysham as I never earned Hawkswood. Because she might even take offence if you were to sell it. And because the unhappy muddle we're now in is my fault and not yours. I didn't marry you to rob you, Ursula. I will not let you sacrifice Withysham; please don't mention it again.'

When Hugh spoke in that tone, he meant what he said and would not be moved. I looked at him sadly. 'Very well,' I said.

For the third time, we turned at the western end of the terrace and began to walk back. It was cold and I felt concerned for Hugh, who was much older than I was and whose health sometimes wavered. 'If only this business in the north could be settled quickly!' I said. 'Then we could go home, at least for a while. I wish we knew what was happening. Surely news must come soon.'

Ahead and below, just visible through the rain haze, we could see the bridge across the river. Suddenly, Hugh's hand closed on my arm. 'I think,' he said, 'that news is arriving now. Someone's coming across that bridge at a gallop.'

I joined Elizabeth's court originally as a young widow after the death of my first husband, Meg's father, Gerald Blanchard. I was in need of money, and when the chance came to earn some, I seized it. That was how I turned into one of the agents employed by Elizabeth and Cecil. Strange and perilous though the business was, it was at least well paid.

And inescapable. I married a second time, and my new husband, Matthew de la Roche, was no friend to Elizabeth. That should have ended my spying days, and as the work had begun to sicken me, I was not sorry. But although Matthew took me to live abroad, the queen, undeterred, found means to draw me back to England. While I was away from him, I heard of Matthew's death from plague.

Again I tried to escape into private life, by marrying Hugh Stannard, but still, now and then, I was called back into service. I still had my lockpicks and my dagger. If you were useful to Elizabeth and Cecil, they used you, whether you wished it or not. Like walking in the rain.

It was more with resignation than surprise that I heard that the messenger from the north, though his principal business was with the queen and Cecil, had asked to see me as well.

The meeting took place in the anteroom to the queen's bedchamber. Elizabeth received us formally, seated on a dais, very much the gracious queen in her pale brocade, her pearls and her open lace ruff, except that her expression wasn't gracious at all, but sharp as a hatchet. The messenger stood facing us, and Cecil stood beside the dais, formally gowned. I waited a few steps back, wondering what all this was going to mean to me. I was worried about Hugh's health and afraid that the loss of Hawkswood might damage it further. I did not want distractions now.

The rain had grown heavier and blew against the leaded windows while the messenger talked. He was a young man, well educated to judge from his voice, not tall but very handsome, with shapely cheekbones and dark, winged eyebrows sweeping outwards and upwards above deep-set brown eyes. His black hair was vigorous, growing strongly from his hairline. His name was Mark Easton, and he was in the employ of Lord Sussex, President of the North.

He had ridden hard from York, changing horses frequently at the royal posting stables and barely pausing to eat or sleep. Tired and wet though he undoubtedly was, he had insisted on delivering his message before taking any refreshment or even removing his cloak and boots, and it was from his left boot that he withdrew his employer's written report. He would have knelt to present it to her, but Elizabeth, with an impatient: 'No need for that!' held out her hand for it, and when he gave it to her, she broke the seal at once and began to read the contents aloud.

They were alarming. The earls of Westmorland and Northumberland, stirred up by wild ambitions on the part of another nobleman, the Duke of Norfolk, had between them mustered fifteen thousand men, and had now ridden into the city of Durham in the north-east '*to raise the standard of revolt*,' read Elizabeth grimly. '*They intend to release Mary of Scotland from her captivity in England and carry her back to Scotland, and then, apparently, they dream of reinstating the Catholic faith in our own country. These are their pretexts for this act of treachery.* So Lord Sussex writes. It turns my stomach.'

She stopped reading aloud, but glanced rapidly through the rest of the letter and then handed it to Cecil. 'Here. See for yourself, Master Secretary. It appears,' she said, addressing the rest of us, 'that Westmorland's wife, Jane Neville, who happens also to be Norfolk's sister, has done much to encourage it all by telling her husband, *and* Northumberland too, that after all Norfolk's urging and his efforts to raise money for this . . . bah! . . . this *exploit* . . . inaction would shame them forever and leave them nothing but to crawl away into holes in the ground. I wonder where Sussex got that item of information from?'

'He has his spies, madam,' said Mark Easton. 'He receives good reports of the enemy's movements and intentions. A shepherd here, a vicar there; a disgruntled butler who overhears the table talk while he's handing the sauce; a tenant who doesn't agree with his landlord's politics.'

'All this,' said Elizabeth, 'springs from the foolish dreams of that foolish man, Thomas Howard of Norfolk. He wants to see Mary of Scotland rescued, reinstated on the Scottish throne, and he hopes to marry her and make himself her consort. Well, well. His sister wants to help him. The next stage, of course, would be an attempt to take my throne for Mary.'

'I have been hoping, all this time, that the revolt would fizzle out for lack of support,' said Cecil bitterly.

'Courtesy of the delightful Jane Neville,' said Elizabeth, 'it has not. I have heard that Northumberland's wife is as bad. The women appear to be worse than the men. What's to be done?'

'Sussex seems to be doing it.' Cecil had by now read through the rest of the letter. 'He says here that by the time we receive this, he will have forces mobilizing in the midlands to make sure that whatever happens, the rebels can't reach Mary.'

'Where is she now, Sir William?' I asked. 'The last I heard, she was at Tutbury Castle. Is she still there?'

'She is indeed,' said Elizabeth. 'On the borders of Staffordshire and Derbyshire. I've never seen it, but I'm told it would be a formidable obstacle to them even if they got there.'

'It stands on top of a hill, and there are marshes below,' said Cecil. 'Mary's been there before, and she doesn't like it. She says it's damp and draughty, and it probably is, but it's certainly secure. I think we have her fast. We've also got Norfolk, nicely mewed up in the Tower of London. The important thing now is to have these wretched earls imprisoned too, as soon as possible, in some other castle and preferably in its dungeons. But for the moment, the matter is in the hands of Sussex. There is little to be done here in the south.'

'Except that Master Easton has asked that Mistress Stannard should be here,' said Elizabeth. 'Does Sussex require the services of my Ursula?'

Here it came. I braced myself. No doubt Lord Sussex wanted me for some secret and probably uncomfortable spying task. Probably, it was something at which a harmless-looking woman was more likely to succeed than a man. Presumably, I was about to be sent north, away from Hugh, with orders once again to listen at doors, read private documents and put myself at risk for Elizabeth's sake.

'Not Lord Sussex, madam,' said young Master Easton unexpectedly. 'It is a private matter. There has perhaps been a little misunderstanding. Lord Sussex knows my business with Mistress Stannard, but it is not official and is not connected in any way with him. I do indeed seek her help, but it's a private matter – a family affair.'

TWO
Old Sins

Windsor was a royal castle, which meant luxury (at least for the queen and the courtiers, if not for the scullions) and also, when viewed from a would-be attacker's point of view, an air of grim impenetrability.

The luxury was on a grand scale: mighty fires, velvet-hung beds, carved furniture glossy with beeswax polish; tables draped in valuable carpets or fine white linen; candles galore to drive back the shadows of night (or the grey skies of winter); fine food served on gold plate for formality and gilt for everyday; music, singing, dancing. Out of doors, one had the terrace to stroll on and the gardens to wander in; there were boats on the river, the busy little town of Windsor with its shops and taverns and a vast park with a herd of deer in it to provide sport and exercise.

The impenetrability was similarly impressive. Grey walls loomed ominously; towers commanded views of every approach. *We are more than just mighty walls and towers,* they said. *We represent the power of the crown, the gold in the royal treasury, the queen's armies and the loyalty of her people. Don't waste your cannon on us.*

In the castle, Hugh and I and our people, therefore, had comfort and security, but privacy and a domestic atmosphere were more difficult to come by. Still, we tried. Because of the link between myself and the queen, we had a good suite of three rooms. They were secluded, at the top of a twisting stair in one of the towers, and were adequate for us all except for Meg's tutor, Dr Lambert, who lodged at the Garter Inn in the town.

Old Gladys rarely left the suite, because she said (or, to be more accurate, grumbled) that the stairs were a struggle, but if anything, this was an advantage, since Gladys didn't get on well with other servants, though she was less of a liability than she had been. A narrow escape from being hanged on a charge of witchcraft – I had managed to save her, but only just – had had its effect. She no longer spat curses at people she disliked, and she washed, these days, without being told.

I had at one time feared that old age was damaging her mind, but it was as though the shock of coming so close to death had jolted her back to normality. All the same, I wasn't sure that she'd stay there, and I felt that the less she mingled with other people, the better.

She did light cleaning and plain sewing for us, for her eyesight was good, despite her age. She slept on a truckle bed in the room where the Brockleys occupied a small four-poster. They didn't like the arrangement, but could hardly complain, for few servants had a room of their own and a curtained bed. To have an extra person in the room was a minor inconvenience.

In any case, Roger Brockley was responsible for Gladys' presence in my household in the first place. Brockley, my groom, manservant, steward whenever we were at Withysham and sometimes my invaluable co-agent, had a chivalrous kindness for the aged. Gladys had been charged with witchcraft more than once. Years ago, when we first came across her on the Welsh border, Brockley, seeing her as a helpless, frightened old woman, had intervened to protect her from a similar accusation. 'So you really can't object to sharing a room with Gladys now,' I had told him. 'She wouldn't be here at all, but for you!'

Within the suite, Hugh and I had done our best to create the illusion of a home. We had given the second largest room to Meg and Sybil, while the main room was ours. It had a vast four-poster and a deep mullioned window bay with a practical window seat which lifted up to reveal a chest below. By moving a table and a couple of settles into the bay, we had created a miniature parlour, and this was where we talked to Mark Easton, after Elizabeth had sent us away to discuss his mysterious family business in private.

He joined us there after a brief visit to his own quarters for a much-needed wash and a change of clothes, and his first comment was: 'This is like being inside a private house. How delightful!'

'We do our best,' Hugh said, leading him to one of the settles in the bay, where they both sat down. 'Will you have mulled ale, or wine?'

For purposes of hospitality, we always kept a cask or two of good liquor in our chamber. Fran Brockley (though I still often called her Dale, her surname before she married Brockley) was by the fire with Gladys, mulling pewter jugs of ale and wine with hot pokers. My daughter Meg was next door, out of the way, at her books with Lambert, but I had called Sybil Jester, who had been with them, in to join us. She was partly Meg's chaperone but very much more my friend. She was in the middle years, and her looks were unusual: her features just too wide for their height, her nose a little splayed, her dark, strong eyebrows stretching towards her temples. Yet there was charm in those distinctive features and in her serene smile. As she came in, following Mark, she gave us that familiar smile, but looked enquiringly at our visitor.

'This is Mark Easton, messenger from Lord Sussex in York,' I said, motioning her to the window seat. 'But he has family news for us, though what it is, I've no idea.'

Easton accepted mulled ale, and Brockley, who had been warming his hands at the hearth alongside Fran, brought it to him. 'I called it family business,' Mark said, 'but it's really to do with friends of Mistress Stannard. One of them, mistress, was formerly your ward, I think. Mistress Penelope Mason, she used to be, I believe, before she married a fellow called Clem Moss.'

'Pen!' I said, enlightened. 'Yes, I was her guardian for a short while. She still writes to me. She had a son not long ago.' I had been glad to hear news of Pen. I was fond of her, but there was no denying that as a girl she had been both highly intelligent and emotionally unsteady. I was most relieved when she took the sensible, strong-minded Clem Moss as her husband. Taking the settle opposite Master Easton, I said: 'I hope you aren't bringing bad news. She and the baby – are they all right?'

'Indeed, yes, mistress. The baby's as bonny a little fellow

as ever I saw. He's been named Leonard after his grandfather. No, this concerns a young lady called Jane Mason – sister to Mistress Pen Moss. You'll have heard of her?'

'I remember her as a child, when I had occasion to visit the Masons,' I said. 'She was about nine, then. I stayed with them for a while and taught the girls embroidery.'

I had also disrupted the household by discovering treason in it. The original Leonard Mason, now deceased, had taken a dislike to me after that, and only his death had made it possible for his wife Ann and myself to become friends.

'Jane is eighteen now,' said Mark Easton. He put his tankard down, and his handsome young face took on an anxious look. 'I met her when I was travelling for Lord Sussex, in Yorkshire, and the Moss household put me up for a few days. Jane Mason was sent to live with her sister some months ago; it seems that the idea is for Mistress Moss to find a husband for her.'

I nodded. I had done the same for Pen. Ann Mason had thought me better placed than herself to launch her daughter into the world and arrange a marriage for her, and an onerous task it had proved to be.

'Jane is . . . a joy,' said Mark. 'I fell in love with her and she with me and there shouldn't be any impediment, not really. I'm not Catholic, as she is, but I wouldn't interfere with her private observances. I'm willing to promise that. I have a good house I can take her to. A steward runs it for me now because I want to make my way in public life; that's why I'm in the service of Lord Sussex. A man needs achievements as well as legacies if he is to amount to anything. My home is in Derbyshire, and I also have a property in Devon. But . . .'

'But?' I said. 'There is a difficulty? Jane's family feel that for some reason the match isn't suitable?'

'They've nothing against me personally,' said Easton. 'But Mistress Penelope wrote to their mother and their elder brother George in Berkshire, asking their opinion, and when the answer came back it was no, and Mistress Penelope said she agreed, and her husband nodded and said that so did he. I begged time off from Lord Sussex to visit Berkshire, to explain things in person. But—'

'What things would those be? You haven't explained,' said Hugh.

Easton looked at us unhappily. He was clearly a young man of means, and he was in a position of responsibility in the service of Lord Sussex. He should have been full of self-assurance. Instead, he now seemed vulnerable, almost desperate.

'They say,' he told us carefully, 'that is, the Masons say, and the Mosses agree with them, that they are sorry for me, and they don't hold me to blame in any way, but there it is. They can't sanction the marriage of the second Mason daughter, my lovely Jane, to the son of a poisoner.'

Dale dropped a poker into the hearth with a clatter. Her protuberant blue eyes were bulging, and the pockmarks of a long-ago attack of smallpox stood out as they always did when she was tired or ill or disturbed.

Even Roger Brockley, who had gone back to stand beside her, let his eyebrows rise, wrinkling his high forehead with its dusting of gold freckles. Which was remarkable, for it took a great deal to shake Brockley. Mark had achieved the rare feat of startling him. He had startled us all. Gladys was gaping; Sybil looked appalled. Hugh had visibly stiffened.

'A poisoner?' he asked. 'Er . . . which of your parents . . .?'

'My father,' said Mark miserably. 'Or so it was said. I didn't tell Jane or her family about it myself,' he added in a bitter tone. 'It isn't the sort of thing one blithely announces across a dining table or when playing cards with one's hosts in a parlour! But Mistress Penelope had heard the story before she met me. She was at court before her marriage, and apparently it was a scandalous tale that the maids of honour still tattle about. She recognized my name and then asked my father's first name and said to me: was he the Gervase Easton who was accused of poisoning a man called Peter Hoxton? He was. I'd have been a fool to deny it – she and her husband could have found out easily enough whether or not I was lying.'

'I didn't hear the story when I was at court,' I said. 'But I suppose I was never there for all that long at a time, and I didn't mix much with the maids of honour.'

'My father was never charged with the crime,' Mark said, 'but that was because he took his own life first. I was only three at the time.' He put a hand inside his doublet and drew out a miniature portrait which hung round his neck on a chain. Lifting the chain over his head, he handed it to me. 'The man he was said to have killed had been making advances to my mother. It was supposed to be a crime of jealousy. This was my mother. Judith, her name was. Look.'

Hugh came over to me, and we examined it together. Sybil slipped off the window seat to look as well. The miniature was exquisite. It showed the face of a young woman, dressed in the style of twenty or so years ago, with a small ruff and a round French hood. The dark hair in front of the hood and the almond-shaped brown eyes were just like Easton's. She did not have her son's upward swooping eyebrows, but her own slim dark brows perfectly suited her face. Her face, altogether, was . . .

Beautiful. There was no other word for it, and the artist, whoever he was, had understood it and paid homage to it. Even in this tiny portrait, he had shown not only the shape and colour of the eyes, but also their lustrousness. He had shown the dewiness of the skin and the lovely bone structure, so clearly defined and yet so delicate, as though the bone were made of polished ivory. He had shown the generosity in the mouth and captured the little tilt of the head, which was not coquettish but enquiring; as though its owner were shyly asking a question. He had wrought a miracle of fine detail in a minuscule space.

'I can't remember my father's face,' Easton said. 'But I was five when I last saw my mother, and I can remember her and she was just like that. It's a good picture. May I tell you the story? You see, I need someone to help me. I have never believed my father was guilty. I want to prove that I'm right, because if I can, then I'll be able to marry Jane.'

The Brockleys came over to us as well, and after a glance at Mark for his permission, Hugh held out the miniature for them to see. 'What a lovely face,' Fran said, while Brockley nodded in agreement.

Hugh handed the picture back to its owner. 'So, tell your tale,' he said briefly.

'I said I had a house in Derbyshire,' Mark said. 'My

father – Gervase Easton – should have inherited it; he was the eldest son. But he fell in love with my mother—'

'Who could blame him?' Brockley remarked suddenly.

'Quite,' said Mark. 'She was the daughter of one of our smallholder tenants and that wasn't the kind of match that his parents wanted for him. But he insisted on marrying her, so he was disinherited. His younger brother, my Uncle Robert, was to have everything; my father would have to shift for himself. So he came south, with his bride. Her family had friends in court service, apparently, and someone helped him to get a place at court. The friends weren't very influential, though, and it wasn't a very splendid place.'

Mark's lip curled, which didn't suit him. His handsomeness was meant for friendly candour. Anything like a sneer sat badly on him.

'Go on,' Hugh said.

'It was 1543,' Easton said. 'In the days of King Henry. He'd just married his sixth wife, Catherine Parr. My father became a Clerk of the King's Kitchen, helping to check larders, collect supplies for the cooks, that sort of thing. He was paid only sixteen pence a day, though I understand that he had hopes of promotion. My mother found work at court too – as a maid to one of Queen Catherine's ladies. Until I came into the world, the following year, in April.'

'And then?' Hugh asked.

'There was another man employed about the royal kitchens, higher up the hierarchy,' said Easton. 'A Clerk Comptroller, though I don't quite know what that means.'

'You seem to know a good deal, even so,' I remarked. 'Yet you say your father died when you were three.'

'People told me things later. Uncle Robert brought me up, and he told me about my father's work and what he was paid. He knew all about it from my mother. I'll come to that in a moment, if I may . . .?'

'Of course,' Hugh said. 'You were speaking of a Clerk Comptroller, whatever that may be.'

'Yes. Peter Hoxton. He had a reputation as a womanizer, I believe, but it seems that he truly fell in love with my mother. He wouldn't leave her alone. He waylaid her and found chances to talk to her and pay her compliments, and it made my father angry. Once, after dark, someone attacked Hoxton in a courtyard here in this castle, and had a fight with him, and put him in bed for four days, and the court gossip said that my father did it.

'Well, it seems that not long after that, Hoxton fell ill. It was still summer – well, early September – but he was caught in a downpour and developed a heavy cold which turned to a fever. The court was still here at Windsor. For a few days, his manservant brought food to his room. The kitchens got it ready for him, and the servant collected it. Hoxton was mending, but on the third day, he fell ill again, with sickness and a kind of madness, and he died two days later. The physicians said it was poison.'

'Wasn't the manservant suspected?' Hugh cut in.

Mark shook his head. 'No. I don't know why not. My uncle did once say that the man had been proved innocent. I think perhaps he was never seriously suspected, though, because . . .' He paused and swallowed. 'Perhaps,' he said at last, 'it was because apparently there were two witnesses who actually saw my father, with a bag, come to where Hoxton's food was waiting for collection, take out a pie from the bag and set it on the tray with the other dishes. Hoxton ate it, or most of it. It was shortly after that that he . . . apparently went insane and began to vomit. Later, he fell into a stupor and never recovered.'

'What was it?' Hugh asked. 'The poison, I mean?'

'Deadly nightshade, so I've been told,' said Mark. 'The berries were in the pie. I believe they look something like bilberries, and it seems he was fond of those. I've never seen either of them.'

'I wouldn't recognize nightshade,' I said. 'But I've eaten bilberries. They grow on wild heathlands in the west of England, I think. They can be stewed and either put in pies or baked under a topping of sweetened breadcrumbs. They're delicious.'

'I don't know what that pie would have tasted like,' said Mark dryly. 'The physicians said the nightshade berries would taste strange, but not foul, and the flavour could be disguised by sugar or honey, and anyway, it seems that Hoxton's nose was so blocked with the rheum that he had lost nearly all his sense of taste and smell. My mother told my uncle all this as well. She attended the inquest.'

'How did the physicians know what it was?' Hugh asked.

'It seems that some of the pie was left, and one of them recognized the berries. He'd used nightshade himself in a medicine – apparently, in very tiny doses, its essence can relieve pain. He knew the symptoms, too. He'd had cases of children eating the berries. Everyone,' said Easton, 'believed my father was responsible. Everyone at court knew he hated Hoxton. Like poison.' He made the very word sound venomous.

'But you believe he didn't do it?' Hugh said. 'Why?'

He spoke mildly, yet the words sounded harsh and Easton flinched. He felt once more inside his doublet, and this time he brought out a folded letter. 'Because of this,' he said.

He gave it to us, and we read it together, Hugh and I, with Sybil and Brockley still looking over our shoulders. It was an old document, the creases deep, the ink faded:

> *My beloved Judith, when you read this, I shall be gone. I have to leave you, because if I do not, I am likely to be taken from you in a worse way, which will leave an even darker shadow over your life than my death by my own act. They say it is sin to take one's own life, but the Romans did it in the name of honour and they had their own wisdom.*
>
> *There is something I must tell you, something of which you must be certain. I did not kill Peter Hoxton. I never touched his food; never dreamed of such a thing. It's true I once fought him and gave him bruises so remarkable that he hid from the world for half a week, but what of it? He made me angry, but men do fight sometimes. That's very different from serving venom disguised as bilberry pie. I do not know who poisoned him or why. But whatever those two women may say, I was not the man they saw tampering with Hoxton's meal.*
>
> *I shall die soon; I swear, upon my hopes of resurrection to eternal life, that this is the truth. I, your husband, am innocent of this thing.*

When our son Mark is old enough to understand, make sure he knows. Keep this letter and show it to him. Assure him that he is the son of an honest man.

Dear Judith, I know well that you truly love me and have been ever faithful to me; that I had no need to fear Peter Hoxton or any other man. When I fought him, it was not because I feared that he would take you from me, but because I knew his pursuit distressed you.

Now and ever, you are my love, my friend, my trusted companion. I regret nothing; not my estrangement from my home, nor anything else that has befallen me because I made you my wife. I only wish I could have given you more, a better way of living. It would have come in time, but for this disastrous chance. Now the only thing I can do is slip out of your life, and out of my own, before the name I have shared with you is stained beyond hope of cleansing. I say it again: I am not guilty. Rest assured of that and hold on to it for such comfort as it can give you. I love you. I always will.

Your most true husband, Gervase.

My eyes stung. It seemed to me that from those words there rose such a declaration of devotion that reading them was like walking accidentally into a room where a couple are making love. I was happy with Hugh, but the loves I had had before him had been more passionate (one of them even stormy). I recognized the feeling in these written words.

There was no hint in the letter that Gervase expected his son to clear his name, only that he desperately wished that Mark would believe it to be clean. Silently, we handed the letter back. 'When did this come to you?' Hugh asked. 'You have never done anything about it before – never made any enquiries? How did your father die, by the way?'

'He drank geneva,' Mark Easton said. 'The spirit made from juniper berries. A lot of it – the empty flask was found by his bed. Then he went down to the river and plunged in. He couldn't swim, anyway. His body was washed ashore later that day. He left this for my mother. She married again, the following Easter. I think she needed someone to provide for her and me; she couldn't manage well enough alone. She was so lovely that she had no difficulty in finding a new husband. Myself, I wish she had taken more time and found a nicer stepfather for me, though. I believe my stepfather is still alive and lives near here. He didn't like me. He used to hit me and shout at me, even though I was so small.'

'But you said you were brought up by your uncle,' Hugh said, frowning.

'When I was just turned five, my grandfather died – the one who had disinherited us. He left Uncle Robert everything, but even though my father was dead by then, my uncle was a good man and he wasn't happy about it. He came to see my mother, to tell her the news, and he saw that things were not right between me and my stepfather. My mother could not leave, being married, but Uncle Robert offered me a home. Mother kissed me goodbye and gave me to him, for my own peace and safety, she said.

'He took me back to Derbyshire. He was married, but no children ever came, and in the end, he made me his heir. He was very prosperous by then – in fact he had just acquired the Devonshire property. He said he was glad to give me a future, that it would put right the injustice my grandfather had done. He said he'd married for love as well, only in his case, the girl was someone his father thought "suitable". She was nice,' Mark said, wistfully. 'Aunt Kate, I called her. She was always kind to me. We lost her to the lung-rot, one bad winter, when I was about eighteen.

'Well, I hadn't been with them more than a few months before word came that I had lost my mother as well as my father. I think my stepfather ill-used her, just as he'd ill-used me. Her belongings were sent to us, but they were put away in a chest and mostly forgotten, until three months ago when Uncle Robert died too and everything came to me. I had to go through his possessions, and I found the chest pushed into an attic, up under the roof. This letter was inside it.'

Hugh said: 'And you believe what it says? Because it would be very natural for your father to want his wife and son to think well of him, to believe in his innocence, even if it were not true.'

'He swears,' said Easton, 'on his hopes of the resurrection. That is a very serious thing. Who would take an oath on that, on the very edge of the grave, unless he spoke the truth?'

He said it with sincerity, a young man evidently unable to believe in anyone devious or cynical enough to play games with oath-taking. Studying him further, I saw that he was essentially a straightforward individual, quite lacking in guile.

But clear-headed. '*Someone* poisoned Peter Hoxton,' he said, 'though I'm convinced it wasn't my father. I want to know who it really was. Mistress Stannard, according to Lord Sussex, who knows something about you, you have a reputation for being able . . . able to find things out. You are said to be clever at it. I would try on my own account, but I have duties which occupy all my time. Will you help?'

'What if it's the wrong answer?' Hugh asked.

'It won't be,' said Easton fiercely. 'I know it won't.'

We were all silent. The fire crackled, and rain spattered on the windows, as though impatient fingers were tapping at them, as if ghosts from the past were trying to get in.

'It will be difficult,' said Easton at length. 'I know that. But if you do uncover the truth, I would reward you. I . . . could sell that Devonshire property. It's leased to someone now and brings in some extra income, but I can do without it. In fact, I already have a possible buyer. My Derbyshire land is profitable. I could give Jane a comfortable life there. I believe,' he added, 'that the value of the Devonshire house and land would be around two and a half thousand pounds.'

There was another silence. I didn't look at Hugh, nor he at me, but we were both thinking the same thing.

Two and a half thousand pounds, roughly, was the present value of the loan for which Hawkswood had so unwisely been put up as security. That amount would cover the interest as well. Solve Mark Easton's mystery and Hawkswood would be safe.

I said: 'But what if I find the truth and it *is* the wrong answer? That possibility can't be just ignored. Or, of course,' I added, 'I might try but fail to discover anything. After all this time, that is the likeliest outcome.'

'I have no doubt that the truth would clear my father,' said

Mark, 'but provided there is no doubt at all that the truth is what it is, I would pay up. I would pay for honest endeavour.'

There was no choice, no question at all about what my reply must be.

I said: 'I will try.'

At least I wasn't going to be forced to travel to Westmorland or Northumberland to foil the schemes of dangerous conspirators. That was certainly a relief.

THREE

Pictures

'S*omeone's coming across that bridge at a gallop.*'

Hugh had said that as we watched Mark Easton thunder across the bridge towards Windsor castle. I had known what he was thinking. The last time we saw someone do that, he was a courier and was bringing a letter for Hugh. I had watched him read it, watched his face change, and been frightened. For some time, his health had been making me uneasy, for he seemed often to be short of breath, and there were times when his skin seemed grey-tinged and his eyes shadowed, as though they were sinking into his head. Now these changes appeared all in a matter of moments, and with them came a terrible look of misery and age.

'Hugh?' I said. 'What is it?'

At first he seemed unable to speak and he avoided my eyes, but when I asked the question again and put out a hand to him, he took it and then, at last, his eyes met mine. 'Oh, Ursula,' he said. 'I'm so sorry.'

'Sorry? For what? Hugh, what's happened?'

It came out, not all at once but in bits and pieces, as though he could only bear to put a little of it into words at a time. I will tell it more simply. I had known nothing of it, but more than a year ago, Hugh had joined with some merchants of his acquaintance in a venture which, said Hugh sadly, had promised fine profits. Two of the merchants imported luxury fabrics from a number of sources, and they had recently travelled to Venice where they chanced to meet the agent of a Turkish buyer who was interested in purchasing modern firearms and seasoned oak timber in bulk. They had come home with an idea.

'The Turkish fellow probably wanted guns and timber for warships,' said Hugh. 'It's a stormy part of the world, the eastern Mediterranean. Maybe he was setting up as a pirate! But my associates didn't worry about that. They were afire with their new scheme, and they infected me.'

The outcome of all that was one of the merchants hastened back to Venice in a hurry to clinch the deal, and in England, the group set about acquiring the goods required. Two ships were leased and crews hired. The plan was that when the arms and timber had been paid for, the money should be used to purchase silk brocades, damasks and velvets in bulk, along with quantities of rare spices and dyestuffs, to be brought home for sale at a healthy profit.

'So – what happened?' I asked.

'We had such great hopes,' Hugh said unhappily. 'I expected to make money; plenty of it. I had visions of buying you fine jewels; maybe purchasing more land. But it all took much longer than expected. The Turkish agent haggled and delayed before he paid up. He did pay eventually, but by then it was autumn. The return voyage didn't start until November. Our two ships sailed in convoy with another, belonging to someone else. It's a long way – through the Adriatic and the Ionian Sea, westward through the Mediterranean, and then northwards towards England and through the Bay of Biscay.'

'And?'

'Biscay is notorious. There was a storm. The ships were blown this way and that and in the end . . . our two were blown inshore and piled up on rocks. The third ship survived to bring the news home. The crew saw the disaster happen, but they couldn't save anyone, or any of the cargo. This letter is from one of my associates. We have lost our investment. And . . . Ursula . . .'

'Yes, Hugh?'

'I didn't have enough free capital for my contribution. So much was involved – buying ships and cargo and getting crews together. I borrowed over two thousand pounds. I shall have to repay it somehow. And . . .'

'What did you use for security?' I asked, alarmed.

'Hawkswood,' said Hugh.

* * *

'Hawkswood!' I said, a single word, my first after Mark had left us and Hugh had shooed the others out, to give us privacy.

'I know.' He drew me to the window seat and sat me down. 'If you could solve Mark Easton's mystery, then, as you say – *Hawkswood*. We would save it.'

'Only,' I said 'how can I possibly go about it? Where do I start? It was all so long ago. I need to turn time back, and no one can do that!'

Hugh was standing up, gazing out of the window towards the low, wooded hills to the north, blurred now by rain into outlines of grey shadow. He was slow to reply, and when he did, it was only to agree with me. 'It's as hard a challenge as anyone could well imagine,' he said.

'I think Mark believes what his father wrote,' I said, thinking it out. 'But he has such good reasons for wanting his father to be innocent. He could easily be wrong.'

'And also,' said Hugh, 'in this castle, we are in a kind of protective imprisonment. If the quest led you away from Windsor, you might not be allowed to go. The queen isn't likely to be sympathetic to a fool like me who took too big a risk, nor to a young man's affairs of the heart. She has other things on her mind, and so, I suppose, have we.'

I, too, turned to look northwards. Somewhere in that direction, armed men were on the move, and in Tutbury Castle on the Staffordshire border, Mary Stuart, who had lost the Scottish crown, was probably dreaming not only of getting it back, but of seizing Elizabeth's crown as well, to adorn her own carefully groomed head. I imagined her, beautiful and charming, her long white fingers working at her embroidery while she brooded on her plans. I saw the armed men marching.

Hugh brought me back to the present. 'But I can think of one or two ways to begin making Easton's enquiries, if you're willing to try.'

'Of course I'm willing! I'll do almost anything to save Hawkswood, and since you refuse to let me sell Withysham . . .'

'I do indeed refuse. And that is final. I can't do that to you.' He still kept his head averted as he added: 'My poor Ursula. I look back and I think: how could I have been so rash? I meant to look after you, and then I bring all this trouble on us.'

I said: 'I have had peace with you. Peace from Matthew's endless plotting, even peace from the fear of childbirth. I nearly died when Meg was born, and again with Matthew's baby, the one that didn't live.'

'The physicians told me,' said Hugh dryly, 'that I could never be a father because I had the swelling sickness as a young man. Most women don't think of it as an advantage.'

'To me, it is. Hugh, hunting for this bygone killer will at least be a distraction from worrying about the trouble in the north. Is there really any danger from the rebels, here, so far away, I wonder? After all, according to Mark Easton's message, Lord Sussex means to get his forces in-between the rebels and Mary Stuart. That means being between the rebels and the south of England as well.'

'We don't know how much support Sussex will be able to raise, and we don't know how strong the rebellion is, either. What if they break through?'

'They'll be hard put to it to get Mary out of Tutbury, from all I've heard of Tutbury. And if they did,' I said thoughtfully, 'there's a Regent in Scotland who doesn't in the least want to hand over power to her. James Stewart of Moray is her half-brother, and even Mary can't bewitch a brother as she apparently bewitches other men. I wonder what plans the rebels and Mary have for him?'

'That woman!' Hugh snorted. 'A fine queen of Scotland she made! She picked a dissolute boy like Darnley as a husband, was almost certainly a party to his murder and then married the noble who was assuredly the ringleader in it. The Scots turn on her and she flees to England, and now we've got her as a hybrid between a prisoner and a guest and she's become a focus for plots to put her back on the Scottish throne and then snatch Elizabeth's! Someone ought to chop her head off and be done with it!'

'Tutbury is secure, surely.'

'I dare say, but there's more than one way of taking a fortress than knocking down the walls with cannon. There's treachery – or alternatively, there's the option of just marching straight past Tutbury and coming directly south to see if they can seize the Tower and Windsor and the person of Elizabeth instead. Or put her to flight. Either would do, I fancy.'

'Hugh!'

'I dreamt of it last night,' Hugh said. 'I've been dreaming of Hawkswood on most nights, but this time I dreamt I was here, at this window, looking out at those hills, and I saw the banners and lances of the rebel force coming towards us, over the skyline there.'

That was a thought so frightening that if it hadn't been for the need to redeem Hawkswood, I don't think I could have undertaken Easton's commission because I just wouldn't have been able to concentrate on Peter Hoxton. As things were, however, I knew I must pick up the gauntlet. 'Your ideas on how to investigate Mark's mystery,' I said. 'What are they?'

'My Little Bear!' said Hugh, and he smiled. Little Bear was his nickname for me, because my name, Ursula, meant a she-bear. Matthew had called me Saltspoon. In a way, my two nicknames said similar things about me. Matthew said my conversation always had salt on it; Hugh's pet name implied, gently, that I possessed a fierce side. But the smile drew us together.

'Well?' I said.

'There's an obvious place to start,' said Hugh. 'But . . .'

He paused, head cocked, and then peered out of the window again. I moved to see what he was looking at. The rain had stopped by now, and the queen had emerged on to the terrace again, amid her usual cloud of courtiers and ladies, cloaks billowing in the chill air but hoods pushed back so that we could see who was who.

Senior ladies walked close to the queen, but bringing up the rear were the maids of honour and a handful of their friends, chattering among themselves. Among them was my daughter Meg. Sybil had joined the group too, but was walking a little way behind Meg. Hugh undid the window latch and pushed the casement ajar, and Meg's voice floated briefly up to us. 'Ooh, you didn't!' The girl beside her giggled. Then they were past and going away from us.

'Damnation,' said Hugh.

'I know. I feel the same, and I hardly know why. Girls are always giggling over things, especially things they shouldn't have done. Mostly, there's no harm in it, but somehow, for Meg, it seems wrong. She's more grown-up than those other girls in some ways, but in others – she's too young to be in their company. I don't feel they're good for her.'

'Ursula, I know I'm not Meg's father. She's Gerald Blanchard's child, and from all I've heard of him, it was a tragedy that you lost him to the smallpox while you were still so young and Meg so little. I have tried to look after you both. I don't feel,' said Hugh with bitterness, 'that I've distinguished myself lately. But I do want to do right by the two of you. I am wondering whether, once we are allowed to leave the court, Meg need ever return to it. Need she ever be a maid of honour? Most of these girls are sent here by their families in the hope that they'll make good matches, but Meg already has one in the offing. If that excellent young man George Hillman remains of the same mind when she's sixteen, they could be married then.'

As so often before, I experienced a surge of gratitude towards this man, with whom I had found so much repose. His ships had found no safe harbour, but I had found one in Hugh himself.

'I have been thinking along the same lines,' I said.

'While we have to stay here,' Hugh said, 'I think it would be best to keep her busy. Did we not, some time ago, talk of having her portrait painted? There's a portrait artist staying in Windsor – a man called Arbuckle, Master Jocelyn Arbuckle.'

'Oh, yes. He's been painting one of the queen's other ladies,' I said. 'It's nearly finished now. I believe he has quite a reputation.'

'Suppose we asked him to paint Meg?'

'Can we afford it?'

'Oh yes. Might as well. If we do have to sell Hawkswood, it'll cover the portrait as well, and if we get Mark's two and half thousand, *that* will cover it instead. I'd like us to have a picture of Meg while she is still a young girl. She'll grow older, and we'll forget how she was at fourteen. She's at a very charming age, you know.

'*And*,' he added, 'if we splice long sittings for Arbuckle on to her Latin and Greek studies with Lambert, and her embroidery and music and dancing, she'll have much less time for chattering with those girls. If you agree, I'll find Arbuckle and sound him out. Meanwhile, about Mark Easton. I think you should start by going to the kitchens and talking to anyone who was there at the time of Hoxton's death and remembers it. See if anything emerges. Though, there are a couple of things to see to first . . .'

The couple of things involved, firstly, drawing up a contract with Mark, which he and I and Hugh all signed, with the Brockleys as witnesses. The second thing meant talking to the queen. I was, after all, about to intrude into her kitchens. It seemed only right to ask her permission first.

Elizabeth was shut away with her councillors for most of that day, but I managed a few words with her while I was helping her undress for bed. I was wary, for I knew she was anxious. Looking at her, I understood that she, too, had pictured the enemy lances appearing over the distant hills and felt, as I had, a small cold snake of fear within her. Elizabeth's face was shaped like a shield and usually protected her thoughts like one, but we were half-sisters and sometimes I could see beneath the shield.

But for all her anxiety, she listened to what I had to say, and if her tone was a trifle acid when she replied, she nevertheless gave me the permission I sought.

'Oh yes, Ursula. By all means. Poke and pry in my kitchens and ask all the questions you wish, provided you are on duty when you should be and don't cause valued servants to give notice.' She paused, propped on her pillows. 'At the meeting I shall attend tomorrow, a clerk will be taking notes. I'll dictate a note to the Lord Steward, saying that you have my permission to prowl in his territory. I suggest you start by talking to a clerk of the Spicery called John Sterry. He's been there since I was a child. He's as grey as a badger these days, but there's nothing wrong with his mind. If anyone recalls anything useful, he will. That's what you want, isn't it? To talk to long-standing servants with long, retentive memories.'

'Yes, ma'am. That's it exactly. It seems my best starting point.'

'From what you have told me, Ursula, I would say that it's your only starting point! Well, Sterry is your man.'

FOUR

The Fruit of Insanity

I waited a day, so that the contract could be signed and Elizabeth's note to the Lord Steward given time to do its work. But the following morning, after chapel, Elizabeth withdrew to confer with her councillors, leaving her ladies free to please themselves. The weather being damp and cold, most of them settled down indoors with their needlework. Hugh, after wishing me well, said he would go into the town and see the artist Arbuckle. Brockley had made the acquaintance of Arbuckle's manservant and knew where they were staying. And I, seizing my chance, plunged into the kitchen regions.

I had never before entered the kitchens at Windsor. I went down steps on which I had never before set foot, through passages I hadn't known existed and into a maze of rooms organized into suites for Larder, Cellar, Buttery, Bakehouse, Pastry, Spicery and other departments. People male and female, mostly in stained aprons, directed me, and after passing through a huge, steamy kitchen full of culinary aromas and sweating cooks, I reached the Spicery.

It turned out to be a cramped room lined with shelves on which stood various boxes and jars, while beneath the shelves were bigger containers: casks, chests and stone amphorae. A row of workers – chiefly male and muscular, but also including two mighty women with rolled-up sleeves and arms like legs of mutton – stood at a stone work-table, pounding spices in pestles, weighing the results and ladling it into bowls. The air was so aromatic that I was half afraid to breathe it. I felt that to open my mouth wide and take in a gulp of it would leave me reeling drunk.

'I'm looking for a Master John Sterry,' I said loudly, to be heard above the crash of the pestles. One of the women left her work, put her head round a door at the far side and called something which brought a man to the doorway. He was advanced in years though straight-backed still, and his short, stiff hair was the iron-grey of a badger's coat, as was his small moustache. 'John Sterry?' I enquired.

Elizabeth's instructions had evidently reached him. 'You will be Mistress Stannard?' he said. His voice was clipped and competent. 'I was expecting you. You have questions that I am to answer, I understand. If you will come this way . . .'

I walked past the work table, where the woman who had summoned him was once more industriously pounding, and followed him through a passage and into what seemed to be his office. It had a table, where papers and ledgers were lying along with a writing set. There were benches on either side of the table. Here, the rhythmic thudding of the pestles was reduced to a faint and distant thunder. We sat down, and he looked at me enquiringly.

'Were you here at the end of old King Henry's reign?' I asked. 'When a man called Peter Hoxton was employed in these kitchens and died?'

'Ah. It's about that old business, is it? Yes, I was here. I've been in the Spicery for thirty years. I remember the Hoxton affair well. It isn't,' he added, 'the sort of thing that happens every day, though it is the sort of thing that sticks in the memory.'

Elizabeth had chosen me a good contact, I thought; one with a businesslike mind. 'A man called Gervase Easton was accused of deliberately poisoning Hoxton,' I said. 'Two witnesses apparently saw him add something to a tray of food which had been set aside for the victim. Do you know who they were? Would it still be possible to find them and talk to them? And what about the manservant, and the physician who was called to attend Hoxton?'

Sterry snorted. 'You're over-hopeful! Some of the folk you'd like to talk to are in the graveyard now. It was nigh a quarter of a century ago, and people die off. There were two physicians, and they're both dead now. The manservant's gone, too. Edwards, his name was. He got another place with someone here, but he had a night off, went out roistering in the town, came back dead drunk, went to sleep it off and never woke up again. He always had drunk too much,' Sterry added disapprovingly.

'But the two witnesses who actually said they saw Easton doing something to the tray?'

'I'm coming to them. One of them was a pestle-woman – you've just come through that department. I don't know where she is now. She left us five or six years back; said the work was over heavy for her now she wasn't so young any more, and she was going to find something easier. She wasn't missed. No one liked her much, for some reason. But I doubt she was lying about Easton. She didn't have anything against him. The other one's still here, though. Madge Dyer, her name was in those days – she's Madge Goodman now. She left to wed, but she was back in three years, widowed and with no wish to marry again, it seemed. I don't know what happened, but I did once hear her say her husband didn't live up to his surname. She's working just across the passage there.' He pointed. 'Making comfits. You want to talk to her?'

I said I did, and once more he led the way.

I somehow expected Madge Goodman to resemble the massive pestle-women. She proved, however, to be small and rosy and slightly wrinkled, like a russet apple which has been kept all winter. Her mild blue eyes were clear, and the hair which her white cap didn't quite hide was still brown. She must have been very young at the time of Hoxton's death, for even now I thought she was under forty, though the lines on her face suggested a life in which there had been considerable wear and tear.

We found her among a group of women who were all using their fingers to stir things in shallow brass bowls suspended over small charcoal fires. It looked dangerous, and when, at Sterry's bidding, Madge left her work and washed her hands in a nearby basin, I saw old burn scars on her fingers.

Sterry led us back to his office to talk. 'Sit down, Madge,' he said. 'Don't worry about your work. This business is official. This lady is Mistress Ursula Stannard, and at the queen's wish, she is enquiring into something that happened many years ago. I'm sure you remember how, when you were young and new to the castle, a man called Peter Hoxton died mysteriously. You were a witness of some importance. Indeed, I believe it was you who found him in a state of desperate illness in the first place.'

Madge, who had been looking puzzled, brightened. 'Oh yes, Master Sterry, 'course I remember. Who'd forget a thing like that? I never saw aught like it! I was that frightened.'

'I'm sure you were. Well, will you tell Mistress Stannard here all about it? Every detail that comes to your mind.'

Madge shot a scared glance at me.

'It's all right,' I said gently. 'No one wants to catch you out. Don't be afraid! A man called Gervase Easton was accused, and his son wants to know more about it. I have said I'll try to find out for him; that's all.'

'Go on, Madge,' said Sterry reassuringly, and Madge, after swallowing nervously, did as she was told.

It was the most dreadful thing she had ever encountered. Madge Dyer was only sixteen, and she had come to the Windsor kitchens to work in the Spicery barely two weeks before, straight from the shelter of her very respectable family. This was far outside her youthful experience, and she had no idea what to do about it.

Maids and lads as far down the hierarchy as she was were often sent on errands not directly connected with their official department in the royal kitchens. They were merely pairs of hands and pairs of legs, to go here, go there, fetch this, collect that, take this to so and so and do it yesterday because you're also needed in three other places now this minute. Madge, seized upon to fetch used dishes from an ailing man's room, because his manservant had gone into the town to buy more medicine for his employer, hadn't dared to protest, but she went upstairs very nervously.

She had her reasons. To begin with, the territory above stairs was strange to her and she was afraid she wouldn't be able to find the right room. She was also afraid that if she did find it, it might contain something alarming. Master Peter Hoxton was not just a Clerk Comptroller, which was in her eyes a very exalted being; he was also a man with a reputation. The word among the maidservants was that he couldn't keep his hands to himself and that if he had a real fancy for a girl, she'd better say yes or she might find herself mysteriously out of a job. His only merit, according to the other women, was that he never got anyone into trouble.

In fact, she found the way easily, though she was puzzled by some curious thuds and bangs from behind the door which she thought must be Hoxton's. The kitchen hand who had directed her had said that there was a tapestry of a hunting scene on the opposite wall, and that seemed to be right. The noises were growing louder. What on earth could Master Hoxton be doing? Doubtfully, she went to knock.

Before she could do so, however, the door was flung open and Hoxton burst out of it. Madge recognized him, but only just, since he was completely naked, and with his face flushed to crimson and his eyes so huge and dark, he looked wild enough to belong in a menagerie.

Madge shrieked and recoiled, appalled by the blatancy of him: the dark fur on his chest and arms; the unconcealed privates; the spittle in his fringe of black beard. He stopped short and stared back at her with those enormous eyes.

'Don't go in there. The ceiling's coming down! It'll squash you flat!' he shouted. He then plunged past her, seized the wall hanging in two very hairy hands, made a noise like an animal snarling, and ripped it off the wall, rending the fabric and splintering the panels as the nails which had held the tapestry in place were torn out. The hanging fell in a heap on to the floor, whereupon he snatched it up, threw it away along the corridor, and whirled round. Thinking he meant to attack her, Madge reeled back in fright, but his target this time was a wall sconce just above his door. He grabbed hold of it and tried to wrest it off the wall.

The stout iron bracket withstood him, and with another snarl he rushed back into his room, knocking Madge impersonally aside and causing her to crash into the doorpost. Clutching at the post, gasping and petrified, she caught a glimpse of the room's interior. And then, for several moments, gaped at it, as much in astonishment as fear.

The ceiling looked perfectly normal, but it was the only thing that did. The place was strewn with items of clothing and also with the bed curtains, which looked as if, like the wall hanging, they had been dragged forcibly down, while the door of the clothes press hung drunkenly, half off its hinges.

A chest settle had been overturned so that the spare coverlet and half a dozen candlesticks which had been stored inside were scattered across the floor as well. Hoxton himself was now tearing the legs off a stool, hurling each in turn across the room. Finally, flinging the mutilated stool away from him, he leapt at the rails which had held the bed curtains and began trying to wrench them loose.

And then, abruptly, stopped short and was sick.

Occasionally, even Madge's healthy family ate things which didn't agree with them, or overindulged in times of plenty. She knew about vomiting. Sufferers usually huddled over a basin and threw up miserably; they didn't stand upright and spew in a hideous arc like the contents of a hurled bucket. At this ghastly spectacle, Madge screamed aloud and fled. She fell over the tumbled heap of tapestry, got up sobbing, and then just ran and ran.

This time, she did lose her way in the unfamiliar upper regions of the castle, until one of the White Staves, the noble and godlike beings who oversaw the counting house and the organization of the royal household, found her wandering tearfully in an upstairs gallery, where no maid from any part of the kitchens had any business to be, and pounced on her.

'You're a wench from the Spicery. I know from the colour of your dress. What are you doing up here?'

Madge, much alarmed by his height, his velvet gown, gold chains, white stave of office and the menacing grip on her arm, which prevented her from placating him with curtseys, gasped out her story.

'His name? The sick man, who is he? I can't send help unless I know. Come, come, girl,' said the White Stave, and then, realizing that she was terrified and that his own majestic mien was making things worse, eased his grip and softened his voice. 'Don't be afraid of me. I am William Paulet, Lord

St John, Master of the Household. Tell me who is ill and I will see something is done.'

'Master Peter Hoxton, sir. He's a Clerk Comptroller, sir. Oh sir, he's . . . I think he's out of his mind! He might kill someone! And such sickness; I never saw the like . . .!'

'I will deal with it. Go back to the Spicery and go on with your duties. You have done nothing wrong.'

'But sir, I can't find the way back! I'm lost!'

Paulet, now patting her arm kindly enough, steered her rapidly to the head of a narrow staircase and pointed down it. 'Turn left at the foot of that, and you'll know where you are. Off with you, now.'

And after that, her responsibility was over, except that later on, when they knew that Peter Hoxton was dead and that the physician was talking about poison, she found herself remembering something that worried her, and she nervously told one of the upper maidservants about it, who passed on the information to one of the sergeants of the Spicery, who at once spoke to a Comptroller, who spoke to Paulet, and much to her distress, Madge found herself in Paulet's office, standing before the great man once again, to answer questions. Concerning a man she had seen on the day of her frightening encounter with Hoxton. A man she had seen putting a pie on the tray which held Hoxton's dinner and was waiting to be collected by his servant.

'It were all just awful,' Madge said, after getting that far with her story. 'Awful. Awful! I won't ever forget it, no I won't!'

Clearly, she hadn't. The shock had been too great. She had been young and inexperienced, and she had never seen a naked man before, let alone a naked man apparently in an advanced state of insanity, and Hoxton's reputation had scared her anyway.

'A reputation he certainly had,' said Sterry. 'He was a womanizer; there's no doubt about that.'

'A young woman like Judith Easton was likely to attract his notice, then?' I asked.

'Very likely! That was the reason why her husband killed him, or so it was said. In fact, with Judith . . .'

'Yes?' I said.

Sterry was frowning. 'It was odd. Mostly, if a girl refused him – and there were those that did – he'd resent it, but he'd turn easily enough to somebody else. But with Judith Easton . . . He behaved as if he were really besotted. Madge, go on with your tale. Tell us about this man you saw putting something on Hoxton's tray.'

Madge hesitated.

'What is it?' I asked.

'Well . . . it'd be easier to show you, like. Show you where things happened and that.'

I glanced at Sterry, who nodded. 'All right,' I said to Madge. 'Can you show us now?'

Madge nodded and led the way, back through the pestle room, through the main kitchen and into a short passage with small rooms on either side, most of them with wide doorways and no actual doors. People carrying supplies in and out, usually with both hands occupied, needed elbow room but could well do without latches.

At the far end, the last two rooms, one on each side, contained shelves where food had been set to cool because it was to be served cold. One had an array of custards and blancmanges, while the other had cuts of meat on wide dishes.

'There are no flies to worry about at this time of year,' Sterry remarked. 'In summer, everything has to have covers or thin cloth over it, otherwise the place fills up with bluebottles.'

'Back then,' Madge said, pointing, 'there was a table there, in that room where the meat is now. While Master Hoxton was ill, his food was put on the table, ready for his man to take. There'd be a tray with dishes on it, covered, and a jug of something with a glass or a tankard alongside. I saw his tray put here on that day – just on noon, it was.'

'How did you come to be here, if you were working in the Spicery?' I asked.

'Well, at that time, the Spicery was through there, to the left.' Madge pointed on ahead to where the passage met a broader one, which crossed it at a right angle. 'I was bringing a tray-load of bowls with spices in, from there to the big kitchen we've just come through. The kitchen wasn't different, just the Spicery. I nearly bumped into a fellow coming from the kitchen with another tray, and he said to be careful, to look where I was going, this was Master Hoxton's dinner.'

'What was he going to eat?' I asked.

Madge shook her head. 'I don't know. It was all under covers.'

'I can remember,' said Sterry. 'I ought to, with all the questions that were asked. Some sort of coney stew, and an egg custard. The man was sick, but mending by then. Getting his appetite back. Then, later, Madge was sent to fetch the used dishes—'

'But I never did. I just forgot all about them when . . . when . . .' Her eyes grew round, thinking about it.

'Quite,' Sterry said. 'And there in the room was a bit of pie that he'd left, a pie that was never made in these kitchens. Paulet fetched help to Hoxton's room – that included me – and we were trying to quieten him when his manservant came back. We sent him off again to find a doctor, and while he was gone, someone found a physician in the castle, tending someone else, so in the end we had the two of them.

'The first one smelt the pie and said the berries weren't bilberries, whatever else they were, and the second one, when he arrived, knew it for deadly nightshade straight away. Children eat the berries sometimes, not realizing they're dangerous. They can make people mad, and make them see things. Poor Hoxton went mad, right enough, and thought he saw the ceiling coming down on him, too.'

'That's horrible,' I said.

'There was nothing that anyone could do,' Sterry said. 'The doctors got people to hold him down, and they tried salt water to make him empty his stomach out completely. Then they tried plain water, to wash out the stomach the other way, so to speak, and then charcoal in water. That's supposed to help with poison cases. But it was no use. He fell into a lethargy, and within two days he was gone. Well, Madge, tell Mistress Stannard the rest.'

'There ain't much more,' Madge said. 'Only, on my way back from the kitchen to the Spicery, I saw the tray still on the table and I saw a man put something extra on it. I didn't know who he was. I couldn't even see him that well. There was sunlight coming through the window, and there was a shaft of light, like, between me and his face. I mean—'

'It wasn't Hoxton's manservant?' I asked.

'No, no, it wasn't Master Edwards, that I am sure of. This fellow was a different shape, like. He had a little satchel on his belt, like Master Sterry now . . .'

'I carry a purse and a slate with notes of work to be done in it,' Sterry said.

I nodded. Like many busy men who needed to keep the tools of their trade handy, Sterry had a square leather bag strapped to his belt.

'He was standing looking at Master Hoxton's tray,' Madge said, 'and as I went past, I saw him put his hand into the satchel and take out a little bundle. He pulled off the cloth it was wrapped in. Inside was a small pie, in a dish. He put it on the tray, and then he went away.'

'What did you think he was doing?' asked Sterry.

'It weren't aught to do with me. I was only sixteen and just a skivvy,' said Madge. 'If I thought at all, I'd reckon a dish had been forgotten and he was bringing it.' Her voice became indignant. 'You see someone doing something to a tray, here in a royal kitchen, and you don't say to yourself: ooh, look, that man's putting a poisoned pie there!'

'That's reasonable,' said Sterry.

'I agree,' I said. 'But Madge, can you describe the man in any way at all? Did you think you'd seen him before?'

'Not that I knew. I told all this to Lord Paulet, then.' Madge was far too humble to tell us candidly that she thought we were fools to be enquiring into a murder which had occurred and been apparently solved a quarter of a century ago, but she couldn't quite hide her opinion.

'Tell us what you can,' said Sterry firmly. 'Try to remember.'

'I said, I couldn't see him that well. Shortish, darkish, I thought. Beak of a nose. Funny, I do remember that. He was dressed in brown. That's all I saw. Lord Paulet made me go and stand by some stairs and look at people coming down them and say if I saw him, but I couldn't. Nothing odd about beaky noses! There're dozens of them. I only saw him a moment, down here, and like I said, there was the shaft of light in the way, and anyhow, I didn't stare! It wouldn't be my place. The other woman that saw him, though – she was coming along behind me though I didn't know it then – she said she knew him and it was Master Gervase someone or other.'

'Susannah Lamb, her name was,' said Sterry. 'But where she is now, God only knows. She could be in the next village, or in far Cathay or her grave.'

'What was *she* like?' I enquired.

Unexpectedly, Madge giggled. 'Not like a lamb! More like a great big ox. She cracked two mortars in her day, bashing away with them great big pestles. I was scared of her,' she added. 'Always shouting and booming and making a to-do, she was. *Sounded* like an ox, come to think of it. Used to be someone's housekeeper afore she came here, but I reckon they couldn't stand her bellowing about the place, either.'

I laughed. Mistress Lamb sounded remarkably like one Cecily Moss, who was mother-in-law to my former ward Penelope, the elder sister of the Jane Mason whom Mark so much wished to marry. Cecily Moss had a good heart, though, for all her resounding vocal powers.

'But she recognized the man as Gervase Easton?' Sterry persisted.

'Oh yes, sir. Very definite, she was.'

'Yes, that's what I remember, too. Well.' Sterry turned to me. 'There you are, mistress. Is there anything more you want to ask – or anyone else here you want to meet?'

'Can you yourself remember anything – any small detail that we haven't talked about? You've obviously got a sharp memory.'

Sterry shook his head. 'All I've told you is all I know. Everyone in the kitchens was questioned, of course, but none of them, except for Madge and myself, are still here. They've all retired or died or gone elsewhere.'

'Why wasn't the manservant looked at more closely?'

Sterry looked impatient. 'Because Susannah Lamb said she'd actually seen Gervase Easton put the pie on the tray, and because Edwards was never alone with the food anyway. When he picked it up, I was passing, on my way upstairs on an errand to Paulet's office, and we went up together. I saw him take the tray in at his master's door. I held the door open for him, and I saw him put the tray down on his master's knees. Master Hoxton was in bed, you understand. Then Edwards went off into the town for some medicine or other his master wanted. They were on good terms. There was no earthly reason why Edwards should want to harm Hoxton. He was well paid and treated with great forbearance, considering the way he drank. I'm sorry I can't help you more, mistress.'

'It's all such a blank,' I said. I felt as though I had come up against a wall. I could see no flaw in the case which had been made against Gervase Easton. Voices that might have given me information had been silenced by death or simply faded away into the wide world and been lost in anonymity. 'I can only thank you both for trying to help,' I said.

'Go back to your work, Madge,' said Sterry. 'Here.' There was a clink as he took a couple of coins from a belt pouch and pressed them into Madge's hand. Her face lit up with pleasure, and for a moment the pretty girl she had once been reappeared. The curtsey she gave us was gracious. Then she was gone, and Sterry once more turned to me. 'Mistress Stannard . . .?'

'Yes?'

'You are one of the queen's ladies, mistress. You're near the heart of things. Down here, it's like an ant-heap full of gossip and there are things we all want to know and aren't told. A lot of new supplies are coming in. A whole herd of cattle was driven within the walls this morning, and wagonloads of all kinds of provender keep arriving. I've seen guns being delivered, and barrels of gunpowder. How much danger are we in? Is it true that there's an army marching from the north and the castle may be besieged?'

'I hope not,' I said. 'Lord Sussex, in the north, is moving against them, to cut them off first and then defeat them, or so we all hope. At the moment, there's no danger.'

'Could that change?'

'I suppose it could. We have to wait for news of Lord Sussex's campaign. But there's no cause for alarm yet. The queen is simply – taking wise precautions.' I smiled at him. 'Hoping for the best and preparing for the worst; that's all she's doing.'

He looked relieved. I hoped that his relief would be justified.

FIVE

Artistic Preoccupations

Sterry's unease made me notice things I might otherwise have missed. On my way back to our suite, I passed a barrow-load of casks with *Salt Fish* chalked on them, standing in a passageway while two leather-aproned men stood scratching their heads and saying that they couldn't put that there in the usual place because it was chock-full of casks of meal already and at this rate they'd soon be storing supplies on the roof.

Just after that, having climbed a flight of stairs into a gallery, I came upon a knot of courtiers talking anxiously together, and round the very next corner met two council members with worried faces urgently discussing something as they walked along and I heard the words *ammunition* and *cannon*.

Fear of what might be coming had permeated the whole castle. What was happening in the north could be the seed from which a most terrible crop might spring. In the kitchens, I had been asking questions about a crime which had happened half a lifetime ago. Now, the fate of Peter Hoxton seemed the least important matter in the world.

The moment I entered our suite, though, there was Hugh, asking: 'Did you find out anything useful?'

'Nothing,' I said, collapsing into a settle. 'Hugh, it's a blind alley. I suppose there never was a real chance that I'd learn anything this morning that didn't come out at the time. Gervase's letter may or may not have told the truth; Mark may or may not be right to believe it. We'll never know. Nor will he. How *can* one find out what happened over twenty years ago? Too many of those concerned are dead or gone away to heaven knows where. It just isn't possible.'

'Don't be too disappointed. You did your best.'

'*Hawkswood*!' I said with passion. 'Just for a little while,

I saw a glint of hope, but now that's gone and it all feels worse than it did before.'

'We'll get over it. One does get over things,' Hugh said. 'Now, I have things to tell you. First, I've seen Arbuckle – Brockley took me there – and I think he's the man we want. Then we came back, and now,' said Hugh regretfully, 'I'm sorry to say that for some reason Brockley and Fran Dale seem to be quarrelling.'

'About Arbuckle?' I said, puzzled.

'I don't see why they should. But I certainly heard raised voices from their room a moment ago – listen! There they go again!'

I got up and made for the Brockleys' chamber.

I found all apparently in order. The room was warm, with a good fire in the hearth. Dale was repairing a torn sleeve of mine, sitting by the window to stitch by daylight. On the other side of the room, with a branch of candles to eke out the grey light of this dismal morning, Gladys was darning stockings with an air of minding her own business. Brockley was grimly brushing one of Hugh's cloaks. He and Dale, however, were not looking at each other, and I had just heard them shouting.

'Is something wrong?' I asked.

'I'm sorry, ma'am,' said Dale in a whisper.

'Our apologies,' said Brockley. 'It isn't important.'

I began to say something about Arbuckle, but Brockley started to shake his head before I reached the end of the sentence.

It was Dale, plunging her needle fiercely into the green satin of the sleeve, who explained. 'It's not to do with Master Arbuckle, ma'am. But Roger says he wishes he could join Lord Sussex's army! Did you ever hear the like?'

'I seem, madam,' said Brockley, 'in the last nine or so years, since I entered your service, to have accustomed myself to being useful in times of emergency. It feels odd, at a time like this, to be doing nothing. If I could volunteer . . .'

'Please don't, Brockley. I value your services far too much.'

'And I'm thankful that we're not all riding north to risk our lives prying into secrets!' Dale snapped.

I considered them both thoughtfully and with compassion.

The three of us had seen many adventures in our years together. The Brockleys had been my comrades in the sometimes dangerous tasks I had carried out for the queen and Cecil. The tasks weren't usually meant to be dangerous, but I seemed to have a regrettable instinct for going beyond my instructions and pressing on when it would have been wiser to turn back and leave the work to others.

I had brought my servants into peril along with myself, all too often. In France, Dale had once found herself in a dungeon, threatened with a charge of heresy. In a Welsh border castle, Brockley and I had once been shut in a dungeon too, and that was an embarrassing memory, for that night we had come close, so close, to crossing the divide between lady and steward and becoming lovers.

I had never spoken of that episode to anyone, but my second husband, Matthew, had sensed the hidden thing between Roger Brockley and myself and been jealous. The same was true of Dale. Yet she had always been faithful. She had complained a good deal (with reason) about the hardships I inflicted on her; she had been at times frightened, exhausted and ill; but she had never failed either me or Brockley. As for Brockley himself, I knew he deplored what he felt was my unfeminine thirst for adventure, and yet he had a strongly adventurous streak himself, which always surfaced when called upon.

'I won't volunteer, madam,' he said. 'Not if you ask me to stay.'

'If *I* ask him to stay,' said Fran furiously, 'he just tells me I don't understand.'

'Fran, I wouldn't go without your consent and you know it,' said Brockley. 'But if only you *did* understand. I think the mistress does, even though she still wants to keep me here.' He looked at me, still holding Hugh's cloak. 'Madam, I was a soldier once, as you know, back in the days of King Henry. When I was twenty-nine years old, I was on campaign in France. I'm fifty-four now and I notice it, but the further away the past gets, the more vivid the memories become. Sometimes, I long to be on a campaign again and I think to myself: soon

I shall be too old. I long for just one more chance to – yes, to see action again.'

'Anyone would think he'd been sleeping in the full moon,' lamented Dale. 'Men are just not *reasonable*.'

'You're mourning your lost youth?' I said to Brockley. 'Is that it?'

'Lost youth and lost comrades, I suppose, madam. That fellow of Cecil's, John Ryder – you know the one?'

'Yes, of course.' Ryder, a retainer in Cecil's employ, had accompanied us on more than one of our missions. He was about Brockley's age and had changed little since I first met him, seven years ago now. I had seen him the previous summer, and except that he was now completely grey instead of partially, he still looked the same, fatherly and reliable. I liked him; we all did.

'I'm as sure as I can be that I met him in France, in King Henry's army. He was a captain there. We had a mutual acquaintance, a Cornish fellow called Trelawny, Carew Trelawny. It's odd. I haven't thought of him for years, but somehow he's been in my mind lately. He was the most resourceful man I ever came across. When we lost touch with our supply wagons once on a march through France, we had to camp out in a wood, in the wet, and make ourselves rough shelters. He had a knack of looking at a tree and saying: *That branch is the right shape for a ridge pole already; all we have to do is lop it.* He'd seen what the rest of us hadn't. And there was the time the mule harness broke on one of the wagons. It was rotten old harness; even knotting it up wouldn't have been any use . . .'

Brockley's voice tailed off a little, and his eyes by now were reminiscent. He was looking back into the past, into his youth. Then he focused on me again and smiled his rare smile. 'But we were near a cottage where someone was growing peas. There were pea-sticks, fixed together with a strong twine, quite a lot of it. Carew saw it straightaway, and in a trice he was over the fence and grabbing the twine. It repaired the harness well enough to get us to the nearest leather-worker. Though,' Brockley added, 'next day, after a skirmish, an old biddy called him all the names under the sun – in French, of course – because he stole a shirt she'd hung to dry on a bush in her garden, so as to make bandages in a hurry.'

'I can't help feeling,' I said, 'that your friend Trelawny may have made himself unpopular with some of the French peasantry! After all, there was one poor man trying to grow peas, to help feed his family, no doubt, and another poor woman trying to keep her husband's clothes clean, and he just walks up and seizes their things!'

'True,' said Brockley. 'But he did have a way of seeing that things made for one purpose can work just as well for another. It came in useful time and again. They were grand days.'

'You're a fraud, Brockley,' I said. 'You are always telling me that I should live a quiet and dignified life, and all the time you're secretly hankering to go on campaign in the rain and steal things from peasants' gardens.'

'Well, there's this,' said Dale, still stitching furiously. 'You've said now that you won't go if I'm against it, and I am! I'll be down on my knees this evening, thanking God for it.'

'Don't thank him too soon,' said Brockley with another sudden grin. 'You never know!'

We were interrupted just then as Hugh came in. 'I think,' he said, 'that it's time to give Meg a rest from her studies. She's translated quite enough Latin for one day. Arbuckle would like to see her, and why not now? Before I went to find him, I called on the gentleman whose wife he has just painted and saw the picture. I was impressed. It was as good as that miniature that Mark Easton showed us – rather like it, on a bigger scale. Arbuckle isn't cheap, but I think he could be worth what he charges. Shall we rescue Meg and set off at once?'

Meg, who had been at her books all morning, was glad enough to leave off, and Dr Lambert, who wasn't young, also looked thankful. In return for taking a note to Mark, giving a brief account of my interview with Sterry and Madge, I gave Lambert the rest of the day off and instructed Dale to brush Meg's hair and help her into a fresh gown.

'Something bright,' I said. 'The orange-tawny, I think.' Meg's dark colouring always rewarded lively hues. 'After all, we're going to introduce her to a portrait painter.'

Except for Gladys, who preferred to stay where she was and not struggle with the stairs ('No better than a ladder, they are, and no good to my old legs'), we were all curious to see a portrait painter on his own territory. We set off in a body: Hugh, Meg and myself, Sybil and the Brockleys, who were interested enough, thank goodness, to put aside their quarrel. Indeed, their interest was greater than mine. I kept thinking of the fear which now haunted the castle and my own unsuccessful efforts to carry out Mark Easton's commission, and I did not look to Master Arbuckle either to help or hinder. He had nothing to do with any of my anxieties. I think I hoped that visiting him might divert me a little, let my mind rest from my troubles awhile.

Which it did, or so it seemed then. It was quite some time before I understood that fate was going to entangle Master Arbuckle very thoroughly in the northern rebellion and the affairs of Mark Easton, and that as I walked with the others along Peascod Street towards this first meeting, I was taking the first steps on a very perilous road.

Peascod Street was and is a long, busy, narrow thoroughfare leading south into the town from the castle's Lower Ward. Master Arbuckle had taken the upper floor of a house halfway along. 'The landlady is a Mistress Browne,' said Hugh as Brockley went to knock.

The door was opened by a faded wisp of a woman who turned out to be Mistress Browne herself. 'Ah, Master Stannard again. Master Arbuckle's expecting you. He's upstairs as usual. Getting ready.'

Her voice had a resigned note. 'Is he a difficult tenant?' I asked. Whereupon, in a flood of speech, she proceeded to tell us just how difficult Master Jocelyn Arbuckle was.

'He pays regular, I grant you that, and his manservant does for him and has all his own utensils, so I don't have to cook or even lend pans, just let the fellow use the kitchen fire. But the *mess*!' She flung up her hands. 'Paint on the floor, and how I'll ever get it off when he leaves . . . and there goes that hammering *again*.'

A banging noise had begun upstairs. 'He does that now and then,' said Mistress Browne exasperatedly, 'and what he's about, I can't think. Making nail-holes in my walls by the sound of it.'

'He does fine work, mistress,' Hugh said mildly. 'I've seen the portrait he's just finished.'

'Oh no doubt, no doubt, but such a disturbance – and the way he goes about it. I've had artists here before, and they weren't like this. The man has all manner of gadgets – silver hoods for candles, to make their light brighter, and mirrors and –' here her pale brown eyes widened and her voice dropped to a near whisper – 'he uses a magic glass!'

'A what?' I asked, puzzled.

'Well, that's what I call it. He's got a glass hanging up that gives me the creeps to look at it. It's not like a mirror; it's got something about it,' said Mistress Browne, 'that makes me think of an *eye*. Witchcraft, that's what I'm afraid it is, and I cross myself, always, before I go into that room. I dursen't say aught to him; he scares me, and that's a fact. I wouldn't let him paint a picture of me, not for any gold sovereigns, no I wouldn't.'

Hugh and Brockley were both impatient with superstition. Hugh, sensing Brockley's irritation, grinned at him in a silent permission to speak, and Brockley addressed the landlady sternly.

'Master Arbuckle,' he said, 'is a man of reputation and has been in his profession for many years. There can't be much amiss with him. Now, may we go up?'

Intimidated, the faded Mistress Browne turned towards a steep wooden staircase and led the way to the floor above.

The hammering, which had ceased while Brockley was talking, broke out again as we climbed. We emerged into a room furnished, decently enough, as a bedchamber, though some shelves next to a door on the opposite side held an array of the silver-hooded candlesticks the landlady had mentioned, along with half a dozen mirrors on stands and bundles of candles. They were all being shaken by the hammering.

Mistress Browne went across to it and knocked, loudly, so as to be heard above the racket. 'Master Arbuckle? The Stannards have brought their daughter!'

'Then let them enter!' called a muffled voice from inside. 'Door's not locked!'

We went in, and Mistress Browne's exasperation was now explained. We had passed on the instant from order to chaos. As we soon came to realize, Jocelyn Arbuckle was an artist whose gifts made him a close rival to the legendary Hans Holbein. He was also, assuredly, the untidiest artist in England, if not Europe.

A trestle table stood before us, under the front window. It was laden with a wild clutter of dishes and bottles and jars, some containing vivid pigments, others full of more mysterious liquids, some with brushes steeping in them. Stained, crumpled cloths lay about, and there was a pestle and mortar, a set of scales and a measuring jug. A number of these assorted objects had overflowed the space on top of the table and were now dotted about on the floor beside it, like an advancing army. Table and floor were indeed copiously splashed with paint, and the air was full of an odd smell, a mingling of the exciting and the soothing, compounded, I thought, of pigments and oils.

There was little other furniture, but there was a stool under a side window and an easel beside it. A folding screen made of wooden panels, painted black, was propped against one wall, while in a corner were some spindly ironwork tables, stacked roughly into a pile.

Beside them, the strange glass which the landlady had mentioned was poised on top of a thin metal stand. It was a lens of some sort, I thought, a thicker version of the lenses which are put into eyeglasses. It did indeed resemble an eye. I wondered what it was for.

The place wasn't cold or gloomy. A lively wood fire burnt in a hearth to our right, with a wood-basket and a stout fire-guard at hand, and the room was bright, because even as we were climbing the stairs, the sun had come out and light was streaming through the side window. It illuminated the muddle on the work table rather well.

Finally, there was Arbuckle himself. He had been nailing a large sheet of white paper to the folding easel, and he had a hammer in his grasp and a row of nails in his mouth, which explained why his voice had been muffled. Master Arbuckle was not prepossessing; nor was he any tidier than his studio. He was tall and lanky, with small dark eyes, badly combed grey locks and a scruffy grey beard adorning a long chin. His gown was made of cheap material, probably from choice because he obviously had no intention of looking after it. It was basically dark, but like the floor and the table, it was splashed with paint. There were even flecks of paint in Arbuckle's beard.

He nodded at us, and then, seeing Meg, his gaze sharpened. He put a last nail to a corner of the paper, hammered it quickly home, swept the other nails out of his mouth and said, in a voice which was deep and vigorous for a man of his obvious years: 'Welcome. Is this the young lady? Bring her into the light. Such as it is,' he added sourly, apparently not impressed by the efforts of the winter sun. 'The climate of England should be forbidden by law.'

Meg came forward a little timidly, curtseying. I understood why his landlady had said she dursen't say aught to him. For all his unkempt appearance, Arbuckle had presence. To Meg, I said encouragingly: 'Don't be nervous, my dear. Slip your cloak off. That's right.'

'Over here,' Arbuckle said as he led her to where the sunlight could fall on her face. He pushed the window open, to get rid of the shadows from the square leads.

'Ah,' he said, in tones of satisfaction.

Meg was very much her father's child, with Gerald Blanchard's square features and brown eyes rather than my pointed chin and hazel eyes. As an adult, she would have a strong face, but it would be beautiful too. In the last year, delicate hollows had appeared under the cheekbones, and if the square little chin was more resolute than some people might say was desirable in a young girl, it was finely modelled, and her mouth was shapely.

Her colouring was warm. She loved the open air, and in summer it was no use telling Meg to keep out of the sun so as to preserve a fashionable pallor. She would walk and ride whenever she had the chance, and always her face bronzed a little, with a soft rose glow on each of those strong cheekbones, and her neat little nose would peel.

I truly adored my Meg and her emerging beauty, but I rarely spoke of it to anyone except Hugh because after all, as her mother, I thought I was bound to be biased. Here, however, was someone who had instantly seen what I saw, and appreciated it. He had with great skill positioned her perfectly, so that the light could pick out the planes of her young features and find the gloss in the waves of hair which Dale had carefully arranged in front of her cap.

'Delightful,' said Master Arbuckle, holding Meg's chin and turning it slightly to the left. 'And with character. It is hard work to depict sitters who have none. Or else the wrong kind, which they want to conceal, and then they resent my painting because I have seen what they would rather I didn't. When my brush is in my hand, I cannot lie. With this young lass, I'll have no need for lies. This is the dress you wish her to wear?'

He glanced at Hugh first, but Hugh said: 'Meg is my stepdaughter. Ursula?'

'Yes, that's the dress,' I said.

'And how will you have her shown?' Seeing that Meg was cold, he closed the window. 'Standing? Seated? With a book in her hand, or some stitch-work?'

'At a table, writing,' I said. 'Meg is studying Latin and Greek, and she does well at them. We want a picture which will help us, in years to come, to remember her as a young girl at her studies.'

'I wish it were summer,' said Arbuckle. 'I see her in my mind, seated by an open window, with trees visible outside and the sunlight streaming in. Perhaps I can create such a picture even now, with December just round the corner. Would that please you?'

'You can do that?' Hugh asked.

'I think so.' He kept his eyes on me. 'I have no example of my work here at hand, Mistress Stannard, but I believe your husband has seen one. I am a capable craftsman. I also use the finest materials. I create my ultramarine myself from genuine ground-down lapis lazuli. I grind it myself in that pestle and mortar there. I have my own formulae for certain other colours too, and they are therefore unique – and subtle. I believe,' he said, 'that I can do your daughter justice. And I see her, as I said, by a window, in June. I see it so vividly that I think I can paint the vision.'

With a pang, I thought of our houses, of Withysham and Hugh's beloved Hawkswood. In each, there was a room which I used as a study for Meg because the view outside was so pleasant. So often, in summer, I had sat watching her at her books, seated by an open window, with fields of corn and tree-grown hills beyond.

I was homesick. I wanted to go home – to one of our homes; either would do, though for Hugh's sake, my preference just now would be for Hawkswood. I wanted it so much that twice, during my sojourn in the castle, I had suffered from migraine, a condition which was apt to descend on me whenever I was unhappy or torn. At that moment the prospect of the war in the north not only frightened me, it also filled me with hatred.

I hated the rebellious northern earls, and Mary Stuart, and the Duke of Norfolk, whose idiotic notion of marrying her, helping her to resume her Scottish crown and putting a royal consort's crown on his own foolish head, had started all the trouble. They were keeping me and Hugh from our own homes and our own lives, robbing my husband of what was all too likely to be his last chance to enjoy Hawkswood, and I loathed them all, with a passion which verged on the murderous.

I pulled my mind back to the present and realized that Arbuckle, a stranger, had taken one look at Meg and not only recognized her beauty, but also understood how best to set it off. I could almost believe that he had picked the image out of my mind. He was indeed the right artist to paint her, and when he had done so, I would have *Meg, by a window in summer*, to look at all my life, long after she had grown into a plump married dame with children of her own.

'It would please me,' I said. I looked at Hugh. 'Do you agree?'

'Indeed I do,' Hugh said.

Arbuckle nodded. 'Since we now have sunshine of a sort, your daughter's first sitting can be at once, if you so wish. I'll need the window open again, but she can wear a cloak, or two if she likes. It's her face I want to capture first.'

SIX

Paint and Embroidery

'I truly hate England,' said Arbuckle, dragging the folded screen into the centre of the room and partially opening it. It had feet and would stand firmly even if opened out straight, like a movable wall. In the middle of it was a large square aperture. 'I went to Florence as a young man and spent years there, and I wish I were there still. Ah, the light! The strong sunlight that one can harness! A thousand curses on these pitiful northern skies, say I!'

'Why did you leave Florence, then?' Hugh asked him.

'Because I came home now and then to see my parents in Hereford, while they were still alive, and they drew me to the Reformed religion,' said Arbuckle, now dismantling the stack of spindly tables. 'Then the Italian states weren't safe any more. You can get arrested for heresy too easily. When Queen Mary was on the English throne, I went to Flanders. The light there is nearly as bad as it is here. To hell with this table; why won't its legs stay at the length I want them? Sometimes I think gadgets have minds of their own . . .'

There were three of the curious tables, and their thin legs were adjustable. Having set their heights to his satisfaction, Arbuckle motioned to Meg to sit on the stool, put the tables here and there close to her, opened the window again and was staring at the whole thing critically when his manservant, who had evidently been out, appeared with a basket of provisions. Arbuckle promptly barked at him to set them down. 'And bring me some candlesticks – no, I think the sunlight will last awhile. I'll use that, pitiful though it is. I'll get an image of some sort, however faint it is. At least God gave me good eyesight. Bring me four mirrors instead.'

The manservant, a placid fellow, clearly accustomed to his employer's peremptory manners, did so. Arbuckle gave Meg back her cloak, arranged the mirrors on their stands and set them on the tables. Having done so, he swore, removed them all again, dumped them on the floor and once more changed the height of the three spindly tables.

Then he moved Meg and her stool, cursing under his breath, and put the mirrors back on the tables. Meg screwed up her eyes and protested as a shaft of reflected sunlight dazzled her, and with a muttered apology, he adjusted the angle of one mirror. After that, he opened the screen out completely, setting it between Meg and the rest of us. Meg, sitting obediently on her stool and clearly as puzzled as we were, could just be glimpsed beyond the aperture.

Next, he fetched the iron stand with the lens attached to it, positioned it in line with the aperture, closed the shutters of the windows overlooking the street and blocked out the firelight with the fireguard, so that on our side of the screen we were in near darkness. After that, he stood there muttering further imprecations, apparently against the English winter, before squeezing round the end of the screen and once more altering the positions of Meg and the mirrors.

When he had finished, we found that, reasonable people though we were, we could see Mistress Browne's point. It really did look like a magical trick. After shuffling the equipment about interminably and rearranging Meg several times, he had her sitting between the side window and the screen, half-facing towards the aperture. Where the sun did not touch her face directly, the mirrors reflected it instead. While the sunshine lasted, her features would be clearly lit.

The easel with the sheet of paper nailed to it had been carefully positioned, and so had the stand with the lens. To our amazement, the brightly lit view of Meg's upper half, through the square opening, was somehow reflected from the lens on to the paper, where it appeared faintly but visibly, and upside down.

'Horrible,' said Arbuckle disgustedly, picking up a thin wooden cylinder and a knife from the work table and, to my surprise, beginning to sharpen the cylinder. 'I can scarcely see it. This *accursed* climate!'

'What is that you're sharpening?' Sybil asked with interest.

'A modern device called a pencil,' Arbuckle told her. 'It isn't as messy as charcoal. It is made of plumbago and clay, in a wooden casing. Now!' Marching to the paper, he began to trace the lines on the paper with the point of the pencil. He worked, I saw, at tremendous speed and with the assurance that is the signal of the expert.

I said: 'But you can only see the top part of your sitter. We would want to show her right hand, and a desk . . .'

'I make studies of each section separately and then combine them all in the finished work. I can seat my subjects higher, by setting the stool on top of boxes, so as to bring, say, a desktop or the sweep of a skirt into view. For a while she will have to do without the cloak while I work on the upper part of her dress, for instance. This is just a way of obtaining fine detail, so that the final result is exact. If the sun goes in, I am reduced to candles in silver hoods. Bah! And now, if you please, let one of the ladies remain here with Meg but the rest of you should leave. It distracts me to have so many people in the room while I work.'

'I'll stay,' said Sybil.

The rest of us, dismissed like schoolchildren at the end of our lessons, left the house and walked slowly back up Peascod Street towards the castle. A couple of wagons overtook us: one laden with live pigs and hens in coops; one full of guns and boxes presumably of ammunition.

Observing these things depressed us all. In silence, we made our way to our suite where we found that Gladys had gone out after all, enticed no doubt by the sunshine, even though it meant negotiating the spiral steps. As we were taking off our cloaks, we heard footsteps coming up, but they were too brisk and too heavy to be those of Gladys. Hugh went to meet them and reappeared with Mark Easton, who bowed, accepted some ale which Dale drew for him from our cask, and then said: 'I came to find out . . .'

'More about my efforts this morning?' I said.

'Well, yes. Your note said you'd spoken to a man called Sterry and to one of the actual witnesses, but that you had learned nothing that was likely to be of use.'

'That's true, I'm afraid,' I said, 'and I admit, I can think of no further way to make enquiries.'

'Nor I,' said Hugh regretfully.

'Sterry did tell me why the manservant Edwards was never suspected,' I said. 'The witness I spoke to is sure that the man she saw put an extra item on the tray wasn't Edwards. And in any case, he was never alone with the tray and couldn't possibly have tampered with it.'

'I see. But,' said Mark enthusiastically, 'I have had another idea! Since I talked to you first, I've realized that perhaps we, or you, should talk to my stepfather. He might remember something useful. Maybe my mother knew something – not realizing its importance – and maybe she told him about it in the time when they were married. It's possible, isn't it?'

'Possible. Not probable,' I said, feeling sorry for him. He was snatching at straws.

'I'm sure he still lives hereabouts.' Mark refused to be discouraged. 'I'd know if he'd died, I think. Uncle Robert was in touch with him sometimes – in fact, I believe my uncle helped him financially more than once. Aunt Kate told me that. My stepfather wasn't badly off, but he drank – rather as Hoxton's man is said to have done. I can remember *that*,' he added with feeling. 'That's when he'd get violent.'

And for a moment, I saw in him the vulnerable small boy he had once been, afraid of a drunken man who wasn't even his own kin.

But I think my first response to Mark's eagerness was to sink further into the grey depression brought on by the preparations for war and my failure to learn anything useful from Madge or Sterry. Poor Mark Easton wanted our quest to prosper so very very much. So did I, but I had little hope of it, and fear for the future safety of us all was sapping my energy. It was Hugh who said: 'What was your stepfather's name?'

'Bowman. Jonathan Bowman. He was a glover. He had a shop in Windsor, with rooms over the top and a little garden at the back.' Mark's eyes were reminiscent. 'That's where my mother and I went to live with him. People are strange,' he said thoughtfully.

'Strange?' Hugh refilled Mark's tankard and raised an enquiring eyebrow at him.

'My stepfather. He could be hateful, and yet there was another side to him. If someone ordered embroidered gloves from him, he didn't hire an embroideress; he did the work himself and did it beautifully.'

I said: 'You don't know where he's living now?'

'No. In fact, I have just been out in Windsor, searching for him. I called on some of his former neighbours. They remember him, but they didn't know where to find him, though one thought he'd seen Bowman in a tavern a few months ago.'

Hugh said: 'We'll make enquiries of our own. Are you staying in Windsor for a while?'

'Not for long. I must carry the queen's answer back to Lord Sussex, though I hope to return soon, I pray with good news!'

'Amen to that,' I said soberly.

Mark finished his ale, bade us farewell and left. A few minutes later, we heard another set of steps coming up the stairs, slow ones this time, accompanied by a low grumbling and gasps for breath.

'Gladys!' I said.

I went to give her a hand up the last few stairs. I didn't dislike touching her as I had once done. Nowadays, Gladys did at least keep my rules about cleanliness. Nothing could be done about the brown fangs which disfigured her smile (or rather, her leer) but most old people have similar teeth, and if you really looked into her eyes, which were almost black, you could see that even now they had a kind of beauty.

She still had a bad temper, however, though she had given up her former habit of cursing people. She arrived in our room, complaining.

'Why must you have rooms up at the top of a damned old mountain, indeed to goodness?' Gladys was Welsh in origin, had a strong Welsh accent and knew all about mountains. 'Half kills me, it do, clambering up and down those stairs, but if I don't do it now and then I'm just a prisoner up here in this tower, like a princess in a legend.'

'Princess!' said Dale with a snort.

I poured her some wine, which she preferred to ale, and handed her the glass. 'Where did you walk?' I asked. 'On the terrace?'

'Nope. Queen was on the terrace, with all the ladies and gentlemen and those giggly maidens of hers,' Gladys said. 'I went out the other way, to the garden. Then it turned out that her majesty didn't have *all* her fine folk on the terrace with her.'

She let out a lewd chuckle, sipping her wine. 'She's missing one of her giggly girls and a young courtier. Saw the pair in the garden stealing a kiss behind an apple tree, I did. Mind you, I don't spoil sport. Going a bit further than kissing, they were, I reckon. You're not wanted here, Gladys, I said to myself, so I dodged back through the castle and crossed the terrace quick-like and took a walk down as far as that cottage below. And then wished I hadn't; it was such a clamber back up, for my old legs.'

Brockley, who had been standing silently at the window for some time, frowning, made an impatient sound. 'Never mind Gladys' legs, madam. She can rest them now. If we truly wish to help young Master Easton, how are we to find out where this man Jonathan Bowman lives?'

'Bowman?' said Gladys.

We all turned to her. 'Yes, Jonathan Bowman,' said Hugh. 'Do you know anything about him?'

'Course I do,' said Gladys, helping herself to a second glass of wine without being invited. 'He's the old fellow lives in that cottage just below the terrace, where I went to just now. I talk to him once in a while, when I get up the strength to go there. Been talking to him just now. He had a glover's shop in the town, till he got old and retired. Then he moved to that cottage, but his savings weren't enough to live on so he's still a glover on and off and still embroiders the gloves himself. Always seems odd, seeing a man embroidering.'

I looked at Hugh. 'I can't really believe that we'll learn anything worthwhile if we visit this Master Bowman, but I suppose we should.'

'We'll go this afternoon,' said Hugh. 'I'd like to take some part in this myself.'

SEVEN

Never Look Behind You

Bowman's cottage, when Hugh and I walked down to it after dinner, stood like an island in the midst of its heathy hillside. It was in poor repair, with warped window frames and old thatch as tufty as though it had been clawed by a giant cat. The garden was fairly neat, but no garden is much to look at in November.

The man who opened the door to us was surprisingly old. The Easton tragedy had happened over twenty years ago, and the man Judith Easton had then married might well, by now, be past fifty, but Bowman, lined and white-haired, with a small white beard and a pair of eyeglasses perched on his nose, looked nearer to seventy. Judith must have taken a husband much older than herself.

'And who might you be?' he said, not very amiably.

Gladys might enjoy visiting Master Bowman, but we had no idea what Bowman thought about Gladys, who wasn't everyone's choice of visitor. We preferred not to mention her. 'We're friends of your stepson, Mark,' said Hugh. 'Did you know he was in Windsor – in the castle, as a matter of fact? He arrived as a courier from Lord Sussex.'

'Did he? No, I didn't know.' Bowman was brusque and sounded grumpy. 'Haven't set eyes on Mark since he was five. Wouldn't know him if I met him in the street. Heard he was working for Lord Sussex, up north. Thought he was still there. If Mark wants to see me, why isn't he with you?'

We had meant to bring him but found that he had set out for the north immediately after dinner. 'He couldn't find you,' said Hugh. 'We found you today, by lucky chance, but Mark himself has already left Windsor to return to his master. We have come on his behalf.'

'Got business of some sort with me, has he? You say you're his friends. But *who* are you?'

'I am Master Hugh Stannard, and this is my wife, Mistress Ursula Stannard, who is also one of the queen's ladies.'

'Oho! Very exalted company Mark keeps these days, it seems! Courier for Sussex; friends with a queen's lady. You'd best come in.'

He led us into a room which seemed to be a mixture of parlour and workroom. There was a fire, though not a good one, and the place was cluttered, mainly with evidence of its occupant's trade. There were shelves piled with spools of thread, sausage-like rolls of cloth, leather and kidskin, and stone jars of what seemed to be dyestuffs, except for one shelf, beside the hearth, which was stacked with cups and flagons, with a small but beautiful silver salt pushed in at one end and two wine casks stowed on the floor beneath. There were a few seats, but these, too, were littered with evidence of glove-making: pieces of material, more spools of thread, needle cases, pairs of shears and a strewing of snippings. A few half-finished gloves lay here and there.

There was a settle beside the casks, jutting out at right angles to catch such warmth as the fire provided. The settle offered a small amount of unoccupied space, and our host threw himself into it. He adjusted his eyeglasses, gathered up a glove in which a needle was sticking, pulled out the needle and resumed the embroidery our arrival had probably interrupted. His wrinkled hands moved slowly, but with astonishing delicacy. 'Well, sit down,' he said, impatiently. 'What's it all about?'

It is customary, when visitors come, to offer refreshments and also to point out which seats are the most comfortable and remove any obstacles from them. Master Bowman evidently wasn't a slave to custom. He made no move to provide us with as much as a glass of ale, and we ourselves moved bits and pieces off a couple of stools. Hugh put mine by the fire, opposite Bowman, so that I could get warm, though the blaze only warmed one side of me. Watching Bowman as he stitched, I saw that he was so close to the hearth that the fire must surely be scorching the back of the hand that held the needle. Anything is better than cold fingers, though, when one is trying to do embroidery.

Coming straight to the point, Hugh said: 'We are here on behalf of Mark, but also on behalf of two other men, long dead. One of them was Peter Hoxton, who died in the castle in September 1547. The other was Mark's father, the first husband of your wife Judith. He would have been accused of killing Hoxton, except that he drowned himself too soon.'

Bowman paused, needle in hand, and looked sharply up at us through his eyeglasses. His eyes were pale blue, the shade which looks as though it has a layer of water over it. They had no film of age, however. Their gaze was bright and searching.

'I know all about that. Could never stop Judith yearning backwards for that first husband of hers. She always said he didn't do it. Nonsense, I used to tell her; 'course he did. Only a guilty man 'ud go drinking himself silly and then jumping in the river. Hated Hoxton, he did. Whole bloody castle knew that. I had customers there; used to go to the castle to call on the important ones. I met the Eastons and Hoxton there. I knew the whole story. I tried to knock the nonsense out of her, but it was no use. She'd just cry and say Gervase didn't do it, over and over.' He looked at his work again and drew a strand of peacock blue silk carefully through the pale kidskin, completing a complex stitch.

'The point is,' said Hugh, 'that Mark doesn't think his father was guilty. Also, his chances of marrying the girl of his choice are being spoiled by his father's apparent crime. Mark is desperate to clear his father's name.'

'Oh, so that's it.' Bowman snorted. 'Love! When a man goes crazy for a girl, he'll convince himself of anything. But the world's full of pretty girls and every family isn't that particular. You'd have done better to tell him so.' He added another meticulous stitch. 'He's young,' he remarked. 'Young folk in love, they lose their sense of proportion. Done it myself in my time. I always had an eye for a good-looking wench.'

He glanced up and suddenly smiled. A smile can be a very revealing thing. Just as, for a moment, I had caught sight of the pretty girl Madge had once been, now I glimpsed the handsome young man Bowman used to be. Handsome and passionate, I thought. For a brief second, when he smiled, his pale eyes had flashed, as though some bygone emotion had been reawakened. It radiated from him to me, taking me aback. This white-haired creature with the swollen finger-joints even now retained the vestiges of a powerful attraction and a capacity for deep feeling.

Hugh, however, was still talking about Mark. 'He does have some real reasons for believing in his father's innocence,' he said mildly. 'We have undertaken to talk to anyone we can find who was here at the time and may recollect the business, in case, somewhere, we discover a clue that points to someone else as the killer.'

'Judith used to talk like that,' said Bowman. '*No one's tried hard enough to find out who did it. I don't believe that woman that said she saw Gervase putting the poisoned dish there. Gervase just wouldn't.* I got tired of hearing it.'

His attraction promptly vanished. I regarded him coldly, pitying Judith.

Bowman seemed to sense it. 'Think I'm a hard one, do you, mistress? Now let me tell *you* something. It's no good looking back. The dead don't return. And the truth don't change, no matter how much you want it to. Judith didn't want to think her Gervase was a killer; Mark don't want to think his father was, but facts are facts. *Judith*!' Suddenly, he dropped his work on to his knees. 'Oh, dear God. When she used to come into my shop in Windsor, why, I thought then that she was a lovely thing and Gervase a lucky man. I hoped he'd do well or make it up with his family; raise the two of them up in the world. But no, he must needs make a fool of himself and go murdering a rival! Silly fellow!'

I said nothing. Nor did Hugh. Bowman picked up his stitchery again. 'Hard I may seem,' he said, 'but I take the world as it is. Never look behind you, that's what I say, but Judith, she just wouldn't give over looking behind her. Thought when I got her with child that that 'ud make her turn to the future, but no; she loses it before its time and dies herself and didn't even seem to care. I cared for her; I wanted to take care *of* her, but all she could see was Gervase. She only married me for a protector.'

Suddenly, there was bitterness in his voice, and pain, as though he hadn't put the past behind him as well as he pretended.

I said: 'Please, Master Bowman – for Mark's sake, will you try to remember? Did you ever hear anything – did Judith ever say anything – that raised a doubt of Gervase's guilt? That might suggest another name?'

'Nothing. Gervase did it, all right.' The bright gaze lifted from his work again and met mine. 'More than once, when I was up at the castle, I'd seen Hoxton hanging about, hoping to catch sight of Judith, and Easton scowling at him and hurrying Judith away. And you should have seen Hoxton after Easton hammered half the life out of him that time. You know about that?' We nodded. 'Looked as though he'd been trampled by an ox, he did, even after he'd kept out of sight for days.'

'Easton admitted to that,' Hugh said. 'But he also said, in a letter he left for his wife, that a fight was a different thing from a poisoning.'

'With most men, I dare say. But Easton was besotted with Judith. Used to be a lot of laughter about it, in the Antelope where I did my drinking. Oh, it was all known round the town. There was never a word against Judith herself, but folk used to say Easton was a donkey and that Judith was a good woman and Hoxton 'ud tire of his nonsense, sooner or later. But Easton – no, he was crazy with jealousy. A man in that state might do anything. Damn it all, I met Gervase once in the Antelope, around that time. He'd had a fair amount of ale, and he was in a temper because Hoxton had sent Judith a nosegay or something of the kind. He was saying that he'd like to meet Hoxton in a tavern and slip something into his drink, that 'ud stop his nonsense for good and all.'

For a moment, Hugh and I were both silent. Then, however, Hugh asked curiously: 'What were Hoxton and Easton really like?'

Bowman put his head to one side, considering. 'Hoxton was a spry, brisk fellow. Fond of the ladies, and they were fond of him, as often as not. Can't think why. He wasn't tall, and he was as hairy as an ape. Funny creatures, women. Hadn't been a Clerk Comptroller long and was mighty proud of his position.'

'What did he have to do?' I enquired.

'Attend in the counting house sometimes – the Greencloth, they call it. There's a table in the middle with a green baize cloth, so I've heard. He was one of those that signed the lists of dishes and ingredients for the day. He was always talking about his work. Used to travel to buy supplies, as well. Easton was thankful when Hoxton was away. So was Judith, give her due.'

'And Easton?'

'Easton was good-looking enough. Stocky, dark, easy-going most ways. Laughed a lot, but had a temper. Oh yes, he certainly had a temper. The mess he made of Hoxton's face proves that!'

Again, Hugh and I were silent. Bowman, however, continued to be reminiscent.

'The end of it – well, it was just disaster. There was Judith with a little boy and no one to look after the two of them. Poor girl. Couldn't even serve one of the queen's ladies the way she used to because by then King Henry was dead and young Edward was king. We had no queen.'

'I suppose she could have gone home,' I said.

'No, she thought of that. Told me about it, one day when she'd come into my shop for gloves for the child – Mark, that is. I had a shop in the town, you understand. Her dad wouldn't have her back, she said. He was old man Easton's tenant, and it was old man Easton that threw Gervase and Judith out of the place for marrying. He'd have thrown her dad out as well, if he took Judith in.'

'Even though her child was his grandchild?' said Hugh, shocked.

'So Judith said. Well, she seemed to like me – said I was a fine hard-working man; smiled at me. And I more than liked her. While Easton was alive, I'd never have said so, but when she lost him, I let her . . .' Again I heard that note of pain, saw that flash of memory in his eyes. 'Let her put her woman's spell on me. Didn't realize that she didn't know she was doing it. My first wife was dead, a good few years since. I was free. I waited till the new year; then I went courting her. I offered her my hand and heart and my name.'

'And she accepted you,' said Hugh.

He shrugged. 'Yes. I thought she'd come to feel what I did. But she was only looking for security, like most women. I was older than she was; reckon that made her feel I'd be a safe haven.' Here, and somewhat impertinently, he looked from me to Hugh, taking in the fact that I, too, had married an older man. *As you did*, was his wordless comment when his eyes met mine.

I stared at him steadily, and he withdrew his gaze.

'Even when I understood, I thought I'd get her to love me, given a bit of time. Only, I never did. Always Gervase, that's how it bloody was. Always Gervase. And him a killer!' said Bowman with a snort.

Worsted, Hugh and I exchanged glances and prepared to take our leave. As we were doing so, Bowman finally awoke to the fact that he hadn't shown us much in the way of hospitality and apologized for it.

''Fraid I don't have the habits of a good host. Ought to look after the place better than I do. Can't trouble myself with dusting and polishing and most of my food's just something boiled, or thrown in a pan with a lump of lard. I used to have maidservants when I could afford them, but . . . bah! I had three altogether and nicknames for all them – Lazy, Saucy, Lightfingers, that's what I called them. Maybe you'd like a glass of wine?' He pointed to one of the casks. 'I make my own these days, from dandelions. It's cheaper, and that's one thing I *do* bother to do.'

The wine was very palatable. He took down the silver salt, which was elaborate for its size, with four spice trays, and offered us nutmeg or cinnamon to flavour our drinks, though we both preferred them without.

'That's a very charming salt,' I said.

'It was part of my first wife's dowry,' said Bowman, helping himself to wine and adding cinnamon. 'Judith had no dowry to speak of, poor lass, except for her beauty. You're a pretty woman yourself, mistress.' The wine was quite strong, and I rather thought he had been drinking it earlier. It had probably influenced him. 'You've a handsome wife, Master Stannard. Wish I were twenty years younger.'

'Indeed?' said Hugh coldly, and as soon as we had finished our drinks, he made our farewells and fairly dragged me out of the place.

'Sheer impudence!' he said crossly as we made our way back up the lane. 'If Hoxton is supposed to have been a womanizer, I wonder what Bowman was like when he was young? And we've learned nothing. There's no chink, anywhere. Can you see one?'

'No, I can't. It's a wall across the road, every time. We'd do better to stop,' I said miserably. Suddenly, I was near to tears. 'I can't bear to keep on thinking that Hawkswood could be saved if we could find a way through when there *is* no way through!'

'I'm sorry for Mark,' Hugh said. 'This girl he wants to marry – Jane Mason. What's she like? You knew her once, didn't you?'

'She was only about nine, then,' I said. 'A sturdy little thing with pretty brown hair and big grey eyes and the clumsiest hand with an embroidery needle that I ever saw. I was supposed to be teaching stitch-work to the Mason girls, and I swear that Jane stuck her needle into her fingers more often than into her work. Anything Jane tried to embroider usually ended up smeared with blood.'

'However, Mark is in love with her. Couldn't we try to talk the Masons round? Have you thought of writing to them?'

'I could try,' I said. The uphill lane grew steeper, and beside me, Hugh was growing short of breath. I gave him my arm.

Slowly, we continued uphill, helping each other on the way. Once we were indoors, I at once got out my writing things.

We were wasting our time on this hopeless quest. There was nothing new to be learned about the death of Peter Hoxton, and for the sake of Hawkswood – and for these two young lovers, Mark and Jane – I must write to my friend Ann Mason,

Jane's mother, and to George, the eldest son, and try to convince them that whatever had happened in 1547, here in 1569, Mark and Jane should not be kept apart.

Whether Mark would regard that as equivalent to clearing his father's name, and clear our debt for us as well, we didn't know, but we could hope.

EIGHT

Unexpected Harvest

Elizabeth had ordered me and my family to remain in Windsor, but our servants could come and go at will. Brockley took my letter to Jane's mother and brother. Their Berkshire home, Lockhill, was only a day's ride away. He left early one morning and was back by the evening of the following day, tired and muddy from riding in the rain, having slept just one night at Lockhill. Ann Mason and George had asked for time to consider. We must await their messenger.

'I don't hold out much hope, madam,' Brockley said to me with regret. 'They were all good manners and good cheer, but mother and son alike have something unyielding in their natures, and that's the truth.'

The next thing that happened was that Mark himself returned from the north with another budget of news; hopeful for the most part. The insurgent earls of Westmorland and Northumberland had marched south from Durham in the far north-east and arrived at the town of Ripon, where they had had mass said in a church. They had issued wordy proclamations, describing themselves as the principal favourers of God's Word and eulogizing the Duke of Norfolk, who had been arrested when the trouble first broke out, as a martyr and a high and mighty prince. There, however, matters seemed to have halted.

Sussex had mobilized his own men and sent word to the midland sheriffs, who had raised forces from their respective counties to fight for the queen. The resultant army was now a formidable barrier between the insurgent earls and both Mary Stuart and Windsor.

Indeed, it was more than a barrier, for it was moving north towards the insurgent earls. In addition, snow was falling, a hindrance to movement on both sides, but as long as the earls were among the hindered, the south would remain safe.

Another of the northern nobles, the Earl of Cumberland, had declared for the queen, and the rebels would find no sanctuary in his lands, let alone reinforcements. Three powerful cities in the far north of England, Berwick, Carlisle and Newcastle, had also announced that their citizens would support Elizabeth. The wives of Westmorland and Northumberland were said to be beside themselves with fury and urging their husbands to greater efforts, but Sussex's report said that, in his opinion, neither of the earls had half the stomach for war that their womenfolk had, and that the whole lot of them would either be prisoners or would flee into exile before Christmas.

Mark came to see us as soon as he had delivered his message to the queen and Cecil. He repeated his news to us in person and on the whole with optimism. 'My Lord Sussex says all these marchings and proclamations are no more than heat and nothingness, like the hot air above a chimney,' he declared cheerfully. 'I must set forth again soon to fetch whatever is the next news. I shall wear the road between here and York six inches deeper if I go to and fro much oftener.' After that, however, his mien became downcast. He sat in our chamber with his hands dangling between his knees and his good padded doublet hanging on him, as though all the toing and froing had made him lose weight.

'I tried to see Jane,' he said. 'I begged two days' leave and rode across Yorkshire to Tyesdale, where she's living.'

'Is it in good order now?' I asked. 'It was very run down when we were there, before Penelope married Clem Moss. But Clem struck me as a hard-working and competent young fellow.'

'He is. Tyesdale is prosperous. I could almost wish it were not,' said Mark glumly. 'When it comes to finding a husband for Jane, her family have too much choice. They wouldn't let me see Jane. They were polite to me, gave me some excellent French wine and told me, quite kindly, all about the well-off people, good supporters of the queen and with no criminals in their ancestry, who have made approaches on behalf of their sons. The Mosses particularly favour one candidate, I understand.'

'I'm sorry,' I said inadequately.

'Just now,' said Mark, 'most of my rivals are in Lord Sussex's militia. Nothing will happen about their marriages until they're home again. Personally, I almost hope that the earls fight back and that the war in the north drags on and on – given that it stays away from Tyesdale.'

Hugh cleared his throat and said: 'We've written to Jane's mother and brother in Lockhill. We've asked them to relent. Then, even if we can't clear your father's name, you would at least be able to marry. But I also have to say that they haven't yet replied and we aren't hopeful.'

'If they do agree,' Mark said, 'I will honour our contract. That is, if you would not be offended by that.'

With an inward sigh of relief, I said: 'We will discuss that when the reply comes – if it's the right answer.'

'If only it is!' I said to Hugh when Mark had gone. 'I'm sorry for him,' I added. 'I think he's one of the type that fall in love once and for all. Steadfastness is a virtue, but it can be a burden too.'

'Yes. Bowman had a point,' Hugh said. 'Many girls are beautiful, and they don't all have families as particular as Jane's. Time can mend broken hearts, if the owners of the hearts will let it.'

'Hugh, you're a cynic.'

'I'm a realist. You've just called falling in love once and for all a burden. It can even be dangerous. It's possible that Mark's father also fell in love once and for all and so desperately that it drove him to murder. Let us talk of something else. Isn't it time that one of us went to see how Meg's portrait is progressing?'

'I've already said to Sybil that I must go with Meg to the studio one day soon. Sybil says that the whole scene is on canvas now.'

According to Sybil, Arbuckle had created several different arrangements, by which various sections of the whole were lit up and visible through the aperture in the screen, to be caught by the lens and reflected on to the paper.

'He makes a detailed study on the paper, using the reflected images, and then copies them on to the canvas,' Sybil had told me. 'The work on the canvas has begun, but he still needs Meg herself to look at, to help him with further details. And to study her character as deeply as he can, I think,' she had added, perceptively. 'There's no harm in that. Meg's character is all it should be.'

Talking about the portrait did make me feel better. I think it cheered Hugh, as well. We got out our chess set and played three games before supper. I won two of them, and Hugh said: 'You are improving.'

I wasn't so sure. It seemed to me that, these days, Hugh was not as sharp at the game as he used to be, but I didn't say so. 'Just good luck,' I told him. 'And I think you're tired. Let's go to supper and then settle for the night.'

We were coming back from supper when John Sterry accosted us, just at the foot of the stairs. Madge Goodman, he said, wished to talk to me again. She had remembered something that might be of use to me. I could see her at any time in the morning.

I glanced at Hugh and saw the hope in his eyes. I felt it spring up anew in me. Perhaps, after all . . .

'I'll see her as early as I can, tomorrow,' I said.

I worried a little about getting away from the queen the next day, but after chapel she went, as so often these days, to talk with her council, and I made my way unhindered through the labyrinth of the castle and down to the Spicery where I found Sterry checking new supplies in.

'I see that the castle is still being stocked up,' I said, nodding at the pile of small boxes he was counting.

'A little madly, in my view,' Sterry said. He no longer sounded anxious; the news that the danger was receding had no doubt reached him. 'These are all peppercorns. It's an absurd quantity, unless we're expecting to be besieged for a year – or we're planning to grind them up and throw them in the enemy's eyes.'

I laughed, remembering what Brockley had said about his friend Carew Trelawny, who had been good at inventing new uses for pea-stick twine and other people's washing. 'Where is Madge?'

Sterry ticked off a line on the list he was holding and said: 'This way.'

Madge was once more making comfits. Pieces of ginger root were piled on a chopping board beside her, along with a steaming jug of some brown liquid from which arose the smell of hot syrup. In her swinging charcoal-heated pan, she was stirring ginger pieces into pools of syrup. Presumably, comfit-making was her main task. I wondered what it was like, toiling at the same dull job, day after day, with scorched fingers the only break in the monotony. Sterry had said that Madge apparently preferred it to her married life, which was a sorry reflection on her husband.

Madge, however, rosy and neat, deftly working her ingredients, greeted us with a smile, looking as though hers were the only job in the world she wanted to do.

'I've brought Mistress Stannard to see you,' said Sterry. 'Finish that panful and then show her what you showed me this morning.'

'I'm sorry I had to ask you to come all the way down here to see me,' Madge said to me. 'But it's that hard for me to get away, with all this to do, and besides, like before, it's best if I show you what I mean.'

'I'll leave you to it,' said Sterry drily. 'I'd better make sure that ninety boxes of peppercorns aren't accidentally listed as ninety-five. A real disaster that would be. We might find ourselves a few boxes short in ten years' time!'

He went away. Madge removed her pan from its hook, wiped her hands on her apron and then took me through the kitchens, back to the little room from which, over twenty years ago, Hoxton's manservant Edwards had collected his master's fatal dinner.

'See, mistress, it was just here that the table stood where the tray for Master Hoxton was put ready.'

She moved into the little room and with spread arms indicated the size and position of the table. 'It's the queerest thing,' she said to me. 'Even at the time, I made nothing of it. I never thought to mention it. I had a picture in my mind of the man

I saw come in here and put something on that tray, but everyone kept asking me what did he look like, so I only thought about that. I only talked about that. I never thought—'

'Never thought what?' I asked. She was rambling, and it made me impatient, but I used a gentle voice because I could see that she was nervous of my position with the queen and she didn't have Sterry to support her this time. 'Come, tell me.'

She came back to stand beside me. 'I was coming from the kitchens when I saw him. I'd got to about here, where we are now, when I saw this man standing by the table. He was facing this way. I couldn't see his face very well, but like I told you before, he took a bundle from his satchel, unwrapped a cloth from it and there was the pie in its dish. He put it down on the tray.'

I was at a loss, but still carefully patient as I said: 'But what exactly is it you've remembered?'

'Well, it's funny, but after you came to see me the other day, I kept thinking back and seeing the picture in my mind, of what he was doing, and it came up so clear; it was as though I were living all through it again, and then I saw!'

'Saw what?' I said, crushing down quite a strong urge to seize Madge by the shoulders and shake her until she talked sense.

'Well, mistress, that he did nigh on everything with his left hand. I can *see* it in my head. He had the satchel on his *right* hip. He pulled out the bundle and put it down with his left hand and unwrapped it with his left. It's as clear as clear, what I remember, like a picture, only moving. Then he pulled the tray nearer and put the pie on it neatly, like, and all that with his left hand too. And then he folded the cloth up and put it into the satchel with his left hand as well. He was a left-handed man. As sure as I'm standing here or there's a God in heaven, he was left-handed. So if you were trying to find out,' said Madge, 'whether it was one man or another that did it, well . . .'

'Find out which was left-handed,' I said. 'Thank you, Madge!'

I didn't shake her. I gave her a sovereign and a kiss. It seemed that my first visit to the kitchens had planted a seed which had borne an unexpected harvest. At last, at last, a fact. A fact that might, just, help.

NINE

A Picture of the Past

To use my new knowledge, I needed to talk to someone who had known Gervase Easton well. I told all the others what Madge had told me. Bowman might help, I thought, and I suggested that Hugh and I should call on him again.

We could not go that day, for I was on duty with Elizabeth. I had to attend her at a series of audiences which broke off for dinner but resumed afterwards. When they finally finished, Elizabeth decided to study her books. She was in the habit of maintaining her Italian and her Latin by reading works in these languages. I hoped for release, but none came. Elizabeth sometimes studied on her own, but on other occasions she liked to have her ladies close by.

However, there was to be another council meeting the following morning. Hugh and I could go to see Bowman then, I thought. When the next morning came, however, he woke feeling unwell.

He looked ill, too, very grey of skin and very sunken-eyed. Gladys, on hearing his symptoms, at once said she would brew some medicine for him. Gladys was clever with medicines and always had a box of dried medicinal herbs with her. Her remedies were often effective.

He was improving by evening, but Gladys, who said she had seen such illnesses before, insisted that he should remain abed.

'And you're not to visit Bowman without me,' Hugh said. 'Send Brockley! He can ask a simple question, can't he? We only want to know if Easton was left or right-handed.'

I sent Brockley. He was back within an hour, looking put out. 'Bowman, madam, was as useful as a cooking pot made of butter.'

'He can't remember?'

'No, he can't. He has not the least idea. Neither, by the way, has Sterry. I went to the kitchen to see him, too. Oh, I brought you this, madam.' He was carrying a package, wrapped in thin paper, and held it out to me. 'It's a gift from Master Bowman.'

'A gift?' I looked at the package in surprise, while Hugh sat up sharply against his pillows. 'What is it?'

'Gloves, madam. He said he noted the size of your hands during your visit to him and hoped you would like these.'

'Oh.'

I took the little parcel from Brockley and began to undo the cord, but Hugh said: 'Give that here!' and when I went to hand it to him, fairly snatched it out of my hands. 'You don't accept gifts from Bowman.'

'I'm sorry,' I said, startled. 'But . . . can't I even look at them?'

'No,' said Hugh. 'Brockley! Take this package and burn it. Then leave us.'

Obediently, Brockley put the package in the fire and left the room. I stood by the bed, gazing at Hugh in amazement. 'I've never known you jealous before,' I said.

'I love you! And I'm not young and I don't know how long I will still be here to go on loving you. But while I'm here,' said Hugh, 'I'll have no nonsense from the Bowmans of this world.'

I could hardly believe my ears. Hugh was aware of the secret link between Brockley and myself and had never shown the slightest anxiety about it. The only time he had ever worried about my faithfulness had been the previous summer, when, quite by chance, we had learned that my second husband Matthew, who was supposed to have died of plague while I was visiting England a few years ago, hadn't died at all. The queen and Cecil had deceived me because they wished to keep me in England.

Understandably, Hugh had wondered then if I would stay with him or try to return to Matthew. Elizabeth, as head of the Anglican church, had declared my second marriage void, because it had been forced on me, and the ceremony was conducted by an unlicensed priest. Also, since Matthew had been similarly told that I was dead, he had, I had learned, married again and had a son. But the bond between us had been passionate. Hugh had not been sure.

I was sure, though. Passion or no, I had had no peace with Matthew. He was for ever scheming against Elizabeth and on behalf of Mary Stuart. I told Hugh that I wished to remain Mistress Stannard, that I valued the life we had built together and that I wouldn't dream, anyway, of intruding like a ghost into Matthew's new marriage.

The link between myself and Brockley, though quite different in its nature from the union of myself and Matthew, was the stronger of the two, had Hugh only known it. Not that it mattered, for neither Matthew nor Brockley were any threat to him. My husband and the safe marriage he had given me were precious, and I would never let them be imperilled. I had believed that Hugh was now certain of this. Apparently, he was not.

'How could you possibly think I would be even remotely interested in Jonathan Bowman?' I said indignantly.

'I don't,' said Hugh. 'But I'm ailing and it makes me feel – lessened. I feel as though I am imprisoned in a failing body, while you are still young and men can be drawn to you. Please try to understand.'

'You have nothing to fear,' I said gently. 'You *know* that.'

'I think I do. But,' said Hugh, 'just keep away from that man. That's all.'

The following day was a Sunday. There was a long chapel service and then I had to ride in the park with the queen and accompany her to an archery competition in the afternoon. Lately, Cecil's man John Ryder, Brockley's friend and mine, had joined his employer at the castle. He and Brockley both won prizes at the contest, which gave me pleasure.

I had told Lambert that on Monday he need not come to teach Meg until after dinner, because she had a sitting with Arbuckle in the morning. That morning, for once, I had some time off. 'Today,' I said to Sybil, 'I'll take her.'

Master Arbuckle was as scruffy and paint-splattered as before, but still exuded the force of character which his unkempt appearance should have wrecked, but didn't. The picture was advancing well. The screen had been folded away, and he seated Meg at a table near the street window, with books and a sheet of paper in front of her, and a pen in her hand. The painting was up on the easel. Arbuckle gave me a seat where I wouldn't get in his way, and the day's work commenced.

For the moment, he had apparently completed Meg's face and was concentrating on her headdress and the upper part of her clothing. He had mixed a range of tints for her gown: hot orange-tawny where the folds were in the light; darker shades for the shadows in between. He was now putting the last touches to these and with a fine brush was dealing with her little white ruff. The lower part of the picture was a matter of faint pencil lines, which I could hardly make out. I was interested, though, in the part which he had virtually finished: the detail of her face.

Detailed it certainly was, down to the tiny shadows under her cheekbones and nostrils and the moulding of her ears and mouth. There was something else, too. It was as though Arbuckle had seen things in Meg which I had not. The face on the canvas was not quite the Meg I knew, but the difference was so subtle that I could not define it. I thought he had made her look a little remote, as though she were thinking thoughts which she would not share with others.

I remembered him saying that some of his clients had resented his work because he had seen things they would rather he had not. *When my brush is in my hand, I cannot lie.* What had he seen in Meg which had found its way out through his brush-hand? Her future maturity, her womanhood, beginning now to surface?

I sat watching with interest, while Meg, with great patience, posed for him. He chatted to her, very pleasantly, about her studies and about hawking, which was a sport she enjoyed. They seemed to be the best of friends.

I sat on my stool, letting my mind drift, until, unexpectedly, something in the style of Arbuckle's work, and the memory of something that Hugh had said, prompted me to ask a question.

'Master Arbuckle,' I said, 'may I ask – was it by any chance you, a long time ago, that painted a miniature of a lady called Judith Easton? It would be over twenty years ago now. My husband told me that the portrait you did recently of one of the ladies at the castle reminded him of that miniature. Judith Easton was very beautiful.'

'She was indeed,' said Arbuckle, delicately placing what looked like a brush-load of bronze into his rendering of Meg's dark hair. I looked at the canvas intently, and then at Meg, and saw that he was right; the sunlight on her hair did create that bronze streak. It is the kind of thing that artists see but other people easily miss. 'Yes, I was the painter,' he said. 'She had a face like a star. Sparkling, bright. Her husband had the miniature made. I wasn't as expensive then as I am now, but he had a job to pay me, I remember. His payment came in bits and pieces, and some of it was in cabbages.'

'Cabbages?'

'He worked in the royal kitchens. Gervase Easton, that was his name. He had perks, and he took them in cabbages that time, for my benefit. I painted him as well, a little later. He didn't pay for that – he had a brother who made a journey to see him now and then. The brother saw the miniature of Mistress Easton and hired me to do a portrait of her husband – a proper portrait, not a miniature. There was trouble in their family, I think, but the brother wanted to keep friends with Gervase and wanted a picture of him. I heard roundabout that Gervase was accused of some sort of crime later and took his own life. You know something of these people? What became of his wife?'

'She remarried, but she died too, soon after that.'

'I am sorry. Very sorry.'

'Master Arbuckle,' I said, 'the son of Gervase and Judith has lately been trying to clear his father's name. It seems that it may be important whether he was right or left-handed. Can you remember?'

'I can't say I ever thought about it.' Arbuckle, intent on his work, showed little interest. I sighed disappointedly, however, and he paused to please me by considering the matter. 'I can't remember, but the portrait showed him as a clerk, with a pen in his hand,' he said. 'That's why pictures are precious; they preserve times gone by, people who are dead, or have changed. That's why your mother is having *you* painted,' he added to Meg. 'So as to keep the memory of you as you are now.' He turned back to me. 'Every portrait becomes a picture of the past. That would give you the answer. The brother may have the picture still.'

Mark would know, I thought. Mark had taken over his uncle's house now; very likely the portrait was still in it! I must ask Mark. I thanked Arbuckle and once again let my mind drift.

This time, it glided towards Bowman and the threats he said he had heard Gervase Easton make against Hoxton. Ancient threats; words thrown off in temper when a man was in his cups and had been provoked – and the enemy wasn't actually there. How much did such things mean?

And how very odd of Hugh to be so jealous.

At this point, a chill unhappiness settled within me. Hugh was not in good health and kept saying disquieting things, such as *I don't know how long I will still be here to go on loving you* and *I feel as though I am imprisoned in a failing body.*

Was he really ill? He was almost twenty years older than I was, after all.

I don't remember much more of that sitting. I was overwhelmed, once more, with homesickness. I wanted to get out of Windsor and take Hugh to Hawkswood to enjoy whatever time he could still spend there.

I should have known. Sometimes I think it's a kind of precognition in reverse, so to speak. Whenever I am away from home and longing desperately to get back, I am liable to find myself being sent further away from it than ever.

TEN

Merry Yuletide

'A portrait of my father?' Mark said, when Brockley sought him out for me and brought him to our quarters. 'And Uncle Robert may have had it? Well, I lived with Uncle Robert from the age of five, but I never saw it. I wish I had. I've never known what my father looked like.'

Mark himself looked harassed. Since his reappearance at Windsor we gathered that he had been kept continually busy, being questioned in detail about events in the north and the movements of troops, ours and theirs. Now he was preparing to leave for York yet again, with letters from the queen and Cecil for Lord Sussex.

'I have a great aunt on my father's side,' he said, 'living up in the north-west. Great Aunt Bess, her name is. My Aunt Kate told me once that after her marriage to my uncle she was taken to see Bess and given a lecture on the Easton family history that lasted two and a half hours. If the portrait still exists, she might know where it is. It's the sort of thing to interest her, by all accounts. She might even have it! I'll send word to her as soon as I can. I can't go to see her – she lives in Westmorland, far away from York and in the heart of enemy territory, too. Her home is somewhere called Kendal, near a great lake.'

'Have you met her?' I asked.

'Yes, as a small boy. I remember we rode through a town – Kendal, I suppose – and came to the lake. My great aunt's manor house was beside it. I can't remember its name, but her husband's name was Edmund Tracy and he owned a lot of land. The rising won't concern her, though. She's a respectable well-off widow now with far too much sense to get involved in any rebellions. If a single one of her tenants has gone to join Westmorland's army, I'll be surprised.'

'She sounds as though she has a strong character,' I said.

'I'm sure she has. According to my uncle, Great Aunt Bess's tenants do what she tells them, and always did, even when her husband was alive. If they don't, she eats them grilled for breakfast. My uncle's own words!' He laughed, lightening his handsome face into something quite delightful. However in love with Jane Mason he was, I thought that she was probably even more in love with him.

Mark, however, was still thinking about his great aunt. 'Uncle said her three daughters always did exactly what mamma told them to do and married the men she chose for them, and she did the choosing, not their father. She's still alive, or was a few months ago. My uncle had a letter from her last spring, and she told him she was in good health then.'

Mark left for York the next morning. He was back a fortnight later. The news he brought was a blank as far as the portrait was concerned. He had been unable to communicate with his great aunt, since no one could be spared to take a private message across the snowbound moors to Westmorland.

But he brought good news about the war. The insurgents were in retreat, stumbling northwards through blizzard and snowdrift, towards the sanctuary of Scotland. Lord Sussex's forces were in pursuit, unable to overtake their prey because they, too, were delayed by the weather, but on the spoor of the quarry nevertheless, baying like a hound-pack. If they didn't catch the retreating earls before they crossed the Scottish border, Sussex would make sure that they'd never dare to put their noses back over it again.

'Ursula,' said the queen, having summoned me to hear the good tidings, 'the danger is past, I think, but you and Master Stannard will stay here for the Christmas celebrations, will you not?'

We more or less had to stay, in any case. Meg's portrait was not yet finished, and Hugh, though now much better, was still not quite well, and the weather was very cold for travelling, even for a fit man. 'We'll spend Christmas here,' he said. 'But in the new year, Ursula, we'll go home.'

Only a few weeks before, Windsor had been tense and nervous, provisioning itself against catastrophe. Now, the extra supplies formed the wherewithal for feasts of unusual splendour, even at a royal Christmas. The queen's ladies and the maids of honour spent hours preparing new clothes and practising new dances. Masques were being created and rehearsed. Passageways through which armaments had been carried were now infested by people carrying musical instruments, clutching scripts and muttering their lines and, sometimes, wearing extraordinary costumes.

In the kitchens, cooks experimented with fantastic new dishes, throwing dramatic tantrums when the said dishes went wrong, trying to blame inefficient underlings for these disasters and on occasion flinging the dishes at the heads of the said underlings.

Mark Easton, weather notwithstanding, set valiantly off to York, with a further letter to Sussex from the queen – this time full of congratulations on his deft handling of the crisis – and a personal gift. The castle hummed and throbbed with excitement and laughter and music.

'I suppose it's relief,' Hugh said to me as we made our way towards dinner on Christmas Eve. 'I think everyone was afraid, whether or not they said so out loud.'

'It was an ugly thought,' I said. 'The idea of armies riding towards us with murderous intent! Mary Stuart is the greatest nuisance God ever made.'

The Christmas Eve dinner was to be a special affair. A whole crowd was converging on the anteroom where we would wait for the meal to be announced. In a wide gallery we came across Sir William Cecil, back at court after a brief visit to his home. He was evidently being troubled, as he so often was, by gout and was walking slowly, accompanied by his wife Mildred, their entourage following. We exchanged greetings. We, too, had our people with us, except for Gladys, who preferred to stay ('Skulk,' said Dale) in our rooms and have her food there. Brockley, seeing John Ryder in the Cecils' party, turned aside to speak to him.

As he did so, another man in the Cecils' group suddenly looked at Brockley and grinned. He was a short, bearded fellow, with a snub nose, slate-coloured eyes and dark hair silvering at the temples. He was not young, but he moved with the fluid stealth of a cat stalking a blackbird, and to our astonishment, as soon as he saw Brockley, he edged sideways to get behind him, using Cecil as a shield. He appeared to have cast my manservant in the role of the blackbird.

Brockley must have been aware of him, but for some reason ignored him, until the stalk turned to a pounce, as the stranger sprang forward, seized Brockley's left arm from behind and jerked it up my manservant's back in a way that looked anything but friendly.

Beside me, Meg let out a squeak, Dale clicked her tongue and Sybil Jester went round-eyed.

'Greetings, Roger,' said the stranger softly, in a marked west country accent. 'How many years is it since we met?'

'Oh, I should have said at once,' remarked Ryder. 'Our old friend Carew Trelawny has joined Sir William's service. You surely remember Carew, don't you, Brockley?' He caught my eye, and added: 'It's all right, Mistress Stannard. Carew Trelawny always greets old friends like that. When he encounters old enemies, we usually have to bury them.'

'Some people,' said Brockley calmly, 'prefer not to associate with him at all. Personally, though, I'm always happy to see my friends, and if you'd let me turn round, Trelawny, I might actually be *able* to see you.'

He then disengaged himself by applying his right elbow to his assailant's ribs in a manner quite as aggressive as Trelawny's assault on him, swung round and embraced him. They were both chuckling. It had all happened so swiftly and quietly that hardly anyone else in the crowded gallery had noticed it.

A memory suddenly returned to me: of my first husband, Gerald, back in the days when we were a young couple in Antwerp, in the service of one of the queen's financiers. Gerald had made friends with a colleague of his own age, and I could recall a wet afternoon when we were all together in our lodgings. In the midst of a good-natured argument – I could no longer remember what it was about – the two of them swooped on each other and rolled round the floor, wrestling and pummelling in a manner only just short of genuine violence, so that I had to get out of the way in a hurry and a small table was knocked over, sending a glass goblet on to the floor, where it broke.

'Moon-mad, both of you,' I said to Gerald afterwards. 'We only have four glass goblets left now, and you've cracked the leg of the table!'

'I'm sorry,' said Gerald unrepentantly, 'but it's a kind of ritual we've invented for dealing with our little arguments. You don't understand men, sweetheart.'

'I understand broken glass and cracked table-legs,' I said.

'We're not paupers. I'll buy you some new goblets *and* another table if you're going to be as pernickety as that!'

The greeting between Brockley and Trelawny, I thought, was a ritual of the same mysterious masculine kind. Sir William Cecil and Hugh, who had clearly understood it at once, were both laughing. Mildred Cecil was shaking her head, but she looked amused too. I allowed myself to be introduced to Brockley's old friend. So this, I thought, was the fellow with the original ideas about pea-stick twine and other men's shirts. A useful individual in a crisis, no doubt, and it was plain that he, Ryder and Brockley were three of a kind and pleased with each other's company.

Trumpets sounded, and those of us still in the gallery made haste to go into the dining chamber before the queen, preceded by her heralds and followed by her day's selection of courtiers, ladies and maids of honour, swept in to take her place. I was able to remain with my family, for I was not on duty at the queen's side that day, although I would have to be there at tomorrow's Christmas feast. This time, standing behind my seat, I had only to sink into the formal curtsey as her majesty entered the chamber.

The feast began, a merry affair, made all the merrier by the brilliant colours worn by the diners, by jokes and laughter, excellent food and fine wine and tuneful music. It went on unabated for two hours, until a small swirl of disturbance broke out among the maids of honour.

The mistress of the maids was no longer Kat Ashley, the queen's friend from childhood, whom I had once known well, for Kat had died over four years ago. Her replacement – whom I scarcely knew but who had the watchful and harried air common to all duennas with lively charges – was leaning over the table and, to judge from her expression, speaking sharply to the girl opposite. I watched with only mild interest, until I saw the girl turn ashen pale, close her eyes and slide from her seat in a faint.

In the midst of all the rejoicing, it was just a minor awkwardness. The mistress of the maids joined two other girls who had slipped to their knees beside the sufferer. She came round, and after a few moments they helped her up and steered her out of the room. There was a mild buzz of conversation about it, and then the next course was served and we all forgot her.

The feast was followed by a masque and dancing in another room, and it was late that day before Hugh and I returned to our suite. To be greeted by a Gladys all agog.

Gladys, it appeared, had not after all stayed in the suite. Growing bored, she had plodded off down the tower stairs and, at the foot of them, encountered a party of ladies half-carrying a sick girl along. 'Deathly white, she were, indeed to goodness,' Gladys said.

Gladys had a vague reputation in the castle for being clever at potions of one sort and another. One of the ladies had asked her to come with them and give her advice.

'Not that it was any use,' Gladys said. 'They got her to her quarters – maid of honour, she is, or was . . .'

'Was?' I said. 'Do you mean . . . is she . . .?'

'Aye.' Gladys nodded. 'There weren't nothing I could do for her, nor any other mortal being. These girls are so silly, look you. They get into trouble and kill themselves trying to get out of it, when if they'd asked me in the first place I'd have told them how *not* to land in trouble.'

'She was miscarrying?' I asked with sympathy, having been through that myself in my time. 'Because she'd taken something?'

'Aye. It was that lass I saw playing the fool with a young fellow in the garden, the day you first took Meg to see that artist. She'd taken something all right – some sort of yew-tree brew, from what she said. I asked her. It was when we first got her on to the bed – before we knew it was too late. Then the mistress of the maids said to her: *where did you get it? The law will have something to say about this.* The girl wouldn't tell her, except that right at the end she didn't know what she was saying and muttered something about a woman with a house on the edge of the town. Then . . . you never saw aught like it. All the blood in her body came out of her, I'd reckon, and a poor sad thing like a big dark-red tadpole . . .'

'All right, Gladys,' said Hugh. 'There's no need to go on.'

'I hate seeing it,' Gladys said, a little unexpectedly, for there was little sentiment in our Gladys. 'It never happened to me, God be thanked. To see a poor thing cast out into the world long before its time, when it ought to be safe and warm inside, in the dark. Silly, silly girl, to let it start and then to go taking potions. A merry Yuletide her parents are going to have, when they hear. Mistress . . .'

'Yes, Gladys?'

'You've been wanting to know who really poisoned a man called Hoxton in this castle, many years ago. You ever thought that whoever did it maybe got advice, or ingredients, from someone else? What if that someone else, and this woman that girl that died today went to, were one and the same?'

I wanted to say: 'Oh no, it's no use, let's not go hunting up yet another dead-end alleyway to bang our noses on yet another stone wall, *please*.' But I didn't speak, and Sybil said: 'But wasn't it just a matter of nightshade berries in a pie? Everyone knows that nightshade berries can kill.'

'Everyone don't know how to find them, or what they look like,' Gladys said. 'And ain't it supposed to be a man that put the pie on the tray? Most men couldn't cook a pie, not unless cooking's their trade.'

'I could,' said Hugh. 'But I wouldn't know how to find nightshade berries. Who would we ask if we wanted to find out? A physician, a gardener, a wise woman?' He frowned, obviously thinking it over. 'If our poisoner pumped a wise woman for information she might remember and be able to describe him – that is, if she can remember anything at all about a man who called on her twenty-odd years ago and perhaps asked some strange questions.'

'Or said he wanted to poison rats,' suggested practical Sybil.

'But it's possible,' she added. 'A woman who's old now would have been only middle-aged then. If he were a stranger to her, he'd probably feel safe enough. A plain woman, not living near the castle, would very likely never hear about Hoxton.'

Half against my will, I found myself being drawn in. The huntress in me was awake again. 'The girl said something about a woman in a house on the edge of the town,' I said thoughtfully. 'We could at least try to find *her*.'

'Best be careful what you say to her if you do,' Gladys said. 'Or she'll take fright. Whoever gave that girl a yew-tree brew is dabbling too deep and asking to be called a witch by them as doesn't know any better.' Her tone was heartfelt. We said nothing, remembering how nearly the rope had had her on that very charge. 'Best ask around among the women,' Gladys said. 'Or ask the Windsor apothecaries and physicians. They might know a name, even if they're pure as snow themselves. If the woman's got a reputation, someone will have heard of her.'

'How *would* one recognize nightshade?' I asked.

'Green leaves, longer than they're broad, pointed at the ends. Purple flowers round about June or July; then the berries come. They ripen to black, same size as cherries, more or less. Bigger and darker than bilberries, but stewing would break 'em down, I suppose. Said to be bitter – I wouldn't know. I've never tried them!' Gladys eyed me, her black eyes glinting with malicious amusement. 'I expect sugar or honey would hide the taste.'

'You know your plants,' said Hugh admiringly. 'And you've given us a new idea to pursue. Thank you!'

'Folk always undervalue poor old Gladys,' said my aged hanger-on, in a whining voice. 'But old Gladys has her uses, indeed to goodness she has.'

'She'll crow over us for days,' Hugh said to me later. 'We'll just have to put up with it!'

ELEVEN

The Last Hope

So, the hunt was on again.

There was, of course, only the slenderest chance that the woman who had so lethally advised the hapless maid of honour had also, almost a quarter of a century ago, been approached by Hoxton's killer. I doubted very much that the killer, whoever he might be, had approached anyone. If I were proposing to poison someone, I said to myself, the last thing I would do was leave a trail by making enquiries about venomous plants.

In fact, I considered the idea so weak that I wouldn't have pursued it, except for Hugh. I kept thinking that if only his unhappiness about Hawkswood could be removed, his health might improve. I feared that distress was making him worse. Though up and about, he was very breathless, especially when he climbed our tower stairs. I tried to get us moved to a lower floor, but could not because the castle was so full.

I knew that my feelings verged on the superstitious, but I couldn't help it. I kept thinking: *save Hawkswood – save Hugh.* Yet I didn't wish to raise his hopes by telling him I was looking for the wise-woman. If the trail led nowhere, disappointment might do him harm. So I hesitated until the mistress of the maids came to see me. She was very angry about the death of the girl in her charge.

'I have no time to go after whoever it was who gave her that medicine. I have enough to do, trying to make sure that none of the other girls get into similar trouble. Young gallants have no morals these days, it seems to me, and young girls have never had any sense. A pretty compliment or two and their heads turn like weathercocks in a high wind. But you, dear Mistress Stannard, have something of a reputation . . .'

I was supposed to be a secret agent. I didn't seem to be half as secret as I should.

'Do you think you could try to find out who it was – before another poor wench gets killed!'

So, after all, I followed that tiny, slender lead. Not that I expected it to prove useful. I didn't. And it wasn't.

I will not describe in detail the efforts I made, assisted by the Brockleys, to trace a dubious wise woman with a little house on the edge of Windsor. None of the women I questioned had ever heard of such a person. Nor were the apothecaries and physicians to whom we spoke very helpful.

One physician said that during the three years he had been working in Windsor he had four or five times been called to women who were having miscarriages which might have been induced, though he couldn't be sure. If the women had used potions, and where they had obtained them if so, he had no idea. Those who had been capable of speech when he arrived had denied it. 'They always do,' he told us.

The nearest we came to a candidate was a name which was mentioned by two apothecaries and one physician, although none of them suggested that Mistress Catherine Mildmay, widow, of Moor Street in the Parish of Windsor, was the person we sought. On the contrary, they were quite sure she wasn't. Yes, she had lived in Windsor for many years, but she was well known and infinitely respectable. She had a herb-growing business and supplied ingredients for accredited medicines, as well as selling culinary herbs to local innkeepers and a few private customers. No one had *ever* suggested that she helped girls who had got into trouble – or even sold poisons to get rid of rats.

I called on her, though, accompanied by the Brockleys, since Hugh wanted to rest. We were frank about our enquiry. We promised that we didn't wish to make trouble for her, but wished to know if, many years ago she had given information about nightshade or supplied its berries to anyone for any purpose. Perhaps for making bait for vermin.

She had been described as *infinitely respectable*, and her appearance bore this out: from the starched white cap to the tightly drawn-back, pale-brown hair beneath it, which looked as if it would have liked to curl but wasn't allowed to; from the pale, humourless eyes to the prim little mouth; from the reddened, work-calloused hands to the decent dark wool gown. Not to mention her outraged expression when she understood what we were asking.

We were challenging her good reputation, and she sprang to its defence like a wildcat whose kittens have been threatened. She had never been asked for nightshade, let alone supplied it. 'I grow only the most wholesome plants, and if I saw such a thing in my garden, and praise God, I never have, it would be uprooted and burnt within the hour.'

Since we were also supposed to be trying to trace the source of a potion that had killed one of the queen's maids of honour, Fran Dale at this point mentioned girls who got into trouble. 'I believe there's a brew that can be made from the yew tree. Have you ever—?'

Whereupon, Mistress Mildmay's wrath became equal to that of two wildcats. '*YEW? NIGHTSHADE?*' She repeated the names with such indignant emphasis that I could see them written inside my head, in very black letters a yard high.

Had anyone ever asked for such things, she said wrathfully, she would have chased them away at the end of a broom! Her garden, she informed us, contained everything any respectable cook or physician was likely to need *and nothing else*. Yes, it was true she had been in business for a good twenty-six years, ever since her husband died when they'd only been wed for a year and she'd had to support herself. She'd not wished to remarry. But she'd been honest, and if anyone had been saying different, we'd better send them to her and she'd pack them off with their ears ringing!

We had dropped no hints about supplying lethal pies. Just as well, I thought.

'I feel, madam,' said Brockley as we apologized and retreated, 'as though I'd just been clouted round the head with a very heavy hand and now *my* ears are ringing.'

'I do just wonder if she's as virtuous as she says she is,' said Dale.

'I agree,' I said. 'But how do we find out? I didn't see anything in her garden that I could recognize as poisonous, but I suppose there's a yew tree in every churchyard and nightshade grows wild. She wouldn't need to plant them herself.'

Meanwhile, Christmas was over and the maid of honour had been quietly buried, with as little scandal as possible, by the queen's own order. The young gallant who had been her lover had confessed and, to do him justice, seemed truly grief-stricken. He came to the funeral, but left the court immediately afterwards. Officially, the girl had had a fatal miscarriage. And that was that.

At court, her memory passed into oblivion and we returned to our own concerns. We had not found her wise-woman, let alone discovered whether she or anyone like her had supplied poison to Hoxton's killer. Once again, as I had feared, we had met an impassable barrier.

'But a reply to your letter to the Masons at Lockhill is overdue,' Hugh said to me. 'You put the matter very persuasively. If only, when it comes, it proves to be the right answer.'

If it did, then Mark could claim his bride after all. Mark had said he would honour our contract if the Masons changed their minds, which meant that he would pay us. *Save Hawkswood – cure Hugh.* The words repeated themselves, over and over, inside my head.

Mark reappeared at court shortly after Christmas, but went straight to the queen's presence and spoke with us only briefly. He said he had brought a sealed letter from Sussex, but that as far as he knew the rebellion was finished. The insurgent earls had fled into Scotland, but at least they were gone, and their warlike spouses with them.

Elizabeth – reacting, I thought, to her fear when we were half-expecting enemy forces to descend on Windsor – was preparing to order savage reprisals against their supporters, especially those who could not buy their way out. Lord Sussex, I heard, disagreed with this policy, and I think Cecil, who was still at Windsor, tried to soften her attitude but failed. I myself feared Elizabeth in this tempestuous mood, and I didn't argue with her. I did her bidding and held my tongue.

Since Cecil was in the castle, so were John Ryder and Carew

Trelawny. When off duty, they and Brockley often made a threesome, playing cards together, practising archery and sometimes swordplay in the lower bailey. When they did this, they were excellent distraction for troubled minds, because any sporting or military exercise involving Carew Trelawny turned into a cross between farce and fury.

He and Brockley were the worst combination. Ryder would just smile benignly when Trelawny hurled insults at him, but my usually imperturbable Brockley revealed a new side of himself, becoming hilarious and excitable. At times, the pair of them exchanged such outrageous aspersions on each other's ancestry, abilities and social status that the riveted onlookers half-expected and probably hoped for genuine murder to be done.

Hugh had decided that a daily walk would relieve his breathlessness and build up his strength. Accompanied by Meg, we were strolling across the bailey together on the last day of December when we came upon Brockley and Trelawny once more ringed by onlookers and performing – there is no other word for it – like paid entertainers, prowling menacingly round each other, swords in hand, exchanging rude remarks while their audience egged them on. Ryder, out of breath from a recent bout, was there but standing aside, leaning on his blade and grinning.

Just as we arrived, Brockley was taunting Trelawny with being too timid to attack. After which, he turned his back, said: 'This is you, my lad,' and minced away in ladylike fashion, glancing over his shoulder to see the effect on his opponent.

'I wish they wouldn't,' I said to Hugh. 'Brockley hasn't practised swordsmanship seriously in years; he always says he's not skilled at it, and look at him – he's as out of breath as Ryder is. I'm afraid one of them will get hurt. They're neither of them young!'

'They would like to believe they were, though,' Hugh said. Brockley spun round, and the sword blades clashed. 'They're trying to hold off the years. Dear, dear. Tut *tut*!'

Brockley, clowning, had caught Trelawny on the hip with the flat of his blade. The audience applauded, and Trelawny, halfway between real and feigned fury, somehow found the spare breath to declare, very loudly, that Brockley's parents should have drowned him in a rain-butt before he was a day old.

'There was a drought that year,' said Brockley. He closed in for another clash of blades, evaded a thrust with a neat sidestep and bawled: 'You send messages with your eyes! Anyone would take them for a couple of royal couriers!'

'I'm just a good liar!' Trelawny retorted, feinting and then changing direction so that this time Brockley seemed within a hair's breadth of being chopped in half. Annoyed, he attacked anew, got under Trelawny's guard again and repeated the clout with the flat of the blade.

'Stop laughing, Ryder!' Trelawny bellowed. 'And what the hell are you doing, leaning on that damn blade like a tired housemaid on a broom handle? Come and help me! Two to one!'

He then launched himself at Brockley with an energy which looked as though it might really turn lethal, and Ryder, accepting the invitation, joined in. Brockley tripped and went down, and for a dreadful moment I thought he was going to be beheaded before my eyes. Even as it was . . .

'At this rate, I won't have a manservant left!' I protested to Hugh. 'Can't we stop this?'

'Oh, but it's so funny!' Meg exclaimed as Brockley scrambled up and knocked Ryder's blade aside with considerable dexterity, so that he could concentrate on driving Trelawny vengefully back to the centre of their makeshift arena.

'Brockley underestimates himself,' Hugh said. 'I wish I were half as fit for my years as he is. He's puffing a trifle, but I'd be unconscious by now if I tried to play such games. I'm eaten up with envy.'

I laughed, though a little wryly. Then I was distracted, for Sybil Jester had come out of the castle to find me. I didn't realize she was there until her voice spoke from behind me.

'Mistress Stannard, I've been looking for you. A letter has come for you with the Lockhill seal on it. I have it here.'

In the arena, Ryder had apparently come to much the same conclusion as I had and was sensibly calling the bout off. I broke the seal on the letter and read it then and there. My heart sank as I did so. It was from Ann Mason, but both she and her son George had signed it. Clearly, they had taken time to study my plea on behalf of Mark Easton. But their decision, though polite, was unyielding.

They had talked it over repeatedly, all through Christmas. They were sorry for the young couple, and they did not hold Mark responsible for any crime committed by his father, but they still did not wish Jane to marry into a family with a shadow over it. She could do much better. There had been approaches from far more suitable prospects.

Jane herself had been told that she must put all thoughts of Mark Easton away. *She is young*, wrote Ann. *Time will erase Mark's memory as long as he keeps away from her. We shall find her a good husband. Her happiness will be considered, believe me, and one day she will thank us.*

That, apparently, was that. We found Mark and broke the news to him. 'I suppose finding the portrait is the last hope,' he said. 'But I can hardly ask you, mistress, to go riding to Westmorland. I will go myself as soon as I'm free, but I can't take time away from the service of Lord Sussex yet. I can only thank you for all you have tried to do.'

The thanks were kindly meant, but they didn't include any money.

I woke up next morning with a migraine headache.

'So,' said Hugh, sitting on the side of the bed and looking down at my wan face and wrinkled brow, 'what brought this on?'

Those who have never had the migraine can have no idea what it feels like. It seemed to me that an iron band had enclosed my skull, crossing my forehead, and was being slowly, relentlessly, tightened, while an invisible demon struck it repeatedly with a hammer, just over my left eye.

Miserably, I said: 'The only lead to the truth about Hoxton is to trace that portrait. If it shows a right-handed man, then Gervase was almost certainly not the one who interfered with Hoxton's food. It could tell us that much. That might even be enough to make the Masons and the Mosses think again! Then

Easton would pay us. He doesn't expect me to travel north, but I dare say it's safe enough now. Hugh, I do believe that if I could save Hawkswood, that would be the best medicine in the world for you. Only, I can't leave you. I ought to go, for your sake, and I ought to stay, for your sake. What shall I do?'

'You stay here,' said Hugh. 'I'm not so sure about the safety of the north. I've been talking with John Ryder and Trelawny. They're Cecil's men, and they hear things. There are some ominous new rumours. When peace is finally established, as he says, Mark can go after the portrait himself. He's well off; he doesn't have to stay bound to Lord Sussex. Once this rebellion is completely over, he'll be free.'

Brockley said: 'I'll go to Westmorland if you and Mistress Stannard will entrust me with the task, sir. I dare say there is some urgency. If Master Easton waits too long, his young lady's guardians may persuade her, or push her, into a different marriage and then there will be no point in him chasing the portrait at all. Perhaps he would give me a letter of introduction to his great aunt.'

'I don't want to send you into danger,' said Hugh worriedly.

'I've spent half my life in danger,' said Brockley, which was true enough, for I had led him into it, time and again. 'I can face a little more,' he added, with that rare grin of his.

I said: 'The portrait is the only hope left. And I think – I sense – that what is between Mark and Jane may well be a real thing.' I looked at Hugh. 'There's that to think about as well as Hawkswood. You know what I mean.'

'Yes, I know,' Hugh agreed. He rarely spoke of his first two marriages, and I knew little of his previous wives, except that both had been called Mary, and that one had died of plague and the other from a wasting cough and fever. Now, however, lowering his voice so that only I could hear, he said: 'My first marriage was arranged. The first Mary and I got on well enough; but my second . . .! We married from choice. Happily, I was acceptable to her parents.' He smiled. 'Only a poet could describe her. She was warm sunshine and mysterious moonlight. I have never talked to you much about my special Mary because I didn't want you to feel that you had to share my heart. But I do know what you mean. More depends on this than just Hawkswood, however dear my home is to me.'

I glanced past him to where Brockley waited silently by the window, and then towards Dale, who was by the fire, stirring the medicine which Gladys recommended for my headaches. She had said nothing, but her lips were pursed. If I sent Brockley north, I would be sending him away from her. My head pounded. 'I don't know what to do,' I said.

There came a tap on the door, and Dale went to answer it. On the threshold was Mark.

He had brought a summons to me, and to Hugh, to attend upon the queen.

TWELVE

Compass Needle

Migraine is a curious illness. It can be born out of mental conflict, and it can be healed, at remarkable speed, by sheer necessity. A summons from Queen Elizabeth amounted to a necessity. The crisis came on within minutes. Hugh held my head; Dale held a basin for me. I threw up, helplessly and miserably, but as they laid me back on my pillows the pain was already beginning to ebb. Presently, as a precaution, I drank some of the brew that Dale and Gladys had made. Soon after that, I was able, shakily, to rise, to let Dale – still a very silent Dale – dress me and tidy my hair, and then, with Hugh and Mark, I set off to the queen's presence.

She received us in a small panelled study, lit by candles because the day was dull. She sat at a desk, informally dressed in a loose, ash-coloured gown. Cecil was present too, standing by the window. He looked at us with a certain compassion in his eyes, which alarmed me.

What the queen had to say alarmed me still more.

The confidential letter from Lord Sussex, which Mark had brought to her, contained disquieting news.

'Sussex has spies,' Elizabeth said. 'And several of them, from different places, have reported the same tale. The earls of Westmorland and Northumberland and their wives are all supposed to be north of the border by now, but it is being said, or whispered – in taverns, at markets – that all four of them have not, in fact, gone. It is being whispered that one at least is still in England, in hiding, with the intention of reawakening the rebellion. We don't know which of them it is; we don't know who else is involved; we don't know what, precisely, is being planned. We don't know for sure if the rumours are true, though they seem to be strengthening. Sussex has supplied a list of houses which are possible hiding places for this hidden ringleader, whether man or woman. But investigating them is difficult.'

'Why is that, ma'am?' I asked. 'If Lord Sussex has so many spies.'

Cecil spoke. 'Dangerous secrets are often hidden well. All the suspect houses are isolated, and Sussex sent spies to them, pretending to be benighted travellers in need of a night's lodgings. The traditions of the north were kept, and lodgings were always granted. But the spies found nothing suspicious. All was as smooth, they say, as a pond in still weather. Two of them, though, say that they were dispatched on their way the following morning with a certain rapidity, as though their presence was not altogether welcome. There is *something* under the surface of that pond, and this is where you come in.'

'Ursula,' said the queen, 'I have taken a great interest in the work you are doing for Master Easton. I hear from him that much may turn on something shown in a portrait, which may well be in northern England.'

'Her majesty was gracious enough to ask how your enquiries were prospering,' said Mark, a little awkwardly.

'A lady,' said Elizabeth, 'with a romantic and truthful reason for calling at various houses, might have better fortune than Sussex's male spies. Our conspirators may be less afraid of you – less careful in your presence – and you have a gift for discovering secrets.'

I had seen it coming, but now that she had put it into words, my stomach, already aching from my recent bout of sickness, turned a somersault. I glanced at Hugh and saw that his face had whitened.

'Ma'am, my husband is unwell. I can't leave him just now.'

Elizabeth's eyes flashed dangerously. And Hugh, though still very pale, said in a calm voice: 'If the queen commands it, then you will have to leave me, my dear.'

He had taken that attitude in the past, even when not under Elizabeth's glittering gaze. I looked at her again and knew that to argue would be in vain. She was the queen, and her realm was in turmoil. She wanted my help and would put all personal considerations aside. Hugh could be on his deathbed and I could be weeping beside it, but if Elizabeth considered that for the good of England I should be dragged away and sent on a mission, then dragged and sent I would be. She had done things to me, just as bad as that, before now. Such as lying to me about Matthew's death, for instance. There was even a part of me that understood. Just as Hugh did.

And if I found the portrait and it revealed what I wanted to know, there would be a chance yet of saving Hawkswood. I was silent.

'Your search for the portrait is your excuse and your entrée to any house,' Elizabeth said. 'You may or may not find it, but who is to know, unless you tell them? You can go to any house and say you have heard that the portrait had been sold on from hand to hand and this or that house had been mentioned. It will be up to you, then, to find out all you can about who is in the house and what they are doing. You are experienced in this kind of work. You're the likeliest person to succeed. I want you to leave immediately. Take your own servants. Master Easton here will also go part of the way with you, as he is returning to York, and Cecil will lend you an extra man.'

Gladys had been perfectly right. When I declared that none of us were going north for any reason whatsoever, I ought to have crossed my fingers. There was no more to be said. With Elizabeth, there never was.

But once back in our rooms and private with Hugh, I wept with rage. 'Why must I go? Why me? *Why must it be me?* Why can't Lord Sussex provide a harmless-looking man with a harmless-sounding excuse? Oh, I know I might find the portrait and then perhaps we'll be glad I went, but I don't want to leave you while you're ill. It's not right. And I'm tired of being a spy. I hate this. I hate it!'

'I shall be all right. I really am better, Ursula. I don't puff so much on the stairs now, not since I've been having my daily walks. I shall be anxious about *you*. You may be going into danger.'

'But the queen has commanded it, and it's for the benefit of the realm. Even you think it's my duty to go. We've had this argument before. You are the most extraordinary husband any woman ever had.'

'You're a fairly extraordinary woman. Come, dry your eyes and begin to consider your strategy. And stop worrying about *me*. Gladys and her potions will look after me till you're home again.'

'I know.' I wiped my eyes and said: 'If I am successful, in my task for the queen, I'll be paid, you know. I don't know how much; I never do know. But if I don't find the portrait, I suppose the money from the queen could be useful . . .'

'Oh, my dear.' Hugh's voice was contrite. 'That the payment should matter so much, because once I was a fool . . .'

'Just wish me well,' I said.

Cecil's extra man was Carew Trelawny. 'You'll be safe enough with him and Brockley,' Hugh said, determinedly cheerful. 'I wish I could come too, but I know I'm not fit enough. Please don't look so unhappy.'

'I'm sorry.' After supper, I had been summoned by Cecil, for a detailed briefing and to be given my list of suspicious houses. Rejoining Hugh, I had begun taking clothes from my press and tossing them at Dale to pack in saddlebags. 'If you fall ill again while I'm away . . . Please don't.'

'I'll do my best!' said Hugh.

I threw a pile of underlinen at Dale. 'I just hope that Brockley and Trelawny don't start fighting.'

'They won't,' said Hugh. 'They're friends, however oddly they show it. Anyway, they'll be on duty. You know Brockley better than that, and at heart, Trelawny is a similar type.'

Dale picked up a filled saddlebag and left the room. I said uncertainly: 'I can't take Dale. She's not getting any younger, and winter travel has always been bad for her. She'll hate it, that I'm taking Brockley . . .'

Even though Hugh knew of the odd relationship between myself and Brockley, we hardly ever referred to it. Nor did we speak of it directly now, but as so many times before, Hugh had thought ahead and lifted a burden from me. 'I've talked to Dale, while you were with Cecil. She knows you must go and that Brockley's presence is necessary and that I have absolute trust in him and in you.'

Just for a moment, his blue eyes bored into me, not questioningly but as one who drives a nail home to make something secure.

'Your trust won't be misplaced,' I said.

'I know. So does Dale. Mistress Jester could go with you, I suppose,' he said, 'but she's a terrible horsewoman and would slow you down nearly as much as Dale or I would. You'll do better without any of us. Ride as fast as you can. The rest of us will wait for you here. Meg's portrait will be finished by the time you return, and that's something to look forward to. How many houses are there on that list?'

'Only four. Well, five in a way, because I'm going to see Mark's great aunt too. I'm tired of riding north,' I added. 'This will be the third time! I feel like a compass needle!'

'You're my Little Bear, and the constellation of the Little Bear is attached to the Pole Star by its tail,' said Hugh and tried to laugh.

We left the next day, in bitter weather. Hugh and I kissed long and hard. Dale wept, but my eyes were dry. For me, the time for tears was past. As Hugh had looked into my eyes, I now looked into Dale's, except that I was not seeking a promise and a message of reassurance, but giving them.

'We all have good horses,' I said to her. 'Roundel is sturdy; so is Brockley's Brown Berry. Trelawny's mare looks almost too well bred, but Trelawny says that she's the toughest thing on four legs he's ever come across. Mark uses Lord Sussex's string of post horses and changes mounts whenever he feels like it. We're taking packs on our backs and in our saddlebags to save being cluttered with a pack animal. I shall race round the northern counties as fast as I can. Mark says that it's possible his great aunt or one of her daughters will actually have that portrait. They're the only members of his family left. Anyway, even if I do have to go from one place to another to find it, some of the four suspect houses I have to visit may be on my route. Why,' I said, brightly, 'we could be back here in three weeks!'

THIRTEEN

She-Eagle

We made good speed to Westmorland, but it was in the teeth of a north wind that cut through our hooded woollen cloaks like a scythe through corn. Twice we rode through snowstorms. Several times, we had to stop so that Brockley could clear balled snow from the hooves of the horses.

We parted from Mark at Sheffield. He went on northwards, to York by way of Leeds, while I and my escort turned north-west for Bolton, Lancaster, and ultimately for Westmorland.

We could have called at Tyesdale, where Jane was living with my former ward Pen and her husband Clem, but I decided to leave that until we were on our way home. If I could find Gervase Easton's portrait and it showed a right-handed man, I would have news that was at least hopeful. Besides, two of the houses on Sussex's list were in Westmorland. I wanted to complete my business and return to Hugh, as fast as possible.

We pressed on, therefore, using the hours of daylight as best we could, avoiding upland paths which were sure to be choked with snow. My companions were steady and watchful, careful of my welfare and that of the horses. Trelawny, I knew from Cecil, was aware of both our purposes and had been informed of my secret work. He gave me odd, amused looks sometimes, but Brockley told me quietly that I need not worry; I could trust him. Both of them used their clowning habits to keep our spirits up.

Brockley, mounted on his sturdy cob, Brown Berry, had a helmet on under his outsize hat, which drew many witty remarks from Trelawny, concerning the size of Brockley's head. Trelawny himself, astride Strawberry, his elegant roan mare, had dressed for a fashionable silhouette. He had a high-crowned hat complete with a long golden-brown feather which he said came from a species of hawk imported from the New World, a well-cut cloak of mulberry wool lined with silk and magnificently puffed-out breeches (I suspected he was actually wearing two pairs, for warmth). He also had a thick quilted doublet, a dignified ruff and riding boots which he polished every night. Brockley said he looked like a dandy.

Sometimes I joined in with the laughing jibes, free now to exchange whatever jokes I wished with Brockley, though I sometimes felt guilty about this.

I learned more about Trelawny as we travelled. Unlike Brockley, he had never married, although I gathered that he had had many a brief romance in the course of a restless existence. To him, soldiering was the best kind of life, and when not in an army of some sort, he had always been employed in a way which offered at least an occasional chance of a fight. He had been a retainer in several households where his main tasks were carrying messages or accompanying his employer as companion and guard, always with a sword on his hip and always ready to use it.

Eight days after leaving Windsor, on a grey and bitter afternoon, we arrived in Westmorland and, because it was on our way, presented ourselves at the first of Lord Sussex's suspect houses.

Nine days after leaving Windsor, as another overcast and savagely cold dusk descended, we reached the second.

Neither turned us away. I introduced Brockley and Trelawny as relatives who were acting as my escort, and we were all greeted with courtesy, given good guest chambers and invited to dine and breakfast with the rest of the household.

In both houses, we took the opportunity of enquiring about pictures, explaining that we were trying to trace a family portrait which had been sold to someone in Westmorland. It made a very handy excuse for our journey. In both houses, we were invited to look at all their pictures (we found no portraits that could possibly be of Gervase), and in neither did we meet anyone who could have been either of the rebellious earls or their wives.

One household was headed by a quiet young woman with two small children and no visible husband. She said vaguely that her husband was away. ('Among the fugitives in Scotland, what would you wager?' Brockley said to me afterwards.) The other was in the charge of a steward because both master and mistress were somewhere else, unspecified.

But in both cases, after our night's stay, if we were not exactly hurried out of the place, we were certainly not encouraged to linger, and in the conversation at the dining table, in both houses, I thought I detected a constraint, a caution. I did not risk raising political subjects myself. I wished I could say that I was the widow of Matthew de la Roche, for he was well known among the supporters of Mary Stuart and a connection with him might have improved my welcome. The fact that he was still alive, however, prevented me. I was not his widow, and his new wife was probably known to be with him in France.

I left those two houses feeling that I had sensed something, but I couldn't be certain what. It was as though the people who lived there were aware of things they would not mention in my presence, and in the house which was being looked after by a steward, there had been an interesting incident.

It happened while the steward was showing me the pictures, which he did in the morning, while our horses were being saddled. He was leading me towards a staircase which he said went to the gallery where most of the pictures in the house were hung, apart from two in the dining chamber, which I had already seen. As we approached the stairs, we passed a room with a door standing slightly open.

Glancing in, I saw that the room was a weaponry, and that two men were in there, one sharpening a sword and the other cleaning a musket. The steward saw me looking and remarked that his master liked everything to be kept in good order all the time. Then he hurried me on, talking volubly about the pictures upstairs, all his master's family portraits, he said. It was a small thing, but it was a pointer. It looked as if further fighting was expected. But when and why, and who would be fighting whom?

On the tenth day after leaving Windsor, with half of Lord Sussex's task now performed, though scarcely with much success, we arrived at the town of Kendal.

'Our next visit is to do with our own errand, isn't it, Mistress

Stannard?' Trelawny asked. 'We're going to see someone's great aunt now, are we not?'

'What is her home called?' Brockley asked me. 'Her name is Mistress Tracy, I think you said?'

'Yes. She's known as Bess, but I suppose that means Elizabeth. Mark couldn't remember the name of her house, but he did say it was big, and it's on the far side of Kendal, beside a lake. Someone in Kendal will have heard of it, I think. We'd better call on the vicar of the largest church we can find. He'll be able to tell us, for sure.'

Kendal turned out to be a busy place with a market in progress. The weather had brightened, and the edged wind had dropped, encouraging the crowds. There was no sign that war had recently raged round the district. The town had no defensive walls, and its inhabitants seemed entirely concerned with their own affairs, which plainly centred round the wool industry. In the market, stalls selling cloths and yarn and pens full of sheep were much in evidence. We found a helpful vicar without difficulty.

'Mistress Elizabeth Tracy? Of course, of course.' He was a cheery, chatty fellow, who didn't look as if he had ever heard the word *war*. 'Just go straight through the town and towards the lake and you'll see the chimneys of her house from the road. It's on the eastern side of the water. Littlebeck House it's called, from the stream that runs through the garden down to the lake. It's easy to find. You are relatives?'

'We're here on behalf of a great-nephew of hers,' I said. 'We have a message for her.'

'She'll make you welcome. She's a fine old lady.'

The house was impressive. Well, no doubt Mark's great aunt would be impressive as well. His recollections of her had been intimidating. *Great Aunt Bess's tenants do what she tells them, and if they don't, she eats them grilled for breakfast*, sounded positively terrifying.

We were admitted by a manservant and shown to a panelled hall, adorned with pairs of antlers from both red and fallow stags and a set of tapestries depicting the story of Helen of Troy. The floor was strewn thickly with fresh rushes, and a luxurious log fire burnt in a big stone hearth.

Our hostess found us clustered round it, standing up, since although there were stools and settles round the walls, there was only one seat near the hearth, an elaborately carved chair upholstered in crimson damask, which somehow we were all afraid to sit on.

Bess Tracy walked with the aid of a stick, but she held herself very erect. She was indeed a fine old lady, but also an alarming one. I never saw another human being who reminded me so powerfully of an eagle. She had all the essential features: strong hooked nose, fingers like talons – though I think that was due to the joint evil in her hands, which she clearly could not use with ease – and an extraordinary headdress like a bonnet coated with brown feathers. No doubt it was warm. What one could see of her hair was white, but her carefully plucked eyebrows were a pale golden-brown, and her round, arrogant eyes were a perfect match.

I introduced us, explaining that I had come on behalf of Mark Easton and once more presenting Brockley and Trelawny as relatives. They bowed graciously. Bess studied us with those remarkable eyes. Queen Elizabeth had golden-brown eyes too, but Mistress Tracy's were much more yellow and they were penetrating as well as arrogant. In a sharp voice which held only a trace of northern accent she said: 'Never heard of any of you, though it's not surprising. Mark never writes, though his uncle Robert did. You say he sent you, mistress?'

I hesitated. After all, since the matter concerned not merely a portrait of Gervase Easton but also his reputation, and since Bess Tracy was his kinswoman, the matter was more than a little delicate. I began with caution.

'I am a Lady of the Bedchamber to the queen,' I said. 'I met Mark, your great-nephew, when he came to Windsor with a message from Lord Sussex, concerning the – er – disturbances here in the north.'

'A charming way to put it,' said Bess Tracy. 'Disturbances, eh? I'm lucky that I don't hold this manor as a tenant of Charles Neville of Westmorland. It's my property, freehold. Though I'd have plenty to say to any landlord that told me he'd throw me off my estate for not betraying my lawful sovereign. His ears would ring, I promise you. And hers!'

'Hers?'

'He has a wife like a she-wolf,' said Bess the she-eagle, seating herself on the damask-covered chair. 'Jane's the sister of Norfolk, that overambitious popinjay. She has twice his strength of mind. But I,' Bess informed us, propping her stick beside the hearth and closing her talons round the chair arms, 'have twice *her* strength of mind. I would have had things to say if either she or her husband dared to threaten *me*.'

I believed her. The Nevilles, I was fairly sure, would have kept well away from Bess Tracy, even if she had, technically, been their vassal. I personally wouldn't have wanted her as an enemy.

'Well?' she said. 'You have a message from Mark?'

'He sends his compliments to you and will be glad to know that we find you well. Should you need anything that he can supply, he is in York with Lord Sussex and we'll take word to him on our way home.'

'And that's all?'

'No,' I said. 'There's something else. It concerns his father.'

'I wondered when you would come to the point. Why hasn't Mark come himself, though, or sent a courier with a letter? A court deputation suggests . . . I don't quite know what, but I scented an ulterior purpose at once.' Her mind was as sharp as any eagle's beak or talons. 'Oh, sit down,' she said impatiently. 'Pull some seats near the fire and let us be comfortable. Hardman will bring wine.'

The manservant appeared at that moment, with a tray. When he had gone and we were all seated, she looked at me keenly. 'So you are here for some reason connected with Gervase. Gervase the poisoner.'

'If he really was a poisoner,' said Trelawny boldly.

Of the three of us, Trelawny was assuredly the hardest to intimidate. He grinned at Bess Tracy, apparently not in the least troubled by her resemblance to a ferocious raptor.

Bess raised her thin eyebrows at him and enquired: 'If?'

'Mark thinks Gervase may have been innocent,' I said. 'And he is anxious to clear his father's name, if that is possible. He wishes to marry a young lady, the daughter of a friend of mine. Her name is Jane too,' I added, 'like the wife of Charles

Neville, but although it's a long time since I last saw her, I think she is a very sweet girl. She and her family are well known to me – and her parents will not agree to the match unless Gervase can be proved innocent.'

'From all I heard, he wasn't,' said Mistress Tracy with a sniff. She sipped some wine. 'Not that I was anywhere near the business. Hearsay, that's all I have to go on. But didn't someone actually see him add something or other to the victim's dinner?'

'There were two witnesses,' I said. 'The one who claimed she actually recognized Gervase has left Windsor and no one knows where she is. The other only saw a man who met the same description, but one thing she is sure about, and that is that the man she observed was left-handed.'

'Was Master Gervase Easton left-handed? Do you know, madam?' Brockley asked suddenly.

'Good God, I don't know. I never set eyes on the fellow. He was my younger brother's son, and he wasn't born till I was wed and had come here to Westmorland. Did you come all this way just to ask me that?'

'No,' I said. 'I understand that a portrait of Gervase was painted – by an artist called Jocelyn Arbuckle. It is said to show him sitting at a table with a pen in his hand. That would reveal, I think, which hand he used for writing. The portrait is not at Mark's family home. He thought you might know where it was – might even have it yourself.'

'Ah,' said Mistress Tracy. 'Gervase's picture. So that's what you're after. I had it at one time, yes. Gervase's brother Robert commissioned it about a year before Gervase died. Robert took it home, but his father – my brother Richard – wouldn't have it in the house. He had a real spite against Gervase for running off with a tenant's daughter. He wrote to me about it. Her only dowry's her pretty face, that's what his letter said. I did hear that he had someone else in mind for Gervase, someone with money and land behind her.

'And quite right too,' added our hostess, staring at us as though challenging us to contradict her. 'Pretty faces don't stay pretty for ever, but property's different. Look after it when you're young and it'll look after you when you're old. I've been none the worse for making a good marriage and nor was my husband, though I hardly knew him before we wed. He stayed at our house once when he was travelling back from Southampton after selling wool there. He had an introduction from someone my father knew. He took a fancy to me, and when he found I had a dowry worth looking at, it was all settled. And settled well, to my mind. Gervase was a young fool.'

My own first marriage had been a runaway match involving, on my part, a midnight escape out of a window and a perilous clamber down a fortunately sturdy growth of ivy to reach the arms of Gerald Blanchard, who was supposed to be betrothed to my cousin Mary. I opened my mouth to say so, caught Brockley's warning glance and held my tongue.

On that subject, at least. Instead, I asked: 'You say the portrait came to you, Mistress Tracy? How did that come about? Is it still here?'

'My brother sent it to me,' said Bess Tracy. 'Richard was a man of culture. He wrote songs and played the spinet very well. He greatly admired painting and sculpture. The letter he sent to me with the picture explained that, in his opinion, it was fine work and the artist had done him no harm; he would not destroy the skilled creation of another man. He could not tolerate a portrait of Gervase in his home, but he hoped I might find pleasure in it. And so I did. I never saw Gervase in the flesh, but his picture showed a fine young fellow. But I never noticed which hand he used to hold his pen.'

'And now?' I prompted, as she seemed to have sunk into a reverie. 'Is the portrait here still?'

She had said *his picture showed* and *I never noticed which hand he used to hold his pen.* Showed. Noticed. Both in the past tense. I waited anxiously for her reply.

'No, it is not. When my youngest daughter Blanche was married – oh, it was over twenty years ago – she asked to have the portrait. She liked it and wanted it to help ward off homesickness.

'Blanche was soft,' her mother added dispassionately. 'I hope she's grown up a trifle since she was a bride. She was nearly twenty-one then, but young for her years, soft as thistledown; nothing like me. She was frightened of leaving home; said she'd pine and she was afeared of the marriage bed. I'd found her a good man, believe me. Hal Winthorpe was kind-hearted and well off, though I grant you he was nothing much to look at. You wouldn't bother to put him in an oil painting. I told her all the pining and so on would pass, within a week, like as not.'

She looked at me and read my face. 'You're wondering if it did or didn't. I don't know. We sent her off with a wagonload of fine things – clothes, jewellery, furniture, tapestries and the deeds of two farms – and I've not seen her since. My rheumatics set in the year after she left. But I let her take the portrait with her, poor toad. She pleaded for it, and I thought, well, if she has a familiar face near her, even just a painted one, maybe it'll help her to settle. I was considering Hal as much as her. Marriage is a bargain, and a pining bride isn't a good bargain in my opinion.'

Mistress Tracy, I thought, hated admitting to any soft feelings of her own, but I suspected that she had some, if in a limited sense.

'She sounded happy enough when she wrote home,' Bess said. 'She said she had a fine house and that Hal was good to her. I fancy she settled all right, and maybe the portrait helped. If so, I'm glad I let her have it. I dare say she has it still. She's never had any children she could pass it on to, any road.'

I began to ask where Blanche lived, but Bess was in full nostalgic spate and cut across me.

'She's widowed now. I did hear roundabout that Hal wasn't as clever with his property as he ought to have been and got into debt at one point. But it can't have been serious; he died a few years back, and though I couldn't get to his funeral, one of my other daughters did, and she told me that the house was in good order and Blanche dressed as fine as a countess. She still lives in the same place. She's never remarried.'

I got my question asked at last. 'Where can we find her?'

'Oh – it's a fair way off, about twenty miles north-east of

Carlisle. I can show you a map with the place marked on it. Ramsfold, it's called.'

'Ramsfold,' I repeated.

Ramsfold was number three on the list provided by Lord Sussex.

FOURTEEN

Pursuit of a Portrait

We reached the town of Carlisle two days later. It was full of Lord Sussex's soldiers, and just inside the gate we came face to face with a gibbet on which a dozen sad bodies swung. Their garments were cheap; they looked like poor men. Elizabeth's orders concerning reprisals had arrived ahead of us, it seemed, and the ugly business had begun.

As one of the queen's ladies, I could have sought shelter for the night at the castle, but I could not agree with either Sussex or my royal half-sister that the wealthy should be allowed to buy their lives, while poverty meant doom. I preferred not to sit at meat in the castle hall with those who had carried out the hangings. 'An inn will suit me better,' I said. 'Let's find one.'

We were lucky in our choice of hostelry, for in it we discovered a man who made his living partly by serving drinks but also by guiding travellers who did not know the locality. Rab Fuller was a stolid, pink-faced fellow with a nearly incomprehensible northern accent, but he knew where Ramsfold was. I had made a rough copy of Mistress Tracy's map, but he had no need of it. He could lead us straight there in the morning, he said. He had his own mule and could go as fast as we could, in these snowy conditions. We could be there before sunset.

Carlisle was in Cumberland, whose earl had declared for the queen, but Ramsfold lay a few miles over the Northumbrian border, in what had been enemy territory. Our guide steered us competently, in a north-easterly direction. We passed through a hamlet, where we crossed a river on a bridge and rode on through land which grew progressively wilder and weather which had turned bitter again. There had been a fresh snowfall the previous night.

It was a lonely district. The few small villages were isolated signs of human life amid hills and moorlands. To the north the land was lower, and we saw dense forest in the distance. Rab told us that we were now in Northumberland, and a few miles further on he said that we had reached Ramsfold land. The country became less forbidding. We passed through a village where a number of people came to their cottage doors to stare. The path led on through a fir wood to emerge at the foot of a knoll, and the track, heavily trodden and covered with slush and broken ice, climbed towards a building at the top. 'That's Ramsfold,' said Rab.

I looked at the place with interest. Like many manor houses near the border, it was fortified. There was no moat, but the gradient to the gatehouse was steep, a defence in itself. Our horses were already tired. They were drooping wearily before we got to the gatehouse.

The porter, when we finally reached him, greeted us with restrained politeness. I explained that I had come from Mistress Blanche Winthorpe's mother, Mistress Bess Tracy. He said grumblingly that he would announce us and that we could come through the gatehouse but must remain mounted and wait in the outer courtyard. Obeying him, we found ourselves arousing interest from some cross-bred hounds in a fenced run to our left. As if they had mistaken us for a dinner which was being unkindly withheld from them, they threw themselves, baying, against their fence. Our horses stamped uneasily. 'I hope they can't get out,' said Trelawny, eyeing the hounds with dislike.

I patted Roundel to calm her and studied the main house, which faced us across the courtyard. Built of yellowish-grey stone, it had a crenellated watchtower at one end and arrow-slit windows. In front of us, at the top of a short flight of steps, was a massive door, shut fast and studded with iron. Even within its surrounding walls, the face which Ramsfold presented to visitors was hardly friendly.

'My, my,' said Trelawny. 'What a merry place this is. Always ready for a siege or a funeral, I'd say.'

'I think the idea is to avoid funerals,' Brockley told him. 'Whoever lives here is determined to defend themselves.'

Trelawny laughed, and the rest of us chuckled with him. Then the gatekeeper, who had disappeared not through the front door but round the right-hand end of the house, came back, accompanied by a groom and a stable boy. 'You can dismount. We'll see to your animals,' he said.

We had gained entrance, at least. We dismounted and handed our horses over. Brockley, who had been fretted by my recent insistence that he should masquerade as my relative, because it prevented him from going with the horses to see them properly cared for, now showed signs of wanting to go to the stables anyway, but I put my hand on his arm. 'No, Brockley. I want help from this Blanche Winthorpe, and I don't know what she's like. Her mother says she was soft as a girl, but she may have changed by now. She may be just like Bess!'

'Did that female peregrine falcon scare you?' Trelawny asked.

'You saw her like that too?' I said with interest. 'I thought of her as a she-eagle. I hope her daughter is gentler!'

Rab said in his broad accent that he would go with the grooms; he wanted to see to his own mule, anyway. He'd have to start back to Carlisle soon, he added, and looked at me questioningly.

'I don't know when we'll leave or quite where we'll go next,' I said. 'We'll find a guide from here when we go. Pay him, Brockley.'

As Rab went off with the grooms, the iron-studded door was opened, although the person who came through it was manifestly not Blanche Winthorpe. This was an upper manservant, very dignified in a black doublet adorned with a gold chain. He also had a face as stony as any outcrop on the northern moors.

'Good day. I am Ulverdale, butler and steward of this house.' He halted on the lowest step, and not at all in the attitude of one who bids welcome to a party of wayfarers. He looked as though he wished to bar our way and, if possible, send us on it.

From the corner of his mouth, Trelawny muttered: 'Dear

God, he's one of *those* butlers. Satan employs a demon blacksmith to forge them on an anvil in hell.'

'Quiet, Trelawny,' Brockley growled, also out of the corner of his mouth.

'My name,' I said to the butler, 'is Ursula Stannard. I am from the court of Queen Elizabeth and have at times served as one of her ladies. If, as I believe, the lady of this house is Mistress Blanche Winthorpe, then I have business with her. I was directed here by her mother, Bess Tracy of Kendal. My companions are relatives of mine: Master Roger Brockley and Master Carew Trelawny. Is Mistress Winthorpe at home?'

'The mistress has been unwell and may not wish to receive visitors.' Ulverdale's northern voice was as dignified as his mien. 'However . . .'

The day was passing, and the wind was sharp, and anyway, in the north of England, it is customary to make travellers welcome even if a wake is in progress. Ulverdale bowed to custom. 'If you will come this way, I will arrange refreshments for you and enquire if my mistress can see you,' he said, turning to lead the way up to the door.

We climbed the steps behind him, following him into a short stone passageway through a thick protective wall. This in turn delivered us to an inner courtyard at a higher level. Here, the snow had mostly been swept out of the way, and chickens scattered before us. A girl shaking a cloth out of a kitchen door to our left, and another drawing water from a well in the middle of the court, paused interestedly to watch us.

The house, which was bigger than it appeared from the outside, was built all round this inner court. From the style of the building, the place was a good century old or more, but some of its inner windows were not depressing slits like the outer ones, but modern mullions, though the ground-floor ones, I noticed, were smaller than those higher up and wouldn't admit much light.

The stables, where the grooms were now tending our mounts, were on our right, and our horses had evidently been brought in through a double-leaved gate on that side. Stabling, harness rooms and hay store occupied the ground floor of the right-hand wing, but the true main entrance to the house was on the left, flanked on either side by mullions, and this was where the butler led us.

Entering on his heels, we found ourselves at once in a big panelled hall not unlike the one at Littlebeck House though much less gracious. It certainly wasn't well lit, for although there were three big iron candle chandeliers hanging from the ceiling, none of them were in use. The shadowy minstrels' balcony which overlooked one end had a forlorn and dusty air, as though it hadn't seen a minstrel for a hundred years, and the slatted wooden stair that led down from it, into the hall, looked rickety.

I also noticed with regret that the white cloth on the big table in the middle was stained and the elaborate silver salt, which stood on the table among other miscellaneous objects such as knives and tankards, was tarnished. A film of dust covered the oak sideboard which stood between two of the mullioned windows, and the pewter dishes and tankards on its shelves looked dull. This was a sadly uncared for place.

It was not unoccupied, for three men in soldierly buff garments were playing cards at a small table near the fire with the help of the only extra lighting in the entire hall, a triple-branched candlestick in the middle of their table. They paused in their play to eye us sharply. As we waited for Ulverdale to show us where to go next, a door opened at the far end, and a woman came in. She entered diffidently, but when she saw us, she hurried towards us, though she detoured slightly as if she didn't want to pass too close to the card players.

'I saw from my parlour window that we had guests. How delightful – in January, too. I am Blanche Winthorpe. May I know . . .?'

I had a strong impression that Ulverdale would much rather she didn't know, but after all, we had been brought in to be presented to the mistress of the house. He introduced us, remembering to say that I was a lady-in-waiting to Queen Elizabeth.

I stepped forward, my hand extended. 'I am happy to meet you, Mistress Winthorpe,' I said, smiling, 'Madam, I am here with the knowledge and approval of your mother, Bess Tracy. I hope I find you in good health?'

'Tolerably, tolerably. The winter is always a wearing time. And my mother? Is she well?'

'You should not have left the warmth of your parlour, madam,' said Ulverdale. He was trying to sound solicitous, but to me he seemed irritated. 'This hall is draughty. Might I suggest that you and your guests withdraw? Joan is with you, I trust?'

'My maid,' said Blanche to me. 'Yes, indeed . . .'

Ulverdale had said she was ill, but I didn't think she was, though I felt that something was amiss with her in some other sense. Blanche Winthorpe was a plump lady with a pile of thick light-brown hair in front of her starched white cap. Her green, quilted satin sleeves were thick with fine embroidery, and her ruff was trimmed with costly lace, which spoke of means and position.

But that swerve as she crossed the hall and the nervous expression in her big grey eyes told another story. Also, when Ulverdale mentioned my connection with Elizabeth's court, I thought I had seen a flash in those eyes, though whether it was of hope or fear I couldn't tell. My companions had seen it, too.

'Something's going on here,' muttered Trelawny, just clearly enough for me and for Brockley to hear him.

'Your mother is well,' I said to our hostess, 'and sends her love. Madam, could we speak to you privately? These gentlemen are family connections, who have accompanied me to guard me along the way and are fully aware of the business in hand.'

'Of course, of course. Come through to the parlour. Ulverdale!' As though our presence had given her confidence, she adopted a more commanding tone. 'Take my guests' cloaks and bespeak some hot food and drink. They must be chilled, riding in this weather.'

Ulverdale bowed politely, and I felt sure that he was gritting his teeth. He took our cloaks as instructed, and we followed Blanche across the hall. Once more she swerved to keep a distance between herself and the card players, although this time she had the three of us close to her. I thought that she didn't realize she was doing it.

She led us through the further door, where we found ourselves in a parlour which was neat and pretty, if somewhat small for the mistress of the house. A young woman, who was sewing by the fire, rose as we came in and bobbed to us.

'My maid, Joan,' said Blanche. 'You may be seated again, Joan. Please, everyone, be comfortable.'

The parlour seemed to form part of a suite, because a spiral stone staircase came down into one corner of the room; very likely, there was a bedchamber above. The room was certainly a pleasing contrast to the bleakness of the hall. There was a bright fire, many lit candles, embroidered cushions and a smell of polish. And, hanging on the panelled wall opposite to the door, there was a portrait.

It was quite big, a good two feet by two. It showed a man seated at a desk, and the fashion of his ruff and doublet suggested that it had been painted at least twenty years earlier, perhaps more. I went straight across to it and looked at the artist's signature in the lower right-hand corner.

Jocelyn Arbuckle.

'Mistress Winthorpe,' I said, 'may I know the name of the man this excellent portrait shows? I have a good reason for asking – it has to do with my purpose in coming here. Your mother knows all about it.'

'That's my cousin Gervase,' said Mistress Winthorpe, sounding surprised. 'I always liked the picture, and my mother gave it to me as a wedding gift. He was her nephew. I believe there was some estrangement between him and his father, who therefore refused to keep the picture in his own home. Ah. Here is Ulverdale with some wine. Now, Mistress Stannard, you can explain this mysterious errand of yours to me.'

I stared at the portrait. So that was Gervase. Mark wasn't much like his father, except for one thing. They both had the same dramatic, sweeping eyebrows, marked enough to remove one question from my mind. I had wondered if Gervase's hatred of Hoxton had been because Mark was not, in fact, Gervase's son at all.

After all, if Hoxton had fathered him instead, then no one could say he was a poisoner's son, though whether the Masons would regard an irregular pedigree more kindly than a criminal one, I did not know. Now, looking at the portrait, I felt that, judging from those eyebrows, the man in the painting had to be Mark's true father.

Otherwise, Mark took after Judith. Gervase was dark, like his wife and son, but his eyes were blue and he had Bess Tracy's eagle profile, which Mark had certainly not inherited. The painted Gervase was looking straight ahead, but on the table before him lay an inkstand and a sheet of paper with writing on it, and he held a quill, as though he had been interrupted while working and had just glanced up.

The hand in which he held the pen was his left.

FIFTEEN

The Scent of Treason

'Did you say,' asked Blanche, 'that my cousin's portrait is connected to your purpose here?'

Silently, I cursed. I had made a bad mistake, the kind which no agent of experience should ever make. I had admitted that to find Gervase's picture was why I had come to Ramsfold, thus spoiling an excuse to ask to be shown round the house to look at all its pictures. Ramsfold was a suspect house, and for a moment I had let myself forget it.

It was too late now to retract. I sipped mulled wine, smiled as pleasantly as I could and told Blanche of the errand on which Mark had sent us. I could least make sure that I sounded candid and innocent.

'Having seen the painting, I now know which hand Master Easton senior used for writing,' I said. 'Alas, it comes near to confirming his guilt. Your cousin's guilt, I should say. I am sorry.'

'Oh, it means nothing to me,' Blanche said. 'I never met Gervase. He never came north, and I have never been anywhere else. I've never cared for travelling. Joan – Master Brockley's goblet is empty, I think.'

Joan, who was sharing the wine and had been put in charge of the tray, rose gracefully and went the rounds with the jug. 'My mistress is happy, living quietly in her home,' she said in a gentle voice.

I drank, wondering what, after so foolishly ruining my most obvious approach, I could do about my second errand. Was Blanche friend or foe? I had an instinctive feeling that conspiracies would frighten her. I ventured what I hoped was a natural and commonplace question.

'Have the recent troubles in the north affected you?' I asked Blanche. 'You are in Northumberland here, are you not?'

It went home. I saw it in her eyes; saw the quiver of her lip. And also saw the quick glance she gave towards Joan who, busy refilling Brockley's goblet, did not notice.

'It has not quite passed us by.' Her tone was flurried. 'Some men went from here to join my lord of Northumberland. I fear they won't come back. They have fled with him into Scotland. I may be fined, though they didn't go at my orders. I am loyal to the queen.'

'Is your home held from the Earl of Northumberland?' I asked. 'If you are his tenant, he could demand that your men join him and you would have no say. You might then avoid blame.'

'It's held from him now,' Blanche said sadly. 'It used to be freehold, but my husband ran into debt. He gambled, you know, and then there was an unwise purchase of a new breed of sheep. The north was too harsh for them, and we lost the whole flock and a whole year's wool. To keep Ramsfold, we had to sell it to the earl!'

'Oh dear,' I said sympathetically. I understood, all too well.

'It sounds funny, doesn't it? To keep it we had to sell it!' Under her forced brightness, I heard something close to hysteria. 'So now I am a tenant, and when the earl demanded that I provide two dozen men, I had to do as I was bid. And more than enough men were willing.'

Joan, who had finished topping up the goblets and resumed her seat, raised her head proudly. 'But, madam, why should they not be, when they were called to help reclaim England for the true faith?'

'Joan is Catholic,' said Blanche. 'I am not. Though she is much attached to me; indeed, she scarcely ever leaves my side.' A flicker of a glance from Brockley told me that he, too, had heard the curious nuance in Blanche's voice. And now, in her eyes, I saw a signal. It was a plea.

Darkness was falling. There was no question about whether or not we would spend the night at Ramsfold. We had no alternative. We were shown to two rooms on the other side of the courtyard, one for myself and one for the men. They were above the stables, but were nevertheless perfectly good, well-furnished guest rooms. Rab, apparently, had already taken himself and his mule off on the road back to Carlisle.

I longed to speak to Blanche in private, but it was all too true that Joan scarcely ever left her side. The maid was apparently bound to her mistress by an invisible fetter. I also wanted to confer with my own companions and found that even this had suddenly become difficult. It was as though we were being kept under surveillance. The house seemed short of servants, but nevertheless, a diminutive lass called Annet was found to act as my maid and Ulverdale himself hovered round Brockley and Trelawny, offering to unpack their saddlebags. As I finished washing and changing, I heard them shooing him out and then Brockley called me, but when, taking a candle, I left my room, tiresome little Annet tried to tag after me.

I sent her back, saying that my things needed tidying, and joined my friends in the narrow passageway which ran outside our rooms. In daylight, this was lit, though none too well, by arrow-slit windows looking outwards. No doubt, in wilder days, the passage had been a standpoint for archers. Now it presented us with a row of closed doors, any of which might conceal interested ears.

Trelawny, who like myself was carrying a candle, put the situation succinctly and in a low voice. 'If there isn't something odd going on here, I'll eat Brockley's helmet.'

'I know,' I said. 'But how do we find out what it is? I've found the portrait, by the way; it's in Blanche's parlour. And I've gone and told her I've found what I came for, so now I can't ask to be shown round the house to search for it!'

'Did you learn anything from it, madam?' Brockley asked.

'I'm afraid so. The confounded man *was* left-handed. But now, how do we go about investigating this house?'

'We keep our eyes and ears open,' said Trelawny, 'and evade our kindly hosts and explore on our own whenever we get the chance. Who knows what we may come across – or who we may find? Let's start by seeing where this passage goes.'

Our first foray along the passage ended in a locked door. Turning back, we tried the other direction and soon found ourselves turning into a wide gallery along the upper floor of the wing forming the rear of the courtyard. It was cold and dark, and I jumped when a lantern glimmered and Ulverdale, ghostlike, appeared from the shadows, to ask if we had missed our way and to tell us that supper would be served in an hour.

'If you would care to go down to the parlour, madam, Mistress Winthorpe would no doubt enjoy your company.' I noticed that this time there was no reference to poor health. 'And perhaps the gentlemen would like to come to the hall for a hand of cards before the meal is served.'

Exploration was decidedly at an end.

Supper had been served to Blanche and myself and the watchful Joan in Blanche's parlour, while Brockley and Trelawny had been asked to sup with the other men in the hall. After supper, Blanche and Joan retired and Ulverdale came to say that my escort were staying in the hall for a game of backgammon. I left them to it, thinking they might draw the men out, and, like Blanche, went to my room.

Annet tried to help me undress and offered to spend the night on a truckle bed in my room, but I declined both services and sent her back to her usual bed among the other maids. I had gathered that there were three others apart from Joan; a very small number for a house of this size, but nothing seemed to be normal in Ramsfold.

Having bidden Annet a civil goodnight, I bolted my door and sat down, still fully dressed, on my bed. I was uneasy and wanted to talk to my companions. I would wait, I thought, until I heard them come upstairs.

There had been a clock in the parlour, and I knew I had retired at about eight. I had a clock candle in my luggage and lit it from the candles already provided so that it would tell me of the passing hours. I waited, listening.

At nearly midnight, I heard the sound of feet along the narrow passage outside. Thinking that this must be Trelawny and Brockley, going to their room, I rose and went to my door, but then stopped. The footsteps had come from the wrong direction, from that of the locked door which had earlier barred our way. They were now receding towards the dark gallery where Ulverdale had intercepted us. There was certainly no sound of a door near mine being opened or shut.

Before I came to my room, someone had been in and closed the shutters. Quickly, I blew out all but one of my candles, put that one where it couldn't shine through my window and quietly opened my shutters again. The window looked out across the courtyard. I glanced at the gallery to the rear of the house, and there was indeed a light moving through it, but something even more interesting was happening in the hall.

I stared. The hall windows had no shutters, and I could clearly see that not only was the hall still lit, but extra lights were being kindled. The chandeliers, in the usual way, had pulley ropes secured to rings on the wall. I could just make out that someone was unfastening one of the ropes. I saw him lower its burden and then use a nearby candle to light those in the ring of the chandelier. New light sprang up. He put his candle back in its holder, released the rope and hauled on the pulley, raising the assembly back to its proper place before knotting the rope into its ring once more. After that, he moved on to another chandelier. It was as though the hall were being prepared for a revel.

I could not see Brockley or Trelawny, but as I peered, trying to discover if they were there, I noticed that the people in the hall were not all men. A female figure had passed across one of the windows. For a moment, I thought: I see. How distasteful, and no wonder Blanche Winthorpe gets out of the way early in the evening. Then I realized that this figure was dignified, stately. Her ruff was vast, her profile lofty. This was no young girl. Nor was it Blanche; this woman was nothing like her. And whoever she was, she looked far more like the lady of a big house than Blanche did.

Somewhere inside me, there was a thud of excitement. Was it possible? Of course it was. Ramsfold was on that list. If I could only see that woman more closely, then I would know.

I was about to close my shutters again when I heard the sound I had been waiting for, that of footsteps going to the room occupied by Brockley and Trelawny. Ulverdale was apparently with them, but I heard him bid them goodnight, and then the sound of his feet retreating. Their door closed, and my ears picked up another small sound. They, too, were unshuttering their window.

The night was cold, and I put a cloak on before I left my room. I caught up my candle and hastened out to tap on their door. Trelawny opened it.

'Something's happening in the hall,' I said shortly. 'I heard you open your shutters. Did you see?'

'We did indeed, madam,' Brockley said as Trelawny drew me inside. 'We didn't learn anything from the men this evening,' he added. 'All the talk was of cards and hunting, hounds and horses. Then everyone said they were going to bed, and when we came up here, we found our shutters closed. But somehow . . .'

'Ulverdale insisted on lighting us to bed,' said Trelawny, 'but when we left the hall, we noticed that no one seemed to be putting any lights out. We thought it odd, and when we got here, we looked out to see what was afoot. I scent unlawful doings. Treason, maybe.'

'We need a better vantage point,' I said.

'The minstrels' balcony,' said Brockley. 'We can probably see without being seen *and* hear, from up there.'

'How do we get there?' I said.

'Back along this passage to the gallery where we went earlier, along the rear wing of the house, madam,' said Brockley. 'From the far end, there's a door to the balcony.'

'During the evening,' explained Trelawny, 'we both made excuses to leave the hall for calls of nature and managed to slip out without escorts. We both – er – missed our way in the process. You could say we did a little sniffing around. Literally.'

He grinned, with a flash of good white teeth from the midst of his beard and a wicked smile. 'The men use a privy in the rear wing, under that gallery where Ulverdale caught us all earlier on. Brockley here found a stair up to the gallery and explored. He now has a good idea of its layout. All I – or my nose – discovered was the wine cellar. There's a grating in the courtyard, and you can smell wine if you stand over it. The way down must be from the hall at the kitchen end – I saw servants coming up that way, with flagons. Odd, but this house has seen a good few alterations in its time, I fancy. Well, Brockley's our guide now.'

'Come on,' said Brockley.

Quietly, we left the room. In a whisper, I enjoined caution. 'Someone went this way earlier. I heard them and saw their light. We'd better blow our candles out or we might be seen. I hope no one is lying in wait in the minstrels' balcony!'

The wide rear gallery had been created to give bygone ladies of the house somewhere to walk in bad weather. We could see our way without candles for the night was clear, if frosty, and there was a moon. It didn't penetrate the passage outside our rooms, but here it cast pale rectangles of light across the floor. 'This is a ghostly place,' I whispered. 'I'm glad I'm not alone.'

'If we meet a ghost, Brockley and I will draw swords on it. Nothing like moonlit steel for separating real spooks from frauds,' Trelawny whispered back.

Brockley murmured: 'There's torchlight ahead. I think it's over a door to Mistress Blanche's bedchamber. It's a room above her parlour, anyway.'

We went warily, keeping to the shadows, but no one stopped us. The light was a flambeau in a wall bracket, illuminating a recessed door which, I noticed, was bolted on our side. 'The little stair I found is just ahead,' whispered Brockley, pointing. 'And the way into the minstrels' balcony is here on the left. Careful, now.'

'If the balcony is empty,' Trelawny said softly, 'we'll creep on to it. Pull your cloaks over your faces, and if anyone looks up at the gallery, shut your eyes. Eyes can glint in even the faintest light.'

He steered us to an archway on the left where we found another, smaller, recessed door. There was no flambeau here, and Trelawny had to feel for the latch. He lifted it noiselessly and inched the door open. 'It's clear,' he breathed. 'If anyone came this way, they went on down to the hall.'

Very quietly, we slipped inside. The hall below was well lit, by all three chandeliers plus numerous candles, and I was alarmed for a moment to see that the nearest chandelier cast a strong light on the middle of the balcony. Then I saw that we were at one end, and both ends were deep in shadow. If we made no noise, and no sudden moves which might catch the tail of someone's eye, we would probably remain unseen.

Carefully, holding our cloaks over our faces, the three of us sank down to crouch behind the wooden railings which edged the balcony. We could see between them, without being dangerously close, and if we couldn't hear as well as we would have liked, we could still hear enough.

What was happening down below was no revel. Those concerned were seated in businesslike fashion round the central table, and their faces were intent, brows furrowed and mouths unsmiling. Their dress was formal: ruffs and doublets; cloaks for warmth. There were six of them: the three men we had seen playing cards in the hall, Ulverdale, a man I recognized as the groom who had taken our horses and the woman I had glimpsed through the window earlier.

The woman was evidently in charge. She had her back to the balcony, but as we were well to one side, we could see part of her face, outlined against the light from a tall candlestick on her right. She was somewhere in early middle life, her head-carriage haughty and her dress imposing: green and gold brocade with a splendid ruff and a jewel-sewn headdress over crimped waves of pale-gold hair. Her voice carried, too; educated and commanding.

As we took our places, she had just interrupted the man on her left. 'Cease repeating yourself, Robby. Obviously, we must choose our moment with care, and our friends across the border must be warned that that Protestant vixen in Windsor intends to send Lord Sussex into Scotland to hale the fugitives back. Ulverdale, where is that map?'

'Here, Lady Anne.' Ulverdale reached under his cloak and produced a scroll, which he handed to her.

Brockley, easing his cloak briefly away from his mouth, breathed: 'Lady Anne who?' into my ear.

I was almost sure I knew the answer to that. The woman below answered perfectly to the description I had been given of Northumberland's wife. I could remember the wording clearly. *Tall, well dressed. Ash-pale hair, commanding manner; clear voice.* This had to be Lady Anne of Northumberland, who along with Jane Neville of Westmorland (whose description was *middle height, plain of face, nondescript brown hair and a shrew*) had been one of the driving forces behind the rebellion. Here was Lady Anne, still in England when she was supposed to be in Scotland. Rumour had spoken the truth.

I turned, meaning to whisper a reply to Brockley, and found that I had a foot caught up in my cloak hem. I edged it free, but as I did so, there was the faintest rustle and a tiny creak from the wooden balcony floor. The woman raised her head. 'What was that? I heard something.'

She looked about her, and then, though only momentarily, up at the minstrels' balcony. As her gaze came in our direction, I shut my eyes against the danger of a fugitive candle-beam and hoped the others had done the same. There in the darkness, we cowered, as still as though we had been turned to ice. Ulverdale said: 'This place has rats, like everywhere else, and houses always creak at night. But I wish, my lady, if you will forgive me, that we had held this meeting in your tower or delayed it until these inconvenient travellers had left.'

'We have urgent matters to discuss, and who knows how long our unwanted guests will stay? Also,' said Lady Anne, quite petulantly, 'I find it tedious to be confined to my tower. I've been there all this evening. One cannot even embroider in winter; candlelight isn't good enough. Being a man, you wouldn't know. I suffered from ennui. This is the second time we have had wayfarers in the house since I arrived. Why do folk journey about in the winter? Though they at least are free to roam. I pity Queen Mary, shut up in Tutbury. I tell you, I welcomed a change of scene tonight. Set the dogs to ratting in the morning. Now, the map.'

We had not been seen. We breathed easily again. Below us, the woman was unrolling the map on the table. Her voice came again. 'Our friends across the border should be urged to seek sanctuary in this direction.' Her left forefinger pointed to something on the map. I saw a wedding ring glint on the same hand. 'They can perhaps then make their way south, get *behind* Sussex's men, cross into England and come here. Blanche's villagers can billet them if they overflow from this house.'

'She won't like it,' said Ulverdale. 'And she's capable of betraying us if we don't take care. There's more of her mother in her than you realize, my lady of Northumberland. Have you met her mother?'

I felt Brockley twitch and, on the other side of me, thought I just detected Trelawny's indrawn breath. They both knew who she was now, without my telling them. There was no doubt either about the nature of the meeting in the hall. It was a council of war.

'I have not met Blanche's mother, but it makes no matter,' said Lady Anne coldly. 'Blanche will do as she is bid or lose her home. She must be kept from private talk with these strangers, however, just in case she risks underhand dealings. One of them is from Elizabeth's very court! Our supporters must not be taken by Sussex. They must return here and regroup . . .'

Ulverdale said something, in which the word *timing* was audible.

Anne made an impatient gesture. 'Of *course* the right timing is crucial. We would be wise to wait until Elizabeth's reprisals are over. They will work for us, if we let her have her head. Let the red mare,' said Anne of Northumberland viciously, 'gallop to her destruction. Let her thunder blindly on over the precipice. All these hangings will breed much bitterness, and that will bring us new support. Cumberland may change his mind and come in with us after all. We shall be upheld by the Pope; I have received word that he proposes to issue a Bull to that effect. That will encourage new recruits.

'Once the north is quiet again and Elizabeth is off her guard, we shall be at our strongest, and then we shall strike. And Scotland will be wide open to Mary's reinstatement. Our queen will have her crown again. Which brings us to item two on this agenda . . .'

'Ah, yes,' said Ulverdale. 'I think we should send two messengers. The one who is to warn our fugitive supporters will have enough to do. The other must go to Archbishop Hamilton of St Andrews. He is the conduit for passing word to the chosen assassin. The sooner that Regent Moray is out of Queen Mary's path, the better. A dead Regent of Scotland is what we want, not a displaced one.'

Up in the gallery, all three of us went rigid. We dared not

turn our heads even by a fraction to look at each other, but we felt each other's rigidity all the same. This was not just the scent, but the stench, of treason. The very air was stiff and noisome with shock.

With his forefinger still tracing lines on the map, Ulverdale said: 'Who would be the best couriers?'

'My two retainers,' said Lady Anne. 'They both come from the border and they both know southern Scotland better than anyone else here – and better than any of the village lads, either.'

'Aye,' said one of the other men. 'The lads still left in the village are good Northumbrians, but none of them have been further than twenty miles from home in their lives. All the more experienced village men are over the border with the earl, along with most of the men who used to serve this house. Lady Anne's lads will do better.'

'Quite.' Lady Anne nodded. 'They had better set out at dawn. Yes, Hankin? You want to say something?'

The groom had cleared his throat. 'They'll have a hard ride,' he said and pointed at the windows.

While we had been huddled in the minstrels' gallery, the moonlight had vanished into cloud. A candle, shining from the sill, showed us that it was snowing. Big flakes, falling thickly.

Beside me, Trelawny breathed: 'The ground will be three feet deep by morning.'

SIXTEEN

Most Hateful Task

I saw, next morning, that although Trelawny's forecast of snow three feet deep had been a little too pessimistic, there had certainly been a heavy fall in the night. I remembered what he had said about the wine cellar grating and hoped that someone had closed it; otherwise the cellar would have snow piled up on its floor by now.

We had waited until the meeting below was over, and then crept back through the long gallery, densely dark now that the moon had gone. We held a brief council in my room, but there was little to decide. Our course of action was obvious. The search for the portrait and our errand for the queen had both ended here in Ramsfold, and the presence of Anne of Northumberland must be reported as soon as possible. We must reach Carlisle, inform whoever was in charge there, ask where to find Lord Sussex and then bear the news to him in person. We had no time to lose.

This morning, from the look of that snowfall, I feared that this might be difficult.

All the same, somebody had ridden out. There were hoof marks in the courtyard, and it looked as if the messengers had left as planned. If they proposed to struggle to Scotland in these conditions, one could only pity them. And hope that they would be delayed so long that our news would reach its destination before their messages could be delivered.

Annet appeared at that moment, and I let her help me dress. Brockley and Trelawny came tapping at my door almost as soon as I was ready, and I determined on a firm line. 'I want to talk to my companions,' I said to Annet. 'We wish to take our leave, but I must ask them what they think of this weather. We are accustomed to talk in privacy.'

She looked a little confused, but she could hardly refuse to obey a direct order. She left the room. Having made sure that she wasn't listening at the door, Brockley said: 'I see that someone has braved the snow, but I don't advise it, personally. It doesn't matter if the messengers to Scotland never get there, but when we set off for Carlisle, and probably for York after that, we *must* get there. We'd best be careful.'

'I agree,' Trelawny said, soberly for once. 'Conditions aren't impossible, but things may be worse in other places. I don't think we should leave today. You can't report anything if you're lost in a blizzard or confronted by a snowdrift taller than you are. Let us hope that that is just what happens to those messengers, and meanwhile, can we make use of the time? To find out more?'

Brockley said thoughtfully: 'There was that odd reference to the Pope last night. Something about a Bull – a statement – which he intends to issue.' He looked at me. A faint, wry smile appeared on his face. He said: 'Madam, there's a task you much dislike, and to be honest, I dislike it on your behalf. It always scares us both half to death. But if Anne of Northumberland has been corresponding with His Holiness—'

'His *Un*holiness,' growled Trelawny, interrupting him.

'If,' said Brockley, interrupting back, 'that terrifying woman has been in touch with Rome, we might find proof of that in her private correspondence. If we could get at it.'

'Well, we can't,' I said, in what I knew were thankful tones. I knew what Brockley had meant the moment he spoke of a task that both of us disliked and feared. One of the duties which an agent has to perform, all too often, is reading other people's papers. This usually means intruding into their private rooms and opening their private document boxes. One is always afraid of being caught.

And rightly. No matter how careful you are, there is always the risk that the owners of the documents will come back unheralded from their dinner invitation, their marketing, their hunting, masque or day's work. They have felt unwell or bored; or it has started to rain. So far I had never been caught, although it had been a near thing once or twice. The fear was always present.

'True,' Brockley said, frowning. 'We heard Lady Anne say

last night that she was tired of being forced to keep to her chambers – I fancy they're in that locked tower at the south-east corner. If that's where her papers are, and I expect it is, then she'll be there with them. I suppose getting at them won't be possible.'

'It's clearly a problem. Unless,' said Trelawny in helpful tones, 'we create a diversion.'

We looked at him, in my case with annoyance. In my view, the fact that the papers were out of reach was a blessing, not a problem, or if it was a problem, I didn't want it solved.

'What kind of diversion?' Brockley asked.

Trelawny gave us his most wicked smile. His eyes were dancing. 'Something to draw her out of the tower, or wherever she is. Suppose,' he suggested sweetly, 'we started a fire?'

I had a sudden vision – which, from what I knew of Trelawny, seemed entirely possible – of Brockley's old comrade, with the best of intentions, blithely burning Ramsfold to the ground. And any incriminating correspondence along with it, too. 'No. Blanche wouldn't like it,' I said repressively.

Brockley cleared his throat, and I let a small sigh escape me. Brockley was for ever finding subtle ways to make me understand that he considered it most unsuitable for a gentlewoman such as myself to keep on getting entangled in plots and counterplots and the ferreting out of secrets. Yet, when we were on the hunt, some instinct for following a quarry to the final end always overtook him. Once his blood was up, he would follow the scent with more determination even than I did, even if it meant thrusting me forward into the very tasks that in the normal way he considered so undesirable for a lady.

'Could we not tempt her out of her tower in a less dangerous fashion?' he said. 'If she is bored, confined to her rooms, I wonder what she would do if she heard something very intriguing going on in the hall? Sound would carry from the hall to the tower, I fancy, especially if we opened a window and made *plenty* of noise.'

'What sort of noise?' I asked.

'Well,' said Brockley, 'Carew and I could practise swordplay. You've watched us doing that before, madam. You know that when we get together with blades in our hands, we tend not to be exactly quiet.'

I said: 'But if she doesn't want to be seen, she'll probably still resist temptation.'

'She might do what we did – go to the minstrels' balcony and stand in the shadows,' said Trelawny.

Before I could stop myself, I said: 'Before you came up last night, I think someone passed my door, coming from the south-east tower – from that locked door we couldn't get through. Perhaps that was Lady Anne, going to the hall by way of the gallery and the minstrels' balcony. It would be a reasonable route for her to take, if she didn't want to cross the courtyard. In such cold weather, she probably wouldn't.'

'Very likely,' said Trelawny. 'Now, if we tempt her out, she may lock the tower door behind her, but Brockley tells me that you can pick a lock.'

'You have your lockpicks with you, madam?' said Brockley, sounding quite proud of me.

'Yes,' I said briefly and gloomily.

'If you find people there,' said Trelawny, 'insist that the door *wasn't* locked and say you were just roaming about to pass the time. Then leave. But if we do our part properly, we may draw everyone out, Lady Anne and any servants she has with her, and give you a clear field. You'd better breakfast with Mistress Winthorpe, and then make an excuse to come back here. Then we'll set to.'

'I could kill you both,' I said candidly. 'It's a most promising idea.'

To begin with, however, I thought it was going to fail, even though the din which Trelawny and Brockley created in the hall was magnificent. The shouted insults, the clashing of blades and the laughter of onlookers poured across the courtyard from the hall windows. No one in the whole house could have missed them. No one apparently did. From my own window I saw servants appearing from various doors and grooms from the stable and watched them run across the snowy court to find out what was happening.

But for some time, it seemed, Lady Northumberland defied

her natural curiosity and stayed put. I alternated between watching from my window and listening at my door for footsteps coming from her tower. Nothing happened, and I began to give up hope. Anxious, though, in case the noise my friends were making had prevented me from hearing her, I finally peered into the passage. I looked towards the tower, and at that very moment its door began to open. I withdrew my head quickly, but a few seconds later, I peered out once more. Three female figures were receding towards the door to the gallery. They all had headdresses on, but I saw the tallest one turn a little to speak to one of the others and glimpsed her profile. I also caught a glint of gold embroidery on her skirt hem. She was assuredly Anne of Northumberland. The other two were probably her maids.

I hadn't heard any sound of her tower door being locked after her. As soon as she and her entourage were out of sight, I went to try it. It was open. I entered Lady Anne's quarters without the aid of picklocks.

I found myself in a first-floor parlour twice the size of the one occupied by Blanche, elegantly panelled and tapestried, with dried rosemary in the rushes underfoot and a bright fire in the hearth. It looked far more like a private parlour for the lady of the house than the one in the suite which Blanche now occupied. Very likely, this tower *was* hers, ruthlessly requisitioned by Lady Anne. It would be in character, I thought.

At this stage, I could still claim that I was wandering about, curing the tedium of being mewed up due to bad weather by exploring Ramsfold House. If challenged, I could say: 'I'm sorry; I've lost my bearings and lost my way. Where in the world am I? I'm so sorry if these are someone's private rooms.'

The tower, however, seemed to be empty. Everyone must have gone across to the hall. In one corner of the parlour there were steps, leading both up and down. Swiftly, I established that the floor below contained storerooms and that on the floor above the parlour there were two good bedchambers with velvet-hung four-posters. Seizing my chance, and with my heart thumping as it always did when I carried out this sort of task, I moved quickly about from place to place, seeking a document box. I examined clothes presses and cupboards, settles and window seats and peered under the beds.

I eventually found what I sought, beneath the lift-up seat of a small chest-settle in one of the bedchambers. The box was also in the form of a chest, a small one, but iron-bound and fastened with a padlock. I shook it and heard the rustle of paper within. I took it to the bed, and now, at last, my lockpicks had work to do.

It was a long time since I had used this delicate skill, and I was nervous, listening intently all the time for returning footsteps. How long could Brockley and Trelawny keep up that performance in the hall? I really did regard this sort of thing as the most hateful task that my curious profession ever required of me. If I were found now, I could make no excuses. I had made the crossing between innocence and guilt. My hands shook as I got out my set of thin steel rods with the hooks on the end, and the first ones I tried were wrong for the lock I was trying to coax. It was several minutes before I found the right ones and the old trick of seeing with my fingers came back to me.

The padlock clicked open at last. I lifted it clear, threw back the lid of the chest and there indeed were Lady Anne's private papers.

They didn't at first seem to amount to anything useful. Most of them were charters and correspondence to do with land, sheep, produce, rents, the sort of thing any landowner would have. I pawed through one document after another, in vain. By the time I reached the very bottom of the pile, I felt that I had spent hours over the business.

But there, at the very bottom, I found it. From the date on the document, which was more recent than those on the letters above it, I thought that it had been put beneath them to keep it as secret as possible.

It was on beautiful vellum, a lovely example of the calligrapher's art. It came from Rome, from the Vatican, thanking my lord and lady of Northumberland for their most pious and generous contribution to the cause of combating the rise of heresy. It assured them that if the restoration of Mary of Scotland did not soon take place, and if she was not made officially the heir of Elizabeth Tudor, then a Bull would be issued freeing all English Catholics from their duty to obey the Crown. Elizabeth would be formally deposed by the one true Church. It would be enjoined upon all true believers in England that they should not obey her or any of her laws, and that excommunication should fall on the heads of those who did so. No Catholics should regard themselves as Elizabeth's subjects.

The Northumberlands (and the Westmorlands, most likely) had been bribing the Vatican.

I held the vellum, so physically beautiful and so spiritually horrible, in a shaking hand. Just a letter, exquisitely penned on a lovely material, but as dangerous as a cartload of gunpowder and monstrously cruel. I knew there were numerous decent Catholics in England who did not consider that their faith obliged them to be disloyal to their anointed queen – honest people who only wanted to worship in the way that they were used to, to hold the rituals they loved and which reassured them in this dangerous world. They wanted to invoke the protection of the saints against fevers and plagues; the deaths of children and the perils of childbirth; the degenerations of age; the miseries of hunger when the crops were bad.

They did not want to be told that they must choose between these reassurances and their duty as citizens. They did not want to be told that they must be prepared to become traitors if they wished for spiritual comfort on earth and peace in heaven.

They were going to be told. The aim of this Bull was to turn hundreds of decent English men and women into potential assassins. And threaten them with damnation if they refused.

The letter did not actually state in so many words that it would then become the duty of the faithful to murder Elizabeth if the opportunity arose or could be made. But the underlying meaning was there.

Someone must warn Elizabeth. Just what she could do, I couldn't imagine, but to be forewarned was to have a chance of taking steps; of preparing an answer to steady the nerves of her people; of arranging protection for herself; of mobilizing her defences.

Still trembling, I reread the letter, memorizing it. Then I put it back in the bottom of the chest, shut it and replaced the padlock, pushing it home until it clicked. I picked up the chest to return it to its hiding place.

In my horror, I had forgotten to listen for footsteps. As I lifted the lid of the window seat, the door of the bedchamber opened and there on the threshold were Lady Anne and the butler Ulverdale.

I had at least not been caught reading the letter. I was only holding the locked chest and standing with the raised window seat in my hand. My lockpicks I had already put away in their hidden pouch. No one could have told whether I was returning the chest or had just taken it out, or guessed that I could open the lock. But it was bad enough. I stared back at them across my indefensible burden, as trapped as a murderer who has been discovered standing over a victim with a gory knife.

'I guessed it,' said Ulverdale, addressing Lady Anne. 'The minute I saw you, my lady, come on to the minstrels' balcony and noticed that Mistress Stannard had not, I thought: this is a ploy. A ploy to create a diversion – to divert whom? Who else but my lady? She has been tempted out of her quarters. Why?'

'You were perfectly right,' said Lady Anne harshly. Standing there, tall and angry, her hood thrown back and her pale gold head high, she was an intimidating sight. 'You did well to fetch me so quickly. Well, well. When Ulverdale told me that a Mistress Stannard had arrived, I wondered where I had heard the name before. I have remembered now. You used to be Mistress Blanchard, and you did secret work for that red vixen you call the queen – except that in time it ceased to be much of a secret. I suppose something has woken her suspicions of this house and she sent you here to poke and pry. Give me that!'

She strode forward and seized the chest, examining it keenly. 'You are a fool. I would never leave my private papers anywhere but in a locked container. I doubt if you would find it very easy to open this padlock. Have you tried?'

Evidently, some of the details of my secret career still

remained secret. 'I've only just found it,' I said in a sullen voice. I looked down at the padlock. 'No, Lady Anne, I don't think I could get through that.'

'You know who I am?'

'I've visited the north before. You were pointed out to me once,' I said untruthfully. On no account must she know of our eavesdropping the previous night.

'I see. You don't deny that you were prying in my rooms.'

'Are they yours? Mistress Blanche Winthorpe is the lady of this house. Everyone thinks you are in Scotland.'

'Lady Westmorland has fled north with her husband, but I remained behind,' said Anne of Northumberland, 'to salvage what I could of our unhappy situation. I am in this house because my own husband is the landlord. Blanche is merely a tenant.'

'Well,' I said, wondering what Brockley and Trelawny were doing and whether they knew I was in danger, 'what now?'

'I think that she and her henchmen had better disappear,' said Ulverdale grimly. 'It's the best thing, though disagreeable. You need not be concerned, my lady. I will take this impertinent intruder away and deal with her and her companions.'

'You mean murder them?' said Lady Anne, though not at all as though the idea scandalized her. She sounded as though she were merely considering alternative methods of cooking a chicken (*would a fricassée be best?)* or deciding on the most convenient route to a friend's distant home (*there is a short cut, but only in dry weather*).

'What else can we do with them?' said Ulverdale reasonably.

'I think,' said Lady Anne, considering me with dislike but also with assessment, 'that we would do better to keep them close for a while. You may not know it, Ulverdale, but now that I realize who this lady is, I can tell you that she is something more than a rather too loyal servant of her majesty Queen Elizabeth. She is also her half-sister.'

'Half-sister!'

'Bastard half-sister,' said Lady Anne calmly. She gave me a grim smile. 'Yes, my dear, that too is now quite widely known. The queen has an affection for you. You would make quite a useful hostage, I think, and the same could even apply to your friends. The queen might well wish to protect them for your sake. No killing yet, Ulverdale.'

'My lady, I feel sure that—'

'Don't argue with me!' It came out like the crack of a musket. 'Shut Mistress Stannard in her room for the time being. I'll order Hankin and the other men to disarm those two lunatics in the hall and similarly lock them into theirs. Then I will consider how best to make use of them. It may be,' said Lady Anne, once again with that grim smile, 'that we have a very pretty hand of cards to play with now.'

SEVENTEEN

Fight for Freedom

I had my lockpicks. Once shut into my room, I thought, I could escape. I couldn't escape from Ulverdale's grip on my arm, and I didn't try. He marched me back to my room, and only when we got there did I notice something I hadn't taken in before, which was that although the door had a keyhole, it had no key. Instead, like the door to Blanche's bedchamber, it had bolts on the outside. Two of them, at top and bottom, and now, glancing swiftly round as Ulverdale thrust me forward, I saw that other doors along the passage were similarly equipped.

It was a curious arrangement, but grimly comprehensible to me. Aunt Tabitha and Uncle Herbert, who had brought me up, had had bolts on the outside of my door, so that I could be locked in when I annoyed them, which was frequently, since my mere existence annoyed them. At that time, far from being recognized as the queen's half-sister, I was the embarrassing love-child of Uncle Herbert's sister, who would not name the father of her child. Had she told them it was King Henry, I sometimes thought they might have been kinder to us both.

No doubt some previous owner of Ramsfold had also been in the habit of locking his children and possibly his wife into their rooms when they provoked him, and found bolts more convenient than keys. Ulverdale bundled me over the threshold and slammed the door after me. I heard the bolts shoot home. My lockpicks wouldn't save me this time.

I went to the window and looked across to the hall. I could still hear the sounds of swordplay and shouting, but even as I stood there, the sounds changed. The clash of blades stopped and then started again, more violently, while the shouts acquired a different note, one of genuine fury.

Then the main door burst open, and out of it, in partnership now, going backwards and fighting as they did so, came Brockley and Trelawny, followed by Hankin and a young stable boy, the gatekeeper and the three men I had seen playing cards, whose names I did not know except that one was called Robby. Several had swords; the others all had daggers. As I watched, Ulverdale appeared, running across the courtyard, drawing a dagger as he did so, and joined in.

I knew what must happen. Brockley and Trelawny were hopelessly outnumbered and tired, too; they were not young, and they had been performing, as it were, in the hall for a long time. They couldn't . . .

No, they couldn't, though they tried. Brockley cut the gatekeeper down in the hall doorway, while Hankin, a moment later, fell to a slashing blow from Trelawny's sword and collapsed on his face, a red stain spreading round him and soaking into the snow.

The stable boy cast himself down beside Hankin, shaking his fist at Trelawny. My two men were stumbling backwards, running out of strength. Then they were overwhelmed and disarmed, and standing helplessly at my window, I saw them being dragged across the courtyard to the door below our rooms.

A number of women, including the maidservant Annet who had been inflicted on me and also Lady Anne – though not Blanche – now appeared in the hall doorway and stood surveying the scene. Brockley and Trelawny were hustled in at the entrance below me, and turning from the window, I heard them being hauled up the staircase to the passage, presumably to be shut into their chamber. My quick glance along the passage had shown me that their door, too, had bolts on the outside. Unless the resourceful Trelawny could invent a way of undoing the damned things from within, I thought bitterly, we were all trapped.

Then I heard the footsteps skid to a halt; heard a startled grunt and an anguished shout; heard Brockley bark what sounded like an order; heard Trelawny laugh and then swear.

Then came some thuds, followed by sounds of scuffling and spluttered curses, and then Brockley, breathlessly gasping:

'Heave 'em through. No, not through *our* door. The one next to it!'

Trelawny snarled: 'Oh, no you don't, sod you!' I didn't think he was addressing Brockley.

A door banged shut, and bolts crashed home. Muffled shouts and sounds of hammering followed.

My own bolts were drawn, and Brockley, sounding out of breath, said: 'Mistress Stannard, are you there?'

'Yes! I'm all right! I'm not harmed!'

The door was pulled open, and there they were, dishevelled, in their shirtsleeves, but grinning broadly. Trelawny had a bloodied dagger. There was no sign of their captors, but their whereabouts was obvious, for the pounding on a door some yards away continued.

'We let them think we'd given in and then attacked at the right moment – when we were here, close to you,' Trelawny said. 'We're a good partnership. We learned a trick or two in France. Listen. We have to get out of this house.'

Catching up my cloak, I joined them in the passage. 'Get some more clothes!' I said. 'You didn't shut those bullies into your own room, I think. You two have only your shirts between your top halves and the weather.'

Without speaking further, they plunged together through their own door, to reappear in a moment, struggling into doublets and clutching mantles. 'But they took our weapons,' Brockley said.

Donning my cloak, I pointed at Trelawny's red-stained dagger.

'Oh, this is Ulverdale's,' said Trelawny airily. 'I snatched it off him. Luckily, we only had three of them to deal with.' He made it all sound simple. 'One each holding us from behind in an armlock and that damned butler prodding me in the back with this.' He flourished the dagger. 'Brockley here rammed his man in the chest with an elbow – you saw him do that to me when we met at Windsor—'

'And kicked backwards at the same time, to get him on the kneecap,' said Brockley. 'It weakened his grip. I wrenched free, turned round and punched him on the nose.' Our captives increased their battering on the door of their makeshift prison, and Brockley eyed it dubiously. 'What a din they're making. Let's get down to the stable!'

'Brockley's efforts,' said Trelawny, grinning, and leading us towards the stairs, 'distracted my two so well that I broke loose too. I twisted round, grabbed the dagger, put an armlock on Ulverdale and stuck the blade into the other fellow. Only into his forearm, though, so I hit him on the jaw for good measure. Down here, quick.'

We were on the stairs. They led down into the stable, close to the door that led out to the courtyard. I was doing a head-count in my mind. Hankin and the gatekeeper were certainly wounded and possibly dead. Ulverdale and two others were locked up. There remained one of the unnamed men and the stable boy, but there didn't seem to be many other men in the house. Most of them had answered Northumberland's summons and were now in Scotland, presumably. We might be able to fight our way out. We had two daggers, for I had a small one in my hidden pouch. If we could find our saddlery and our horses . . .

Shouts had broken out outside. Looking warily out, we realized that the captives had stopped assaulting their door and were bellowing for help from their window. Over by the kitchen, a couple of women servants were staring, and a boy who had apparently just come in by the side gate with a donkey cart, bringing supplies of some kind, was standing beside his vehicle, gaping at the scene. But others were more active. We had been seen, and a menacing phalanx was advancing across the courtyard.

I had been foolish. I am a woman myself, yet in my calculations I had sadly underestimated my own sex. Leading the reinforcements, striding masterfully, was Lady Anne. Close behind her were five women servants, Annet and Joan among them, together with the stable boy and the unnamed man. Both the males had swords, but Annet and two other women had brooms, Joan had a businesslike meat-chopper and Lady Anne had armed herself with a terrifying whip.

We were facing superior weaponry, and we were outnumbered.

'The donkey cart,' Trelawny said. 'If we can get to that, I'll deal with the boy and I'll make that donkey move . . .'

'Keep together,' said Brockley. '*Keep together*!'

'Here they come!' growled Trelawny.

Here they came indeed. They rushed us, and the scrimmage was over in moments. Brockley was downed by the men and two of the women. I tried to reach for my dagger as Lady Anne's whip struck at me, but I wasn't quick enough. Having thrown back my cloak in order to get at my pouch, I took the force of the lash across my right side and heard myself cry out as a broom handle crashed into me from the left. Annet, who for all her tiny stature was remarkably strong, seized hold of me, aided by a powerful capped and aproned kitchen wench, and between them they threw me to the ground, whereupon Lady Anne's lash landed again, the pain cutting through my clothes like a knife blade.

Trelawny was the only one who evaded them. Through a haze of anguish and tears, as I struggled uselessly against Annet and her sturdy colleague, I saw him knock Joan's cleaver arm up, seize her bodily and throw her at Lady Anne, which made that ferocious noblewoman stagger backwards before she could use her whip on me again, and then he ran for it, making for the gate and the donkey cart.

The boy in charge of it sprang to meet him, met Trelawny's fist instead and went down. My captors turned me over, ramming me nose first into the snow, but from the corner of my eye I saw Trelawny leap into the cart, and I heard the clatter of wheels and little donkey hooves as he fled, pursued by a chorus of curses. I wondered how far he would get and if he would come back with help.

My cap had fallen off. Someone seized me by my hair and hauled me to my feet. I found that Annet was doing the hauling and that Lady Northumberland now stood before me, glaring. I tried to get free of Annet, and my skirt, with its hidden pouch inside, struck against her knee.

'What's this?' she said, reaching down with her spare hand, and a moment later, my dagger and my lockpicks had been pulled out and tossed on to the snowy cobbles.

Lady Anne stooped to pick them up. 'You carry strange

objects about with you,' she said. 'A dagger, for fear some man should press his attentions on you, I suppose. But what are these?' She held up the slender lock-picks with their hooked ends.

I tried to think of a convincing explanation other than the truth. Lady Anne ran her thumb ominously along the handle of her whip. I wouldn't withstand much of that, and knew it. 'Lockpicks,' I said in a sulky voice. 'I'd have got into that locked box of yours if I'd had more time,' I added, snatching the chance of a convincing lie. Better, I thought, if Lady Anne felt quite sure that I hadn't read her Vatican correspondence.

'Well, well. You really are a well-equipped spy, are you not? You must be highly valued. You'll make a *very* useful hostage, and this time you won't escape. You won't get out of the wine cellar, and here's a reminder not to try. Pull her cloak off, Annet.'

Annet obeyed, and Lady Anne used the whip again, twice. I cried out, and Brockley, unable to help me, swore furiously in his captors' hands. Then Lady Anne said: 'Bring them!'

'Quite like old times, isn't it?' said Brockley, obviously trying to be cheerful. 'Reminds me of Vetch Castle, this does. Only, this one's just a little more hospitable. We shan't die of thirst, at least.'

He was referring to the Welsh border castle whose dungeon we had once experienced. That one certainly had been worse than this. I looked at the wine casks round the walls of our prison.

'I suppose we could drink ourselves to death,' I said. I shivered, crouching where I had been thrown, huddling my knees into my chest. Someone had flung my cloak down after me, probably because a live hostage is more useful than one who has frozen to death. I didn't imagine it was an act of kindness. I was still grateful to have the cloak and pulled it round my shoulders. 'Where's the light coming from? And the draught?'

The faint, pale light which enabled us to see each other seemed to come from the same source as the chill stream of air which made the place so cold. The effects of Lady Anne's whip and the serving maid's broom handle were subsiding a little, but nevertheless, for the moment, I preferred not to move too much. Brockley, however, was prowling about, examining the door, the walls and the vaulted roof above us.

'They both come through this grating,' he said, pointing upwards. 'I think it's the one Trelawny mentioned, in the courtyard. I imagine it's there to let in light, and I expect the grating can be undone so that barrels can be lowered through it. This cellar seems to be partly under the hall and partly under the courtyard.'

'I can see that the door has a lock,' I said dismally. 'But Lady Anne has my lockpicks. We're trapped.'

'Yes, madam. I think we are. We can suppose ourselves lucky that you are known to be the queen's sister; otherwise I fancy they would have disposed of us by now. They may yet dispose of me.'

'Dear God, I hope not! But look, Trelawny's got away! I suppose he'll make for Carlisle.'

'How long will it take him, though? And will we still be here if he brings help? In Lady Anne's place, I'd move us to another hiding place. We might be hard to find.'

I said: 'I hear footsteps. I think someone's coming.'

EIGHTEEN

Pewter Plates and Olive Oil

What was arriving was food and, to our surprise, blankets. Annet and Ulverdale carried them, but with them were Lady Anne, Robby and the other man who had been briefly captured by Brockley and Trelawny.

'We do not intend to harm you,' Lady Anne informed us. I could still feel, all too well, the places where her whip had landed but Anne of Northumberland probably didn't regard that as harming me. Indeed, the expression in her chilly eyes was very much that of a cat which knows it will never eat the pretty bird in the cage, but would dearly love to all the same. I was very much afraid of her.

'Because you could be useful to us,' she said, 'we have to feed you and make sure that you don't die of cold down here. Tomorrow,' she informed us, 'we shall move somewhere else and take you with us. Mistress Winthorpe will be glad when we're gone, though she may be lonely. When I took over the house I made her send her own servants away, though I didn't let her explain why.'

Some had probably guessed, I thought. Here, perhaps, lay the origin of the rumours which had alerted Lord Sussex and fastened suspicion on Ramsfold. I felt better. Inefficiency in an adversary is always cheering.

'When we go,' said Lady Anne, 'she'll be on her own. She may be able to persuade some of the villagers to come and sweep her floors and cook her meals, I dare say. She's a poor thing,' said Northumberland's unpleasant wife disdainfully.

'Where is she now?' I asked. With an effort, I stretched for a blanket to pull round me, over my cloak. The warmth was wonderful.

'Locked in her chamber,' Lady Anne said. 'Don't look to her to rescue you. You will find enough food on the tray, I trust. There are also two goblets. You have my permission,' she added with a thin smile, 'to help yourselves to any of Mistress Winthorpe's wine which appeals to you. However, we have also supplied a flask of well water.'

That was the end of the visit. Lady Anne, having said her say, turned away and they all left us. We heard the key turn in the lock.

'Let's see what they've given us,' said Brockley.

There was bread, a bowl of bean soup, a stew with a reasonable amount of meat in it and a spoon each. There were goblets and the promised flask of water, too.

'They do value you, madam,' said Brockley. 'They may even be a little frightened of you and your influence in Windsor.'

'Lady Anne isn't nearly frightened enough,' I said, pressing my hand to my side where her whip had left its memory.

'Did she hurt you much?'

'It could have been worse, but only because my clothes are thick. I hate that woman. I want something painful and undignified to happen to her, as soon as possible.'

'Amen to that,' said Brockley. 'We'd better eat this,' he added. 'Before they change their minds!'

We ate, drank some of the water and then prowled round the cellar to get ourselves some wine, though I had to move gingerly. Brockley, in a cleverly judged mixture of deferential manservant and loftily knowledgeable courtier, made absurdly pompous remarks about the rival merits of various wines. He even managed, once or twice, to get me to laugh. Brockley always denied that he had in him the makings of a strolling player, but he would have made a very good one.

'After all,' he said when we finally settled down again, blanket-wrapped and as far from the draught as we could manage, to sip our final choice of canary, 'we're not in mortal danger, and Trelawny is free. If only he gets safe away and gets help. Every time I hear a sound from above, I wonder if he's been caught and they're bringing him back.'

'I hope he's somehow exchanged that donkey cart for a horse,' I said. 'He won't get far with the cart.'

Brockley said: 'Wherever he is, he'll need shelter soon. The night will be cold.'

The day wore tediously away. As darkness fell, we tried to sleep, without success. The blankets were little protection from the rough paving of our prison floor, and my bruises ached anew. Moonlight shone through the grating, casting a criss-cross pattern of black and white on to the paving stones.

We were both still wide awake when a shadow obscured the moonlight, something clinked against the grating and Trelawny's voice said softly: 'Mistress Stannard! Roger! Are you there? I've got your dungeon key.'

'How in heaven's name . . .?' Brockley, shedding his blanket, was under the grating at once, his face upturned. 'Trelawny? But how did you get back? What was that about the key? Where . . .?'

'Here,' said Trelawny, and with some difficulty pushed a big iron key through the bars of the grating.

Brockley caught it. 'But how . . .?'

'You went off with the donkey cart!' I said, ignoring my stiffness, throwing off my blanket and coming to Brockley's side.

'No, I didn't. I jumped into it, drove it off, fast as I could, round to the outer court and the gatehouse – which was open, I suppose to let the cart in in the first place. Anyway, I sent the donkey tearing through it and down the hill – those hounds in their pen were making hell's own racket and the poor ass was only too glad to gallop away – while I jumped off and dodged into the gatekeeper's quarters. It wasn't too safe, but it worked out well. You chopped him down, remember, Brockley? I wasn't sure he was dead, but I thought they might bring him back there anyway, to tend him or lay him out, in which case I'd hide under the bed and hope for the best. As it turned out, no one came in. It seems you and I killed both him and Hankin. Later on, peeping from a window, I saw them carry the bodies out of the front gate. I dare say they were local men with kin in the village and our charming Lady Anne didn't want to be bothered with the burials. So there I was, nice and snug in the empty lodging. Very satisfactory.'

'We thought you'd get right away,' I said, astonished. 'Why did you stay here?'

'I wasn't going to abandon you. Certainly, I've been here. One should always,' said Trelawny sententiously, 'make use of what is to hand. I once saw a comrade cornered in the parlour of a house we were looting at the time and killed outright by an enemy soldier. He'd lost his own sword in a skirmish outside, and he just never noticed that the parlour was practically a weapon store. There was a cloth on the table that he could have flung over the enemy's head; there was a five foot iron candlestick with four candleholders on top and an ornamental spike in the midst of them, sharp as a spear, fit to run a man through. But he just backed up against the wall, shouting: *Quick, Carew, I've lost my blade!* and I couldn't reach him in time. I slew the soldier from behind, but my poor mate was dead by then.'

'Carew, will you stop burbling and tell us what now?' Brockley growled.

'I stayed in the lodging for quite a while,' Trelawny said imperturbably. 'I think some of our delightful hosts went chasing after the donkey cart. They must have been annoyed when they found it empty. I dined off the gatekeeper's food. They did him well. I had cold chicken, new bread and some really good quality ale. I've had my sword taken away, but I found a spare dagger among his things. And I found his keys.'

'How do you know this is the right key?' Brockley asked. 'And how did you know where we were?'

'I heard someone say so when they were going out, chasing my donkey cart. *Where are the prisoners now?* one of them said, and another laughed and said: *my lady's shut them in the wine cellar.* As for the key,' said Trelawny, 'I don't think the gatekeeper could read. But he could draw. Each key hangs on a hook with a dear little picture drawn on the wall beside it. This was labelled with a picture of a cask. I reckon it's the one. I grabbed a few other useful-looking ones as well, including the key to the hall and the gatehouse.'

'Didn't anyone come into the lodging to get them when it was time to lock up for the night?' I said.

'One must take chances sometimes,' said Trelawny cheerfully. 'However, the angels seem to be on our side, for a change.

Nobody came for them. Ulverdale locked the gate. He's got his own set of keys, I fancy. The big door at the top of the steps opposite the gatehouse has bolts on the inside and no lock at all. It was unbolted during the day, but I reckoned they'd fasten it at night, so before dusk I found a chance to slink in and hide in the hay store. Once I reckoned everyone was in bed, I prowled round and through the grating, I could hear you fidgeting and grunting so I knew you really were there.

'Your cellar door opens into the hall, so to let you out, I needed to get into the house and I couldn't. The key to the hall door was no use because that's got inside bolts as well – this is a maddening house, bolts all over the place – and when I forced a window and tried getting in through that, I nearly got stuck. The lower mullions are all too narrow to crawl through. Thank God for the grating.' He shook it. 'At least I've got your door key to you.'

'But how do we get away from here?' Brockley demanded.

'Easy. The stable and the harness room aren't locked. I've already saddled our horses, and I've been able to open the side gates – they have inside bolts, but I *was* inside, after all. In the dark, I slipped through, went round to open the gatehouse and then slipped back. The hounds made a to-do, but they've been upset all day because of all the disturbance. No one paid any heed. We can ride straight out.'

'Madam,' said Brockley, turning to me, 'we're wasting time. Let's be away.'

I made for the door and tried the key. Trelawny had made no mistake. It turned at once. I locked it again once we were through. Movement was mercifully easing my stiffness now. In front, just visible in the gloom, were the steps up to the hall. We emerged into it at the kitchen end, and Brockley, pointing, said: 'That way. We can open the door to the courtyard from inside.'

We moved forward. By moonlight and the glow from the dying fire, we could see the central table, which still held a number of items carelessly left over from supper, and the dull gleam of the dusty pewter on the sideboard. We were halfway to the courtyard door when we heard a sound from the minstrels' balcony at the far end, and then a voice thundered: '*Stand!*' and on the instant, the gallery was full of people and light.

Halting in alarm, we looked up, to behold Lady Anne and Joan, both wrapped in fur-trimmed bed-gowns and holding up flaring torches. Between them, with a cloak over his own nightwear, stood Ulverdale, and in his hands was a crossbow, wound and ready to shoot.

'Shoot the man. Not the Stannard woman!' Lady Anne snapped, and the crossbow bolt shifted as Ulverdale trained it on Brockley.

Next to the sideboard, a window banged open and Trelawny's face appeared. 'Lackwits! Use what's there!' he shouted, pointing in frenzied fashion at the sideboard and the table.

In the same moment, Ulverdale loosed his bolt. Brockley seized hold of me and flung us both sideways, and the bolt missed. We collided with the sideboard, rattling the dishes. Brockley snatched a pewter platter from a shelf, and like a boy bouncing a stone on water, he launched it spinning, edge on, at the butler. It struck Ulverdale's upper arm as he was reloading, with so much force that the butler yelled and dropped his weapon.

The crossbow went over the edge of the balcony and crashed to thc floor of the hall, somersaulting towards us past thc tablc. Brockley caught it up and threw it through the open window. I glimpsed Trelawny retrieving it and running off across the courtyard. Lady Anne let out a most unladylike oath, and she and her companions ran to the slatted stairs and jostled down them, intent on seizing us.

And then something happened, as strange as magic, as magnificent as the victory of Agincourt and beyond my understanding, then or now. I can only say that I will never, till the day I die, forget it.

Brockley and I were suddenly overtaken by a wild and unreasonable exhilaration, almost a hilarity, and at the same time, it felt as though our brains had fused into one. In the hectic minutes that followed we exchanged only the briefest of words, but we threw ideas from mind to mind as easily as though we were shouting them aloud. Trelawny had told us what to do, and now we did it as if we were one entity.

As our enemies ran down the stairs, Brockley seized one end of the sideboard and with a violent heave overturned it, scattering pewter plates and bowls and tankards across the floor. Then he veered round and in one powerful movement yanked the cloth from the table, tumbling more assorted objects including knives, spoons, half a dozen goblets and the silver salt on to the floor as well.

Whereat, and in response, I truly believe, to a picture in my mind which had sprung direct from Brockley's brain, I snatched up a fallen knife, kicked a rolling goblet out of my path, leapt to where the pulley rope of the middle chandelier was attached to its iron ring and slashed at the rope. The chandelier plummeted down, smashing into the edge of the table and crashing down to the floor.

Our pursuers, who were now off the stairs and running up the hall to reach us, stumbled on the strewn dishes and found their way blocked by the sideboard. The two women dropped their torches, which fortunately went out instead of setting fire to the rushes. Near darkness, relieved only by the uncertain gleams of moonlight and embers, at once engulfed the hall. Lady Anne slipped on some stray object, landed on her back and for a moment was helpless, flailing and cursing amid the debris and the tangled skirts of her bedgown.

Joan and Ulverdale kept their feet, got round the sideboard and ran at us, but Brockley still had the tablecloth in his hand and threw it over both their heads at once. Unable then to see where they were going, they fell headlong over the chandelier. Exclaiming with pain and struggling to free themselves, they collided with Lady Anne as she was getting up. She staggered and sat heavily down again. I saw that Brockley was scooping up things which had rolled from the overturned sideboard, and I did the same. In the scramble I dropped the knife I had used for the chandelier rope, but I grabbed half a dozen pewter dishes and drinking vessels, before fleeing back with Brockley towards the kitchen end of the hall.

Here the shadows were deeper, and for a desperate moment we blundered about, trying to find the kitchen door. Behind us, the enemy disentangled themselves from cloth, chandelier and skirts and came hotly in pursuit, but the strange, united instinct which had hold of us had apparently made us read the future too. It had made us arm ourselves, even before we knew why. Turning, we held them off, making them duck and shy by bombarding them with our booty, once more spinning the plates to make them better missiles.

I threw all my pieces of pewter within seconds, but Brockley said: 'This one's sharp, madam,' as politely as though he were serving me a new wine sauce at dinner, and thrust a platter with an edge like a blade into my hands.

'Thank you, Brockley,' I said with equal graciousness and whirled the dish at Ulverdale. It spun through the moonlight to hit the butler in the mouth, producing a muffled but – from my point of view – entirely satisfactory bellow.

At the same moment, Brockley sidestepped to avoid treading on something on the floor and I realized that the silver salt, which had the usual containers for extra spices including pepper, had come to pieces when it was flung from the table. Brockley had nearly trodden on the pepper pot. It lay in the moonlight, identified by the pattern of little holes in its silver lid. I suddenly remembered Sterry, joking that surplus supplies of pepper might be thrown in an enemy's face. Catching up the pot, I wrenched its lid off and directed its contents at the foe.

We both sprang away, holding our noses. The enemy reeled about, sneezing, eyes streaming. Flinging the last of our dishes and vessels at them we turned again, this time saw the door to the kitchen in front of us and ran through it.

Like the hall, the kitchen was lit from moonbeams and the glow of a banked fire. And still it held, that mysterious union of our minds. The things we saw, we saw in a new way. They were such objects as you find in any kitchen: knives, graters, skewers, spatulas and tongs, mostly hanging on wall hooks; pans big and little; colanders, cauldrons and trivets; pestles and mortars; basins and jugs, some with lard or olive oil or pottage in them. We judged everything now by its potential as a weapon.

The door we had come through had no lock or bolt, but

setting it ajar, Brockley sprang on to a stool. Without a word spoken I handed him a bowl of pottage, a colander and two pairs of tongs, which he balanced on top before jumping down, grabbing two sheathed knives from their hooks, handing me one and thrusting the other into his belt. I shoved the one he had given me into my hidden pouch. Some of the pepper must have landed on us, for Brockley sneezed. We found ourselves laughing.

Together, we ran to a little door out to the courtyard. This was bolted, but on our side. Brockley tore the bolts back while I, seeing a jug of olive oil on a nearby table, seized it and hurled the oil in a stream across the flagstoned floor.

Then we were out, just as, behind us, our pursuers, still sneezing, rushed in. Sweet in our ears was the crash of our booby trap and the sound of feet skidding on the oily floor, and the shrieks and curses (mingled with continued sneezes) which these joyous events produced. As we raced past the window of the kitchen, I risked a tiptoe pause to glance in and beheld Joan and Ulverdale both flat on their faces, while Lady Anne of Northumberland was sitting on the floor with her feet stuck out in front of her, a look of mingled rage and pain upon her face, cold pottage splashed all over her and an upturned colander on her head.

I was avenged for her whip. It was a glorious spectacle: one of the most splendid moments of my life.

Trelawny was waiting for us. In the interim, he had opened the stable gate wide and brought the horses out of the stable. 'Couldn't find Mistress Stannard's side-saddle. You'll have to ride astride, mistress. There's been a bit of thaw during the day; likely enough we'll get through now.'

'Where's that young groom?' Brockley asked, seizing the bridles of his own horse and mine. 'And what did you do with that crossbow?'

'I threw it down the well. As for the stable lad, I found him asleep in a stall. I knocked him out and then tied him up. I was sorry to do that to a sleeping man, but times are desperate.'

'Blanche!' I said. 'We can't leave her here. Can't we—?'

'No, we can't.' Brockley seized Roundel's nearside stirrup and thrust it under my nose. 'Push your foot into this and get into that saddle. We can't stop for Mistress Winthorpe or anyone else. We have to get away from here! Up with you!'

He had forgotten he was my manservant, forgotten to address me as madam, but because our minds were still linked I knew that he was intent upon saving me; indeed, on saving all three of us. I did as I was told.

As our pursuers recovered themselves and burst out of the kitchen door, we rode out of the side gate. Hooves skidded as we made the sharp turn to go round the corner of the house and Roundel nearly came down but miraculously regained her balance. At a gallop we emerged into the outer courtyard between the main door and the gatehouse. The hounds burst into a noisy howling, but we ignored them. The gatehouse doors appeared to be closed, but leaning from his saddle, Trelawny seized the big iron handle of the right-hand half and dragged the leaf back. As he had said, he had undone them in readiness. His horse snorted and reared as the heavy door went past its nose, and as soon as the gap was wide enough it plunged through. Brockley and I followed. An instant later we were racing downhill, hoping that our mounts would keep their footing on the slush and snow underfoot.

'We're away!' I said.

'I hope so,' Brockley answered grimly, and at that moment, I saw that the moonlight around us had been augmented by a faint orange glow, so that we cast weak shadows ahead. I twisted round and saw that our foes had made contingency plans. Knowing that Trelawny was loose, they had feared that he would attempt a rescue. They had put a beacon on the watchtower. It was flaring into the night sky, signalling to someone, somewhere, to intercept us.

We could do nothing but ride for it. My bruises were throbbing again, but it had to be borne. We sat down hard in our saddles and drove the horses on downhill at the best pace we could manage. The path levelled out when it reached the belt of fir trees, and there we went faster, galloping through the wood and on through the village.

But it was more with alarm than astonishment that we saw,

as we passed the last house in the village, that the beacon had done its work. Someone had been on watch for it. Blocking the track, where it narrowed between high banks, were ten or so mounted men, two of them holding torches aloft the better to see us coming.

The torchlight showed us their rough clothes, their small shaggy steeds and their haphazard weaponry of kitchen knives, a couple of daggers and one ancient sword. These were Blanche's villagers. Plainly, not all the able-bodied men had followed their landlord to war, but some of those who stayed behind would nevertheless be supporters of the rebellion. Others might have their doubts, but feared for themselves and Blanche if they disobeyed their fellow villagers or Lady Anne, their landlord's wife.

'What now?' I gasped as we automatically slowed our pace.

'Ride straight through them,' said Trelawny tersely, and then, startling us with a shout of '*Laissez les allez!*' as though he were a marshal launching knights into the lists at a tournament, he once more threw his horse, regardless of the slippery going, into a gallop.

Brockley shouted: 'You're moon mad!' but at the same time he, too, drove his horse forward, and so did I. Madness it certainly was, but it was our only chance. The horses answered us gallantly. In a moment, we were charging the enemy headlong. Crouching over my pommel, I smelt Roundel's sweat and her mane blew across my face. An icy wind sang in my ears; mud and snow splashed over me, spurting from her hooves. Trelawny was on one side of me and Brockley on the other. Three abreast, the horses reaching for the ground as though they were trying to consume it, we tore on towards the row of waiting men, and I should have been terrified, except that the wild exhilaration of speed had wiped fear away.

As we neared our enemies, Trelawny shouted: '*Keep galloping! Faster!*'

Brockley cried: '*Knives out!*' and from his belt jerked the blade he had snatched from the Ramsfold kitchen.

Fumbling in my skirts, I brought out the knife he had given

to me, and I saw the gatekeeper's dagger appear in Trelawny's fist.

We bore down on them. I can imagine what we looked like; an oncoming charge which was clearly not going to slow down, let alone stop. The ponies our adversaries were riding had not been trained for war and shied, squealing, half climbing up the banks, taking their riders with them. We simply thundered through them.

From the corner of my eye, I saw someone wave a dagger at us, but Trelawny lunged with his own blade, and with a scream, the man fell from his saddle. Brockley and I brandished our knives, but we never had to use them. We were through and racing onwards, the hooves of the horses drumming and splashing. Our steeds were much faster than those we had left behind. Glancing back, we saw that we were not to be pursued. Trelawny burst into a soldier's song.

It was all quite crazy. I was still full of the exhilaration of speed and triumph. As we galloped on, I shouted: 'That was marvellous! Let's go back and do it again!'

Trelawny stopped singing and began to laugh, doubling over his pommel. We all began to laugh. The horses shook their manes as if in wonder at the insanity of their riders. We were free. We were exhausted, our feet were going numb in their stirrups and our ungloved hands on the reins ached with cold, but we had escaped. We had the night and the moonlit snow to ourselves. We had information which must be delivered as soon as possible to the right quarters, but deliver it we would. We had no doubt of that.

Sobriety did not return until, when we had slowed down again to let the horses breathe a little, Brockley noticed that Brown Berry was moving unevenly. Carefully sheathing his knife and putting it back into his belt, he stopped us while he got down to examine the cob's near fore. 'It's only balled snow again,' he said. 'Wedged between the frog and the shoe. I can get it out . . . There we are. That will make you more comfortable, my boy. I think we can take things more steadily now, anyway.'

'I wouldn't be so sure,' said Trelawny.

Brockley, still stooping over Brown Berry's hoof, turned his face upwards in surprise. I looked at Trelawny too, puzzled.

'Listen,' he said. '*Listen.*'

We did so. It was faint, but even as we cocked our ears, it grew louder. It was the baying of the hounds of Ramsfold, on our scent.

NINETEEN
Black and White

The cry of hounds is exciting when you're following the hunt. When you're the quarry, it freezes your veins and sends your bowels into terrified spasm. In a quavering voice, I said: 'Whatever do they want hounds for? We've left tracks enough in the snow!'

'They want to bring us to bay and hold us till the pursuit from Ramsfold House can get to us,' said Brockley. He released Brown Berry's hoof and remounted. 'The dogs will probably outdistance their horses. Or ours.'

We could do nothing but ride on, as fast as the conditions and the strength of our mounts would allow, over empty moorland terrain we didn't know, in the cold and inadequate moonlight. There had been no further snowfall that day, and the air did not seem quite as bitter as it had been, but the going was still quite bad enough. Soon we realized that although we were still going westward and therefore towards the border with friendly Cumberland, and although we still seemed to be on a track of some sort, it was the wrong one. We had missed our way.

It wasn't likely that the chase would worry overmuch about crossing the county boundary, but our best chance of finding help nevertheless lay across that boundary. We needed a friendly village – or better still, a friendly castle – and had no idea where to look for one. All we knew for sure was that there were many lonely miles between us and the sanctuary of Carlisle.

Sanctuary. I said the word aloud. My companions turned their heads. 'On the way here,' I said, 'didn't we see churches in some of those little hamlets? There's an ancient right of sanctuary in churches.'

'I wonder if they'd respect it?' Brockley said, glancing back.

'Local vicars might be annoyed if anyone tried to drag fugitives out of their churches,' said Trelawny. 'We must be near the Cumberland border by now,' he added. 'We've been riding westward long enough.'

Brockley said: 'There's a river ahead.'

The track was going downhill. At the bottom, there was indeed a river, and a ford, thinly iced over but usable. The horses crunched their way across and started the scramble up the slope on the far side. Behind us, the hound voices were louder. At the top of the climb we emerged on to a further wilderness of moonlit moorland. The shadowed vales, where the hamlets and churches would be if they were anywhere, were deep in blackness. If there were dwellings there, we couldn't see them.

And then, with infinite thankfulness, we did see just one.

By sheer good luck, sometime in the past, some pious lordling had honoured his creator by building a church on a hill. Brockley saw it first and pointed. Very likely, the villagers it served grumbled about the climb to their place of worship, but there it stood, its square crenellated tower clear against the starry sky and glinting in the moonlight.

'That's surely the path,' said Trelawny, pointing, and there indeed it was, ahead and to the right, branching off from ours. Like ours, it was a sunken lane between banks – snowbound, but with its entrance visible in the moonlight – and suddenly we saw that there were hoof marks and wheel prints in both tracks, proving that habitations were close. We veered towards it. The hound voices were very loud by now, and behind them, faintly, we could hear shouts.

We came to the village first. The baying noise had woken some of the inhabitants, and as we cantered through the main street, lights were appearing in cottage windows. Then an authoritative figure, waving a cresset and shouting, burst suddenly from a doorway ahead of us and ran into our path. Perforce, we pulled up, looking down into his face.

He was very much a northerner, with pale-blue eyes and white eyelashes; a descendant, no doubt, of Norsemen, and his voice, too, was broadly northern. It was also furious.

'What's all this to do at this hour o' t'night? I am Thomas

Dennison, vicar of this parish of St John's-On-The-Hill. Stand and explain thysen!'

Villagers were emerging into the street, but by the sound of them, the hounds would be in the street too, at any moment. 'We seek sanctuary in your church!' I said. 'I am Ursula Stannard, lady in waiting to Her Majesty Queen Elizabeth. I and my escort have been about her business in Northumberland, and our pursuers are remnants of the rebellion who don't want us to carry news of their doings to Lord Sussex in York. Are we in Cumberland yet, and if so, is Cumberland still true to the queen or not?'

'Aye, you are, and aye, Cumberland is.'

I looked over my shoulder. The first hounds were in sight, and I glimpsed riders behind them. I heard a woman's voice. Anne of Northumberland had joined the hunt.

'We need shelter!' Brockley snapped at Dennison. 'Now, quickly!'

Thomas Dennison, mercifully, did not have one of those bucolic, parochial minds. He responded without hesitation. 'The church isna locked. Get up to it. Take t'horses in with you. I'll hold back t'chase! I'll ask questions later, mind!'

'That's quite in order,' Brockley told him.

Dennison stepped aside, and we urged our mounts past him, driving them, tired and blowing though they were, to the last climb up thc hill. Thcy had had cnough, poor things, fetched from their warm stalls in the depth of the night and forced to gallop for miles through the snow.

The path slanted across the hillside, and we could watch what was happening below simply by glancing to the side. Dennison had made the people in the street form a line across the road, checking the hounds. As the riders caught up, we heard him command them to halt.

They did so, but not for long. There was a brief altercation, and then our pursuers spurred their horses forward. Villagers on foot had little chance against determined horsemen brandishing drawn swords. The chase broke through, and their hounds came with them, bounding up the hillside ahead of the horses, yelling as they came, to encircle us just before we reached the church door so that we could not enter.

Trelawny, controlling his frightened mare as best he could with one hand, leant from his saddle and killed the biggest dog with his dagger, but two more sprang at him, snarling, while a couple of other brutes were baiting Brown Berry. The cob was kicking and squealing, and Brockley could do nothing but cling on, unable even to spare a hand to pull out his own blade.

Roundel, just as terrified, was plunging beneath me, and a lean grey dog, half lurcher and half mastiff by the look of it, but agile as a greyhound, was nipping at her heels. I had managed to get at my knife and tried to attack the beast with it, but I couldn't reach. The riders – Ulverdale, the three Ramsfold men and Lady Anne – came up, laughing.

They called off the hounds, but the pack remained close by, circling like wolves while their masters closed on us. We fought. I scored someone's arm, and Brockley, who had finally succeeded in wrenching his weapon from his belt, jabbed it into someone else. Anne of Northumberland, manoeuvring her horse on the outskirts of the struggle, shrieked encouragement to her men, urging them to kill both Brockley and Trelawny. Ulverdale drove his horse towards me, shouting: 'I'll have you now, my lady!' and stretching a gauntletted hand to drag me from the saddle. At that moment Brockley regained control of Brown Berry, broke free of his assailants, saw a gap in the ring of hounds and drove Berry straight through, to clatter up the church steps, which were fortunately shallow. At the top, leaning from the saddle, Brockley wrenched the door open and shouted to me and Trelawny to follow.

I seized the opportunity and went after him. Roundel didn't like the dark archway and baulked at the top, but a hound bounded after her, snarling, and with a rush she dashed into the church. Brockley, waiting just inside, leant out of his saddle, and his knife spitted the hound as it sprang after her.

The hound had a collar. Brockley somehow caught hold of it and threw the dying animal out of the door and down the steps. I swung Roundel so that I, too, could face the door and see what was happening. Trelawny was still beleaguered at the foot of the steps. I did not want, anyway, to go further into the church, for I felt uneasy at having a horse inside a holy place myself, even though we had the vicar's consent and, after all, God made horses as well as people. Brockley, however, only cried: 'Carew! Come on! Come up here!'

But it was too late. Even as Brockley shouted, Trelawny was dragged from his saddle. He was on his feet at once, standing on the steps, holding off an attack from our pursuers, led by Ulverdale. Ulverdale looked half mad. His mouth was ugly, darkly stained, presumably with blood as a result of the sharp dish I had flung at him in the hall, and he was driving his attack home with a sword which he clearly knew how to handle. Trelawny was fighting hard, but a dagger is a poor answer to a sword, let alone three, and though one of the Ramsfold men was out of the fight, clutching his side, the other two had driven their horses one to either side of the steps and were striking upwards at him.

One of them – the one I had wounded – was dripping blood, but it only seemed to make him more savage. Our friend was outnumbered, and Lady Anne was shouting: 'Kill him! *Kill him*!'

Someone obliged her. A sword blade took him in the neck, and before our eyes, he fell.

I remember thinking how strange it was that in that snowy, moonlit world, there was no colour. None at all. Blood on moonlit snow isn't red but black, and his upturned face, which not so long ago had been joyously creased in exultant laughter, was white, death white, surrounded by a spreading, inky stain.

TWENTY

Bearers of Ill News

Trelawny's fall, and the fact that Brockley and I were indeed on hallowed ground, did create a pause: a breathless, furious hiatus in the struggle. I sat in my saddle, dumb and sick, but Brockley shouted '*Murderess*!' at Lady Northumberland, who rose in her own saddle, gripping the pommel to pull herself up, and retaliated by screeching the one word:

'*Heretics*!'

I had never before heard such hate in anyone's voice. She was no dignified sight, in flung-on clothes and with the stains of splashed pottage still on her hair, but she was frightening.

The loathing that she felt for us came at us in a wave. 'That is all you are! You deny the faith! Your lives are worthless!'

My dumbness passed. I found that I, too, could shout. 'And *you* want to bring back the Inquisition! To bring back the days of Bloody Mary and her heretic hunts! *Murderess*!' I screamed, echoing Brockley.

I had seen by this time, and so had Brockley, that help was on the way. After we left his village next day, we never again met Thomas Dennison, vicar of St John's-On-The-Hill, but I think he was a man both loved and respected by his parishioners, for they had turned out in force to aid him. The figures we had seen making a line across the street had now become a crowd, and at the moment when Trelawny fell, their pastor was leading them up the hill on foot and many of them had weapons.

Dennison was furious, berating Lady Anne and Ulverdale and their companions the moment he was within earshot, threatening them all with both earthly and spiritual calamity for killing a man on the steps of a church and demanding that they should surrender their swords to him.

They didn't, of course, but the weapons in the hands of the mob on Dennison's heels included pitchforks, billhooks and rakes, as well as quite a few old pikes and swords. Our foes were the outnumbered ones this time.

Anne spat something at Dennison, calling him a traitor to God and to the lawful queen (she clearly didn't mean Elizabeth), but by then, a bristling line of pitchforks, pikes and the like had formed up between our enemies and the church. Defeated, she and her companions fled, galloping perilously downwards, the horses slithering and throwing up plumes of snow as they bucketed down the slope. The man Brockley had wounded was swaying in his saddle but clinging on. Someone blew a horn and the hounds went too. We were thankful to see them go.

Brockley and I dismounted and led our horses down the steps. A villager had caught Trelawny's mare, Strawberry, and now took our mounts' bridles as well, so that we could kneel beside our friend in the hope of finding life still in him. But there was none.

Brockley closed the blank eyes and drew Trelawny's cloak over his face, and we stood up. Without thinking about it, or finding it in any way strange, we turned silently to one another, and for a brief moment we stood in each other's arms, glad of the comfort. Then, still silently, we stepped apart and turned to Dennison.

It was he who now took charge. He brought Brockley and me to his vicarage for the rest of the night. He gave us hot soup and rye bread, water to wash in, pallets to sleep on and, in the morning, a breakfast of ale and porridge. He put the horses in a stable behind his house and gave them warm bran mashes. He also had Trelawny placed on a trestle in the church and promised that he should be laid out with decency.

I didn't expect to sleep, but exhaustion overtook me. Despite the dreadful images of Trelawny's last moments, despite the throbbing of my body after that long ride through the snow and Lady Anne's whip, oblivion came. I had stiffened anew in the morning, but it improved again when I moved about; sleep had begun to heal me.

We were grateful to Dennison and always will be. He was

a Cumberland man, but so close to the Northumbrian border that he was in a position to hear news from the neighbouring county. His instant championship of us made me think that in Dennison we could have come across another of Sussex's informants. I didn't ask, however. I had learned from experience that if one is an informer, the fewer people who mention it, the better.

While we were breaking our fast, he fetched two men who turned out to be, respectively, the village carpenter, which also meant the local coffin-maker, and the sexton. Yes, said the carpenter, he had a coffin or two in stock; and yes, said the sexton, there was a grave ready. 'I allus delve out a couple afore winter sets in, for folk give up and die easy when nights get long and cold, and it's trouble, trying to dig when the ground's frozen. I likes to get ready while the work's easy.'

By noon, Carew Trelawny, who last night had doubled up with laughter over his saddle pommel, who had rescued us from our dungeon and called us lackwits for not seeing at once what splendid weapons sideboards and tables and chandeliers and pewter plates could be, was in his coffin and the sexton was filling in the grave from the pile of frosty earth beside it. One sword-stroke had wiped him out of the world.

Urgent though our errand was, it was impossible for us to leave that day. Brockley and I were exhausted, and so were the horses; and poor Brockley was heartbroken at the loss of his old comrade. During the committal, tears ran down his face. 'And to think I *wanted* to fight in the north and upset Fran saying so!' he said.

I wept, too, for him as much as for Trelawny. As during that wild and half-hilarious retreat through the hall and kitchen at Ramsfold, I felt my mind unite with his, and this time it was his pain I shared.

Dennison sent us off next day, however, with three of his villagers as guides, mounted on the sturdy dun ponies which were the local breed. We led Trelawny's mare. The weather was markedly warmer, with the thaw setting in in earnest, and we made good speed to Carlisle. We went straight to the castle this time, anxious to pour our news into authoritative ears at last. It was the right thing to do, for we found Sussex there. He had battled personally through the snowdrifts to join the northward pursuit and was on the eve of setting out for Scotland. 'To smoke out the hornets' nest of rebels over the border. Queen's orders, and if I have to ride into Scotland to get at them, I am to do so.'

When he had heard our story, he sent men at once to Ramsfold. We learned later that they found their quarry gone, servants included, and Blanche Winthorpe free but roaming bewilderedly through her otherwise empty house. At her request, they took her to her mother in Kendal.

Sussex, though, was chiefly concerned about the schemes we had heard Lady Northumberland making, especially the threat to the life of the Scottish regent. Thomas Radcliffe of Sussex was not young, but he was still spare and active and very conscientious, though he had an air of one who for years had striven against unfair odds, which in a way was true.

I already knew him a little, having met him at court in the past. He was one of Elizabeth's most devoted councillors, though at times a bewildered one. I was aware that he believed, quite mistakenly, that Elizabeth, like most other women, longed for marriage and children. He had striven to promote her marriage to this suitor or that and been repeatedly surprised and disappointed by his failure. His short hair, his little, slightly untidy, beard and small ruff, somehow suggested a man forever trying to solve an enigma, with no spare time or energy for elaborate barbering or clothes.

In straightforward practical matters, however, he was at home and alert. 'When did Lady Northumberland's messengers leave for Scotland?' he said. 'Early on the sixteenth of January? This is the eighteenth, and it's nearly evening. They've had three days to get there, so far. The roads are bad but not impossible, and the weather's improving. I know where the Regent is now – he's at Linlithgow, near the head of the Firth. It's eighty miles or so from Carlisle in a straight line and much the same from Ramsfold, I'd say. A resolute rider able to get fresh horses on the way could do it in three days. The message was for Archbishop Hamilton, you say? He's to arrange an *assassin*? Is there no end to the madness of these rebels?'

'One message was for him, Lord Sussex,' I told him. 'The

other was for the escaped rebels you're chasing. We overheard plans being made to tell them they were being pursued.'

'It doesn't matter if they've been warned as long as I know of it. I can outflank them. It's the Regent I'm worried about. Hamilton's in Linlithgow too, I believe. If he has a pet assassin at hand . . . Dear God, the Regent could be dead already. I'll send a warning, but we may be too late. And now . . . tell me again, what you learned about the Papal Bull.'

I recited, as well as I could from memory, the gist of that dreadful letter from the Vatican, promising to release all English Catholics from their duty to Queen Elizabeth and in effect making it lawful for any of them murder her. That meant: any who could come within range of her with a loaded musket or a sharp dagger. Any who feared damnation in the hereafter more than they feared a traitor's death.

Sussex understood. His face was grim as he listened. He said what I had been thinking all along. 'The queen must know of this. I will have to spare men to ride to Linlithgow and others to go south to the queen, though there is time in hand in the latter case. The Bull won't be issued instantly, from what you say. Not until the outcome of this rebellion is known in Rome and has been mulled over. Mistress Stannard . . .'

'I'll carry the news to the queen,' I said.

We went by way of Tyesdale.

It wasn't far out of my way, and it had been in my mind, ever since I set out for the north, that on the way back I should visit my former ward Penelope and her husband, and see Jane Mason, too.

The portrait of Gervase had told me nothing helpful, and I was bearing only ill news to Jane, but I wanted to see what she was like now that she was grown, and to assess her feelings for Mark. I wondered, too, how marriage suited my former ward. Penelope really had been a difficult girl, and a plain one as well, with her high, bulging forehead and mousey hair. She was intelligent and practical, though, qualities which Clem Moss had had the wisdom to recognize. I hoped that all was well with them, but I wished to see for myself.

If I sensed that Jane cared for Mark as he did for her, I

would, I decided, try to talk a little sense into Pen, who might in turn be able to influence her mother. I liked Mark and felt that Jane had made no mistake in falling for him. Pen had a far less admirable record, for until she met the sensible Clem Moss, she had been wildly in love with a whole succession of completely unsuitable men. My former ward, I thought, was in no position to preach to her sister.

There were maps in Carlisle, and Lord Sussex helped me to study the route. In such unsettled times, Sussex wasn't happy to see me travel with only Brockley as a companion. The villagers from St John's-On-The-Hill could not be asked to travel further from home, but Sussex seconded two men to go with us. We stayed two clear days at Carlisle because both we and our horses still needed time for recovery and, having left most of our belongings at Ramsfold, there were things we needed to buy. Sussex found me a woman who salved my welts and bruises and was comfortingly shocked to see them; Brockley kept apart and dealt with his sorrow as best he could. Then, once more, we were on our way.

It was a fairly easy journey now that we and our mounts were no longer burdened with baggage. We were taking the mare Strawberry with us, so that Cecil could return her to Trelawny's next of kin, if he had any, and we bought a pack-saddle for her so that she could carry our belongings. No one had been able to find a side-saddle for me, but I had acquired some breeches, which made riding astride more comfortable. We were not a talkative party, however. Brockley was still very quiet, and I knew that his grief for Trelawny was unabated. Only the weather encouraged any cheerfulness. The thaw had continued, and the sun was out. Trees dripped and sparkled; now and then a few birds sang. At noon on the fifth day, Tyesdale came in sight.

It had been Pen's dowry, and when it came into her possession it was in a very poor state. However, Mark had reported that matters were now improved, and I knew that good coal deposits had been found on the property, which should have made a difference.

And so it had. We saw it at once. Stone walls had been repaired; ditches dug out; paths cleared; fields ploughed.

Smoke streamed cheerfully from the chimneys. Tyesdale had a real moat, which had been stagnant the last time I saw it. Now it was clean, with a little broken ice on the surface, and as we crossed the bridge to the gatehouse I looked down into the water and saw the silvery flicker of a fish in the depths.

'I hardly know the place!' I said to Brockley and was glad to see him smile.

'I knew the lass had good sense, at heart,' he said. 'For all her goings-on when she was a girl.'

Pen's goings-on, as he put it, had considerably annoyed Brockley at one time, I remembered. For the first time in days, I laughed. 'Clem wouldn't put up with goings-on,' I said. 'And here they are!'

We had ridden into the courtyard and there they were indeed, Pen and Clem together, hurrying down the steps from the main door to greet us, exclaiming that they had seen us from a window. On their heels, also exclaiming, came their housekeeper, Agnes Appletree, looking just as I remembered her, a tiny figure with a red face, red hair and a crimson dress that clashed horribly with both; and round the corner of the house, barking lustily, came two big grey dogs, though they sat down obediently when commanded by Clem, thumping their tails in welcome.

Clem hadn't changed, either, beyond that indefinable air of maturity which contentedly married men acquire. Otherwise he was just as I remembered: a big, powerful man with round blue eyes and an amiable expression.

The greatest change was in Pen. All her waywardness and awkwardness had gone. This new Pen was self-possessed and charming. Her businesslike dark-blue gown suited her. The grey eyes, which had always been her chief beauty, met mine with a new, calm assurance. She came gravely to meet me as I dismounted and dropped a curtsey.

'Mistress Stannard! Oh, my dear Mistress Stannard! And you, Brockley! How are you? How is Fran Dale? Is she not with you?'

'I'm well, mistress, but for once we left my wife behind. You know how Fran hates travelling.'

'And in this weather, who can blame her? Come you in;

t'parlour has a fine fire, and Mistress Jane's settin' there, playin' wi' t'baby, and I've a rabbit pie in t'oven that'll just do for us all for dinner . . .' Agnes Appletree was voluble with delight.

'It's so good to see you both.' Pen led the way towards the front steps. 'Only, we had no word that you were coming north, so we've had no chance to prepare! What brings you here?'

'The queen's business,' I said evasively. 'But I wanted to know how you and Clem were and see your baby . . .'

'You'll hear him before long! He has such a pair of lungs, has my Leonard, and when he's hungry, he roars like a lion in the queen's menagerie! He's well grown for five months. He takes after his father.'

'And I wanted to see Jane, too.'

'You're mighty welcome, advance warning or not, mistress,' said Clem, in his slow, warm voice. 'These'll be your escort?' He nodded towards Sussex's men. 'We'll see to t'horses. Brockley, now, thee knows thee can trust me with them. You go wi' t'mistress and get warm by t'parlour fire.'

We were led inside by Pen into the familiar hall, although it was hardly recognizable as the uncared-for place I recalled. Then, it was full of scratched furniture and tapestries with moth holes in them. Now, new tables, benches and stools, gleaming with beeswax, stood about on the rush-strewn floor; the hearth fire crackled merrily; fresh modern tapestries hung on the walls.

'I take it,' I said, 'that the coal deposits weren't a disappointment?'

'They certainly were not,' said Pen. 'As you see! Not that we've been extravagant. A new plough and younger oxen for the farm; they came first. Those tapestries weren't the most costly, either, believe me. Here's the parlour. Jane! Jane!'

Jane Mason didn't get up from her stool as we entered the parlour, for the good reason that she had a lapful of an infant who was certainly well grown for five months. I looked at Master Leonard Moss and concluded that if ever there was a child whose paternity was written all over him, he was that child. He was Clem in miniature, with the same round blue eyes and sturdy limbs which would one day have Clem's ox-like power. Clem's mother was big too. It must run in his family.

But it was the girl who was holding him, his aunt, who interested me most. I looked at her, smiling. 'I haven't seen you for many years, Jane. Nine, isn't it?'

Pen took the child so that her sister could get to her feet. I saw that Jane was still the stockier of the two, and rounder of face, lacking Pen's high, bulging forehead. Jane's eyes, like Pen's, were grey and beautifully set, but where Pen's hair was mousey, Jane's was a rich beech-nut brown, and when she curtsied to me, the hands which lifted her skirt hem were shapely and, as far as I could see, not adorned with pinpricks. The clumsiness of childhood had vanished. And there was something else.

Maturity had brought her a great sweetness. When she smiled, I saw it: saw how gentle and how perfect was the moulding of her mouth, and how those fine eyes smiled along with it. I saw, in fact, exactly what Mark Easton must have seen, and loved.

And realized, in the same moment, that I did not know whether he had ever been able to tell her that he and I were trying to clear his father's name. If she hadn't heard of my investigations, perhaps it would be kinder to say nothing.

'Dear Mistress Stannard,' she said, rising from her curtsey and holding her hands out to me. 'Thank you for all you have tried to do. Mark Easton wrote and told me about it.'

'What do you mean?' Pen interrupted her, with frowning brows, and must have accidentally tightened her grip on her son, because he let out a protesting yell. She soothed him, but looked severely at Jane. 'He had no business to write to you! Clem and I forbade it! Ursula, we have had an approach from a family we know near Bolton. They are interested in Jane as a wife for their son. He is heir to a good property, and he's as personable a lad as you ever saw. He's away with Lord Sussex just now, but when he's home, we'll arrange a meeting. If he takes to Jane, she'll be a lucky girl and no one will be able to say that we haven't done well by her. Why are you so ungrateful, Jane?'

'I'm not ungrateful. But I see myself as betrothed to Mark,

and he *has* written to me.' Jane spoke mildly, but without apology. 'He found a messenger among Lord Sussex's men, who was bound for Carlisle but willing to pass this way, and he managed to get the letter to me.'

'How? Has Agnes been conspiring with you again? Smuggling letters to you? If I have told her once, I've told her a dozen times—'

'Pen,' I said, and for a moment I was once again the guardian who was capable of being stern with her. 'Pen, leave it. Go on, Jane.'

'In the letter,' said Jane, 'he told me, Mistress Stannard, that you were trying to find out the truth of Master Hoxton's death, that he had asked you to do so. He said you were being very kind and were doing your best. Have you news for me? Is that why you have come?'

'I have news,' I said, 'but it isn't what you want to hear, alas.'

As her face crumpled, I took her in my arms. Holding her, I contemplated Pen's angry eyes and hard line of a mouth and shook my head at her. 'Pen. I know Mark Easton,' I said. 'Has it never struck you that you may be doing him a grave injustice? Do you ever wonder if it is fair to burden the son with the sins of the father, if sins there truly were?'

'You say you have bad news, mistress.' Clem had come in with us. 'Does that mean Gervase Easton did it?'

'It means that I cannot prove he didn't. That's not the same thing,' I said defiantly.

Pen turned away, joggling the baby in her arms. 'Jane, why did you mention Mark? Mistress Stannard has barely come into the house, and before she has even taken a seat by the fire, or a glass of wine, you trouble us by talking of Mark and making us all angry. Why will you not let be?'

'Because I think Mistress Stannard came here on his account!' Jane said sadly. She drew herself away from me, and we both sat down. She looked at me. 'I want to know whatever you can tell me. Please.'

'Well, we do not!' Pen refused to back down. 'Jane, go and tell Agnes that we want wine and whatever refreshments she can find, and let this business of Mark alone.'

I intervened. 'That can wait,' I said. 'Pen, I have indeed come to tell the tale of my researches to Jane. I may as well do it now.'

'I'll find Agnes, madam,' said Brockley, and departed.

Pen looked exasperatedly at Clem, who said good-humouredly: 'Ill news is better out than in, in my view. Best do it quick, and if it means tears, get them shed and dried. Let Mistress Stannard talk, my love.'

Clem's greatest virtue was his common sense. Pen sank down on to a settle and said: 'Oh, very well. But Jane, I am angry with you.'

'You know something about being in love, Pen,' I said. 'Be a little tolerant. Now, Jane . . .'

I talked. The wine came, brought in by Agnes and Brockley and accompanied by some sweetmeats made of nuts and honey. I went on talking, for after all, it was a longish story.

At the end of it, Jane, who had listened in silence and with great attention, said: 'In all this, Mistress Stannard, there has been one vital person who may still be there to be questioned, but has not been found.'

'And who would that be, mistress?' Brockley asked, surprised.

'Why, that woman who said she saw Gervase Easton put something on Hoxton's tray. Not the one called Madge, but the woman Susannah Lamb. Mistress Stannard, could you try and find her? Could you? Because Mark says his father didn't do it, that he wouldn't have lied on the point of death and that what he told Mark in his last letter has to be the truth. Yet this Susannah Lamb says she recognized him. There's something there that needs explaining.'

She turned to Pen, her head high. 'Sister, I love you and am grateful for your kindness in looking after me here, but there are things I can't do even for you. I have said this before, and you didn't listen. Now I say it again, with Mistress Stannard here as my witness. Please believe me. Unless I marry Mark, I marry no one. I mean it. I wed him and no other. I ask you, not for the first time, to say as much to the family near Bolton. I don't want to meet their son, for his sake, in case he actually does take to me! I wouldn't like to disappoint an honest young man.'

She spoke with calm resolution, but without aggression or defiance, as though, even at eighteen, she were already too adult, too sure of herself, to need such things. Again, I knew I had recognized what Mark had recognized: not just sweetness this time, but something beyond it, an honesty and a strength.

I found myself responding. The combination of our need to save Hawkswood, if we could, and the appeal in Jane's eyes was powerful. 'If you think it will help,' I said, ignoring Pen's attempts to shake her head at me. 'I will look for Susannah.'

TWENTY-ONE

A Pretty Pope

Heavy rainstorms set in the next day; and anyway, our hard-worked horses again needed rest. We were obliged to stay two clear days at Tyesdale, just as we had at Carlisle. I tried to use the time well. I talked to Pen and Clem and to Jane herself, about Jane's future.

Whenever the matter was raised, Jane, throughout, whether she were speaking to me or to her sister or brother-in-law, held to the statement she had wanted me to witness, and strengthened it. She would not, she said, marry Mark against her family's wishes, but she would ally herself to no other and she would never change her mind.

It was plain enough that she would never do what Gerald Blanchard and I had once done, which was to elope at midnight. Such lawless actions were not in the nature of Jane Mason, and if they had been, I wouldn't, nowadays, have encouraged them. I was in my mid-thirties. I was no longer the rebellious girl I had been at twenty.

It seemed to me, though, that her feelings for Mark were deep and strong, and I tried to explain them to Clem and Penelope. Clem was prepared to listen and agree that they should at least not try to thrust Jane into a betrothal she didn't want. Pen, however, was obstinate.

'Do you propose to force her into marriage?' I asked her angrily, having called her to my room on the eve of our departure, in order to make one last try. '*You* were nearly forced into marriage once, against your will. How did you like it?'

Pen, standing before me in her dark-blue gown, her hands linked in front of her, every inch the dignified young housewife, suddenly flinched. For a moment she looked young and vulnerable. I felt compunction. The episode in question had arisen originally from a mission I had carried out for Elizabeth and had then been helped on its way, as it were, by a wayward love affair on Pen's part. The whole debacle had ended in bloodshed and left a scar on her mind which I had no wish to prod.

It was as well that Brockley wasn't present. Brockley had been so thoroughly exasperated by Pen on occasion that he had recommended me to treat her more harshly than I was willing to do. I knew too much about harsh treatment, having had it from Aunt Tabitha and Uncle Herbert. Had Brockley been there, he would have been more ruthless than I was.

He had already asked me if I had told Pen or the Masons about Hawkswood and the chance of payment from Mark. I had not; not so much out of delicacy of feeling, but out of the certainty that none of them, however sympathetic towards Hugh and myself, would countenance what they saw as an undesirable marriage for Jane in order to rescue us. From what Jane had told us concerning Mark's letter to her, he hadn't mentioned money at all. I felt it would be better if I didn't, either.

Without Brockley, however, Pen was better able to stand up to me. 'It isn't the same thing,' she said protestingly. 'The young man we have in mind for Jane is decent, from a respectable home. You'd like him. So would Jane, if she would give herself a chance.'

'Pen,' I said patiently, 'give Mark Easton a chance. Or give me a chance at least to search all the avenues that might lead to the truth. Try to see things from Jane's viewpoint.'

'She is being foolish, just as I was when I was a girl,' said Pen, to my annoyance. Opponents who surrender a point to you and then somehow turn the surrender into a weapon are very annoying indeed.

Once more, as on the day of our arrival, I drew on the strength of old authority. 'Pen, as your former guardian, to whom I think you owe some respect, I ask you to hold back on this matter of Jane's betrothal until you hear the outcome of my quest. As soon as I return to the south, I mean to search for the woman who claimed to have recognized Gervase Easton as the culprit. Give me time. If Gervase's name can be cleared,' I said, 'would you and your mother and brother then object to Mark as a suitor for your sister?'

'No, we wouldn't,' said Pen, fairly enough. 'But with this shadow . . .'

'And if I remove the shadow?'

'As I said, everything would be different then.'

'Then give it a chance to be different. Let me complete my enquiries.' I spoke with all the assurance I could muster, but even as I did so, I remembered the left-handed man in the portrait at Ramsfold. A sinking in the pit of the stomach told me that, at heart, I now feared that Gervase, after all, was guilty.

Pen must have seen something in my face, for she said: 'But you're not sure of the outcome, are you?'

'I want to *be* sure. One way or the other.'

'If Mark's father had fought this man that he believed had cuckolded him and killed him in a duel, Clem and I, and mother and George too, would accept that as honourable. But poison is another matter.'

'I know.' In this, I had to admit that Pen was right. To trick a man – in this case, an ailing man – into eating poisoned food was a hateful deed, and there were no motives to excuse it. 'But that,' I said, 'is precisely why we need to know the truth.'

'Is it? If it's the wrong answer, will it help Mark to know it? Does he,' said Pen acutely, 'really want to know for sure that his father did such a thing?'

'He has asked me to find out.'

'But he doesn't believe you'll find that his father was guilty. He talked to us about it, you know – when we first taxed him with being the son of a notorious man. You could give him a terrible shock if, after all, you prove him wrong.'

She had become a very dangerous opponent, had my Pen. She had lit up my own innermost doubts and fears.

At length, I said: 'While there is still a chance that the answer may be the right one, I must go on. Mark is not a fool. In fact, for years – before his uncle died and Mark found that letter – he did think Gervase was guilty. He has lived with that knowledge before. He started me on my quest, and he will have to deal with anything I find. And I ask you, Pen, to leave Jane be until I send word to you – to say either that I have discovered the truth and here it is, or that the truth can't be found. Then you must decide whether it is right to bind the father's guilt on to the innocent son.'

It was a fine, noble note on which to end, and it had an effect on Pen. She said: 'Very well. I agree. But there must be a time limit. Three months?'

'All right. Three months.'

I didn't add what I was thinking: that if I found no answer, or the wrong one, I sincerely hoped that Mark and Jane would somehow, after all, find the courage and the ingenuity to elope. They would have a chance then of happiness. Even if Hawkswood . . .

I didn't want to think about that.

'A pretty Pope,' said Elizabeth bitterly, striding angrily about the private room in Windsor Castle where she had given me audience. 'A fine Christian, this Pope Pius the Fifth. Without a twinge of conscience, he is prepared to torment honest men and women by telling them that they must be either cut off from the love of God or else turn traitor to their lawful queen. Who does he think he is, I wonder, to speak with such assurance on behalf of God? If I were God,' said Elizabeth with fury, rounding a table and spinning to face me, her satin train sweeping the rushes like a broom. 'If I were God, I would strike Pope Pius dead with a lightning bolt! What was the wording again?'

I have a good memory, but I had taken the first opportunity I could to write down what I remembered of the appalling letter I had found among Anne of Northumberland's papers. I had read those notes through several times before coming into Elizabeth's presence and had them at my command. With reluctance, I embarked once more on the recital.

'The letter said that if the restoration of Mary of Scotland did not soon take place, and if Mary should not be made your heir, then a Bull would be issued freeing all English Catholics from their duty to obey the Crown. It added that true believers should not obey your laws and any who did would be excommunicated. It said that the one true church would . . . formally . . .'

Here I faltered, as I had done during my first recital, and Elizabeth, who had now halted facing me, regarded me in an ironical fashion. 'Go on, Ursula. I told you the first time – I won't chop your head off. It isn't your fault.'

'Would formally depose you,' I said in a low voice.

'It means,' said Elizabeth, 'that the Catholics in England, whether they wish it or no, may not look on me – or even refer to me – as their sovereign and also remain Catholic. Bah!'

She began to stride furiously about once more. However, although the table had a number of small objects on it, and although my royal half-sister was quite capable of throwing things at people who had aroused her wrath, she had never yet thrown anything at me and didn't do so now.

'I see,' she said, halting in front of me once more. 'Yes. I do see. Dear God. I have striven to look after my people. At one of my first Council meetings, I told my Councillors that corrupt judges must be dealt with; that I would not seek to peer into men's minds and question their most private beliefs. And I have cared for my people. I *have*! And now, many who trusted me, whose welfare I have safeguarded, are to be told that their trust is a mortal sin in the eyes of the Almighty. And many innocent, ignorant souls will believe it!'

'Perhaps not so very many,' I said, in an attempt at reassurance.

'I have made this land solvent. I have kept it – until now – a land at peace. I have given my people a country in which they can *live*; in which they can marry and rear their children; work at their trades, enjoy their sports; entertain their neighbours with good food and music and dancing; sleep in safety; sleep, at the last, in quiet and hallowed graves. Pius, it seems, puts no value on these things. He would prefer a land where blood streams in the ditches and people who chance not to agree with him, on this or that, scream in the flames. A fine Christian!'

'I would kill him if I could get my hands on him,' I said.

'I shan't send you on *that* assignment, Ursula,' said Elizabeth, ferociously humorous. 'There is trouble ahead, my sister, but I hope to hold it at bay. I will see that my vengeance for this last rebellion makes it clear to my subjects that Elizabeth, here and now, is more to be feared than any invisible God. As for that Northumberland woman; she did well to flee to Scotland. She'd be wise to flee further still in case I snatch her out of her refuge even yet! I and my Council will discuss this proposed *effusion* from Pius, and we will be ready for it. Proclamations will be prepared, to warn anyone against thinking that they owe him more allegiance than they owe me; I shall have land and sea forces ready in case of risings here or attack from outside – from Spain, for instance. More, I cannot do. As it is, we have been caught wrong-footed in one respect.'

'Ma'am?'

'Oh yes. Your warning to Regent Moray was carried north with all speed, but still, it wasn't swift enough. Lady Northumberland's message to the Archbishop of St Andrews must have got through the snow and arrived first. Regent James Stewart, Earl of Moray, was assassinated ten days ago. He was shot with a musket from an upper window. The news came yesterday.'

'I think he was shot to clear the way for Mary Stuart's restoration,' I said slowly.

'Yes,' said Elizabeth bitterly. 'I think so too. Well, Mary Stuart shall have no crown: not Scotland's, and not mine. Crownless she is, and crownless she will stay. Mewed up in England, in Tutbury Castle, is where she will stay as well!'

Beneath the fury, I detected a great hurt. It is hurtful, to strive hard to give justice and protection and to have these things dismissed as worthless, and that by a man who had never set foot in England and yet apparently considered himself more its ruler than its own queen. I looked at my half-sister with compassion, and she looked back at me with a small half-smile.

'You have done well, my Ursula. You have carried out, excellently, the errand on which I sent you. I will give you your reward personally. I have it ready.'

There was a box on the table, and from this she took a purse. 'Four hundred pounds, in sovereigns,' she said. 'It will be useful, I hope.'

I curtsied and thanked her. It was not a disappointment, for though I knew that I had earned a good fee, I also knew that she had had to break into the assets in her treasury to finance the campaign in the north and the preparations to defend the south, and that my careful sister would probably be only moderately generous to me.

We had made sure that she did not know about Hawkswood. I wished for a moment that we had told her, but at heart I knew it would have made no difference. Hugh had said she would not be sympathetic towards someone who had been as unwise as he had been. This payment wouldn't save us. It would be useful, of course. We would not have to open our coffers to pay for Meg's portrait, and we could use the rest to improve her dowry. For that, I could be grateful.

Elizabeth, saying that she wished to confer with those of her Council who were to hand, dismissed me with a kiss. I left her and went to our rooms. Brockley and I had arrived at the castle only an hour before. As yet, I had done no more than greet my household, see with thankfulness that Hugh was safe and indeed seemed better than when I saw him last, and let Dale help me change my dress. I hadn't even looked at the finished portrait of Meg, though Hugh said it had been delivered.

I found them all anxiously awaiting me. 'Brockley has told us nearly everything,' Hugh said as he drew me in. He closed the door with one hand and hugged me with the other arm while the Brockleys tactfully gazed out of the window, Gladys poked the fire with great attention, Dr Lambert drew Meg's attention to something in a book he was reading and Sybil sat serenely smiling. 'What a time you have had! Thank God you are safely back!'

I looked thankfully round at them all. I had never been so relieved to see Hugh, never so glad to be safely among my own again. Meg, I could swear, had grown a little, and from Dr Lambert's cheerful and approving mien, she had been attentive to her studies in my absence.

'I've been paid for my work for the queen,' I said. 'For eavesdropping on treason, being beaten and locked in a cellar and riding for my life through the snow.' I handed Hugh the purse.

He examined it with a sigh, but then laughed. 'We expected no more,' he said. 'Well, we needn't look on *that* as an extravagance now!'

He pointed. Against the wall at the far side of the room, standing on wooden legs but with a cloth cast over the top of it, was what looked like some kind of frame. Hugh went over to it and whisked the cloth away.

'Oh!' I said. 'Oh! That's . . .!'

Arbuckle had performed a wonder. However strange his methods, with his screens and mirrors and his extraordinary lenses, they produced astonishing results.

There was Meg, seated at a desk, quill pen in hand, face grave. Behind her, an open window gave a glimpse of green trees and distant hills, but it was Meg herself who commanded one's gaze. Unquestionably, the portrait was that of a girl of fourteen, untouched and vulnerable as only the young can be vulnerable, and yet with a latent maturity. I already knew that Meg possessed it; I had recognized something similar in Jane Mason. But Arbuckle, lacking my knowledge of my daughter, had nevertheless sensed her unusual quality and illustrated it in paint. The woman that Meg would become was there, her petals folded in the bud but revealed through the wealth of fine detail: the tiny lines and mouldings; the light and shade of her face; the subtle shape of the young body beneath the orange-tawny material of her gown.

Her betrothal to George Hillman had never been made formal, but Hillman had asked for her and Meg herself had said that she liked him, the little she had seen of him, and would be glad to know him better. Hugh and I approved of young Hillman and would gladly welcome him as our son-in-law. He lived in Buckinghamshire, but when we could, we meant to invite him to visit us and further his acquaintance with Meg. When he saw that portrait, I thought, he would see for himself not only what Meg was now, but what she would be like when she was his wife.

And he would surely be delighted with the prophecy. I hoped he wouldn't change his mind because the loss of Hawkswood had made Meg's family poorer, and I was thankful that her dowry, at least, would now be more than adequate.

'It's . . . beautiful,' I said. 'Hugh, whatever you paid Jocelyn Arbuckle, you should pay him extra. We can afford that, thanks to the queen! I can hardly believe it. It's Meg, and yet it's more than Meg. What do you think of it, sweetheart?' I added, turning to my daughter herself.

'I scarcely recognize myself, Mother, and yet it *is* me! I think it's wonderful, too, and Stepfather has already paid Master Arbuckle extra. We thought of that ahead of you!' said Meg, laughing.

We were all still admiring the picture when a tap on the door interrupted us. Sybil opened it, and Brockley said: 'Madam, while you were with the queen, I went to the kitchen and asked Sterry to come here. He was busy but said he would come shortly. I think he's arrived.'

'John Sterry?' I said. 'You asked him to come here? Why?' But then Brockley's eyes met mine, and it seemed that the extraordinary linking of minds which had taken place that night in the hall of Ramsfold House was still there.

I knew the answer to my question even before he said: 'We have to trace Susannah Lamb, madam.'

Then John Sterry was standing before me. 'I believe, Mistress Stannard, that you want to ask me something?' His voice, as ever, was brisk and clipped. Sterry, I thought, was a man who disliked wasting time. He would go on being brisk until the day he died, and he would probably do that with despatch, as well.

'I . . . yes.' After that audience with Elizabeth, it was a wrench to make my mind concentrate on Gervase Easton and his son's thwarted romance. During the last month, indeed, I felt as though I had been bounced like a tennis ball between the very public crisis in Elizabeth's realm and the private ones in the lives of Mark and Jane and ourselves. 'Master Sterry,' I said, pulling myself together, 'you remember that before Christmas, I asked you questions about the death of Peter Hoxton, and asked who the women were who saw a man put an extra dish on the tray intended for him.'

'Yes, Mistress. Madge Goodman and Susannah Lamb.'

'You said that Susannah Lamb had left five or six years ago.'

'Yes. So she did.'

'And you've no idea where she might have gone? Surely she had plans of some kind and told someone? One of the other women? I know you said she wasn't popular, but even so . . .'

Sterry said slowly: 'After you came to the kitchens, Mistress Stannard, I did some thinking. It's odd. When you really try to think about the past, you do find yourself remembering things. Since you came to my kitchen to talk to Madge, mistress, I've often called Susannah to mind, and I've talked further to Madge myself. She's the only one who was here in Susannah's day. All the women who worked with Susannah have left, same as she did. People come and go, at jobs like the pestle and mortar. We often find ourselves short-handed. That's how we came to take Susannah on. She was big and strong, and I'd have employed her even if I'd known that there was talk that she'd left her last employer because she'd been caught out in some sort of dishonesty. I didn't know – not then. Madge told me that two days ago. It was women's gossip, you see, that I don't listen to, but Madge did, of course.'

'Dishonesty?' I said. 'What kind?'

'I don't know. Nor does Madge. Madge said it maybe wasn't true, that Susannah was big and noisy and enough to make any employer tire of her. According to her, Susannah had a sharp tongue as well as a loud one and it was likely enough that people might gossip unpleasantly about her. None of the gossip need be true – it could be just spite repaying spite. She left here of her own free will, anyhow.'

'And when she left, she never said where she was going?' I persisted.

'No, she didn't. Madge says she never heard a word about that, but she does have an idea about where Susannah came *from*, if that's of any use. She says Susannah came from Abingdon. She was widowed, and the story among the other women was that she had to find work after her husband died and came to Windsor as a servant in the household of some well-to-do family who moved about between one home and another. According to Madge, once Susannah was in Windsor, she left that family and found another post but was dismissed

– perhaps for dishonesty, perhaps not – and then her next post was here.'

'Abingdon . . .' I said thoughtfully. 'That's not far . . .'

At almost the same moment, Meg, who had not been listening but had been gazing at her portrait, suddenly said: 'Mother – why has Master Arbuckle painted me as left-handed? Look, in the picture I'm holding my pen in my left hand, but I never did that in my life!'

TWENTY-TWO

Light-Fingered Servants

It was too late that day to call on Arbuckle, and in the morning, Hugh admitted to feeling tired and disinclined to go traipsing through Windsor.

'In any case, madam,' said Brockley, when I explained the situation to him, 'you and Master Stannard are Arbuckle's customers; his patrons. It is for him to wait upon you. I'll fetch him.'

Brockley told us afterwards that Arbuckle had taken a good deal of fetching because he didn't seem to be aware that an artist is the subordinate of his customers. Brockley apparently arrived at the painter's premises to find him in the midst of a sitting, which he refused to interrupt, and even when it was over, he said he wanted to go on adding fine detail to the work. He had done with Meg's portrait. He had handed it to Hugh and been paid and that was that . . .

'If I'd pulled a dagger on him, he'd have shouted for his landlady to fetch the constable,' said Brockley wryly. 'So I pointed out, madam, that you were influential in the court and that a good word from you was most likely worth a couple of commissions, while a bad word might wipe them out. And then, instead of a dagger, I pulled out my purse, madam, and I'm grateful for the good rate of pay that you give me. The sight of three gold angels in my palm clinched the matter. He's a man of business.'

'I'd better reimburse you!' I said.

The three gold angels, at any rate, enabled Brockley to return to us at the end of the morning with Jocelyn Arbuckle at his side: paint-stained, untidy and irritable, but there. We calmed his annoyance with a glass of wine and then led him to the portrait of Meg.

'It's beautiful,' I assured him. 'We're so very pleased with it. But we have noticed a strange thing, and there is a link between that and a very serious affair which I have already mentioned to you. It concerns the good name of Gervase Easton, whom you once painted, and whether or not he was right or left-handed. How does it come about that you show my daughter as left-handed, when she is not?'

'Ah. That.' Master Arbuckle was quite unconcerned. 'That's an effect of the lens I use to obtain an image which will give me precise and accurate detail. You saw the equipment. You did not observe that the image appears in reverse? I never think of it as important, myself.'

I said: 'No, quite. But how long have you been using such lenses? For instance, when you painted Gervase Easton, over twenty years ago, did you use lenses then?'

'Gervase Easton. He was the fellow, was he not, whose brother wanted a portrait of him. How do you expect me to remember, so far back? I was experimenting with various methods of working at the time – mirrors and lenses of different types. But lenses weren't as well made then as they are now, and I found it difficult to get a clear image. I gave up experimenting with them and worked with a particular type of mirror, until a year or two ago, when I found that much better lenses could be bought.'

'Please try to remember,' said Hugh. 'Did you try out a lens when you painted Gervase Easton?'

'I may have done,' said Arbuckle, almost pettishly. 'Does it really matter?'

'Yes, it does,' I said. 'We asked you once before whether Easton was left or right-handed, and you didn't know. But I've now seen the portrait you did of him, and it shows him with a pen in his left hand. Master Arbuckle, Easton died because he had been accused of a crime. If he were right-handed, then he is probably innocent, and his son badly wants to know. *Needs* to know! Please!'

Arbuckle frowned. He turned to gaze at Meg's picture, as though he thought it might inspire him. 'I didn't use a lens for the miniature of Mistress Easton, which was shortly before I painted her husband. Ah! I think I remember buying a lens just after I'd finished painting her, though! Yes! Yes, you're right. I did try the lens technique out with Master Easton! And with one or two others as well.'

'So . . .?' I said.

'He was probably right-handed. I suppose he must have been. I misled you when we talked of this before – I'd entirely forgotten that I used the lens technique when I painted him. Yes, it would have reversed his image.' He spoke quite casually. Even now, the dedicated portrait painter had clearly not grasped that, to us, this testimony was vital; that enormous emotions were involved. Arbuckle lived in a world of light and shadow, facial planes, pigments, mirrors, lenses. He could lay bare the human soul, but he needed a brush in his hand first. He would probably stay in that world all his life, like a walled-up anchorite. He did dimly realize, however, that he had caused confusion. 'I'm so sorry, Mistress Stannard,' he said.

After that, tracing Susannah Lamb seemed to be more vital than ever. Her testimony contradicted that of Arbuckle. Also, something had begun to nag at my mind: something which I could not identify, but which I knew was important.

I had had this maddening experience before. It was as though, deep in my brain, was vital knowledge which would not surface into the light. The feeling seemed to stem from the conversation I had had with Sterry, but as yet I could go no further than that. I could only press on along the road that lay clear before me.

'We have to get to the bottom of this now,' I said to Hugh. 'If only we can once find out the truth! I don't want to leave you again, but . . .'

'I'm reasonably well at the moment,' Hugh said. 'Just tired at times, and my joints will always be too stiff for riding in future, I think. I wish I could come with you, but my coach is at Hawkswood, and even if I had it here, the roads may well be too boggy for it. But Abingdon isn't far, as you said yesterday, and if there's a chance of solving Mark's mystery . . .'

'I know.'

It was a winter afternoon, already grey and shadowy, already candlelit. It was too late now to set out for Abingdon, which must wait until tomorrow. Hugh and I were alone together. I studied his face. He did seem better than he had when I left for the north, but there was something else to disturb me. He looked so unhappy. For the first time, ever, I saw the shine of moisture in his eyes.

'I am prepared to send you from me again,' he said, 'because there is a chance, just a chance, that you might yet save Hawkswood for us. Oh yes, for you and for Meg as well as for me. It's part of the inheritance that I'll leave behind me – I hope. I am not a sentimental man normally, Ursula, but Hawkswood is part of me. I've known it from childhood. I know every cranny, every stone. I've seen trees grow from saplings into a tall chestnuts and beeches; I've coaxed and nurtured the rose garden and brought in cartloads of clay because roses like clay . . .'

'And Hawkswood's soil is chalk,' I said. 'Yes. I even helped to spread the clay soil once or twice.'

'Every room in the house has its memories,' Hugh said. 'Boyhood studies, my father teaching me how to play chess, family Christmases, wedding parties, funeral gatherings, the gallery where two of my father's female cousins – who didn't like each other – were unbelievably rude about each other's taste in dress and one of them stormed out of the house in a temper; the hall where a dog belonging to a very influential guest was chased in at one door and out of another by our enormous, bad-tempered old tomcat . . . it took half an hour and about a gallon of our best canary wine to restore our lordly visitor's temper . . . so many moments, so many. The thought of losing it horrifies me. That's why I'm willing to let you go away again – in fact, am virtually sending you. I wouldn't, otherwise. But don't run into danger this time, Ursula, *please*! I suppose we're all free to leave Windsor now, but I can't travel anyway until my coach is brought from home. Meg and I will wait here for you.'

This was wise, in any case, for Windsor was closer to Abingdon than either of our homes were. Abingdon was on the Thames, upstream, thirty miles or so in a straight line, but further if one used the river. I had decided to do so, for I wanted Dale with me as well as Brockley. Dale hated horseback travel so.

Though horseback travel remained a possibility.

'If Susannah has been in Abingdon but moved on,' I told Dale, 'and we have to go after her on land, we'll hire horses there and you'll have to make the best of it. If it comes to it, please don't tell me that you can't abide riding in the cold, unless you want me to put you on the first barge going back to Windsor.'

Brockley hired a barge for us. He did more. He also went to see Sir William Cecil and begged the loan of John Ryder as an extra companion. 'In case we have trouble with Susannah,' he said. 'The more impressive we look, the better. Sir William says, madam, that we can have Ryder for a week, but please will we bring him back in one piece, since the last time he lent us a man, we didn't manage to bring him back at all.' For a moment, his mouth twisted with remembered grief.

Sir William Cecil did at times have a dark sense of humour.

The barge that Brockley found had a covered cabin, which gave us shelter from the weather. The day after we had talked to Arbuckle, we set out, upstream.

Abingdon was a small place, but when we first arrived, we were at a loss. Where did we begin to look for a widow called Susannah Lamb who had lived here long ago, gone away and possibly – only possibly – returned five or six years back?

'We could be on completely the wrong path,' I said glumly. 'We don't *know* that she came back here.'

'Try the church,' said Brockley, pointing towards a slender spire. 'We could start with the vicar, the way we did in Kendal. If Susannah is here, she could be one of his flock.'

The vicar of St Helen's, as the church was called, wasn't immediately available. We began by going to the church itself, where we found the sexton scything the grass between the graves. He told us that the Reverend Bell was conducting a wedding at that very moment, would be going on to the feast and would stay to bless the bridal bed in the evening.

We took rooms at an inn and tried again the following morning.

This was not immediately successful either, for the vicar turned out to have a dragon-like housekeeper, who said that her employer couldn't receive us until noon. 'He was late to bed last night,' she explained, in disapproving tones.

When we did eventually come face to face with him, the Reverend Arthur Bell proved to be a round little man with a bald crown, tufts of ginger hair sprouting above his ears and a face which was probably pink as a rule, but just now was unwontedly pale.

'I'm sorry to have kept you waiting,' he said, peering at us as though his eyes found the light painful. 'I was at a feast yesterday, and I am not accustomed to drinking wine . . . Even a little has such an effect . . .'

The good vicar, in fact, had a wine-headache. Avoiding details, I explained that Susannah might have useful testimony which could help to solve a crime.

Bell shook his head regretfully. 'I'm temporary here. The usual vicar has had to go away for a while – the death of a relative – and I am on loan from another parish. My curate is looking after my own church for three weeks. I know little of the parishioners here. However –' he brightened – 'Mistress Freeman, the housekeeper, may know. She goes with the vicarage, so to speak.'

The dragon-like housekeeper, when summoned, recognized the name of Susannah Lamb at once. And stiffened.

'Oh yes. I know of *her.* She came back from Windsor – a bit over five years ago I think it was – to live with her kinfolk. Not parents – they were dead and gone – but she had a brother here, Master Hayward. He was a lot younger than she was, and he'd wed late, I think. He had a wife and some children not yet grown, and Susannah more or less pushed herself into their house.

'But not for long,' said Mistress Freeman with satisfaction. 'They couldn't put up with her, and that's a fact. I knew the wife quite well; she often brought flowers for the church here. Kate, she was called. She said Susannah was loud-mouthed, spiteful and kept on clouting the children.

Well, Kate's gone too now; died in childbed, like so many women. I've never married, myself, and I'm glad of it. Kate Hayward wasn't a bitter woman as a rule, but on the subject of Mistress Lamb, well! In the end, the brother found a post for Susannah, as a cook-housekeeper somewhere in Nettlebury.'

'Nettlebury?' Brockley enquired.

'It's a village a few miles away,' said Bell. 'Not far. To the north – a mile or so off the main track to Oxford. I can give you full directions. You might find her there, I suppose.'

'We'd better talk to the brother,' I said. 'And ask him the name of her employers. I suppose he'd know.'

'Oh, he's left Abingdon,' Mistress Freeman said. 'When Kate died and left him with a brood of children to look after, he went to live with some cousins who had children too, or so I heard, roundabout. I don't know where. Oxford, was it? He was a tailor by trade; that's work a man can do anywhere.' She noticed my disappointed expression. 'I am sorry I can't tell you more, but I don't pay much attention to gossip,' she told me primly and, I suspected, inaccurately.

Brockley said: 'What's the best stable for hiring horses?'

'Quiet ones,' said Dale.

'At reasonable prices,' added John Ryder.

We were on our way to Nettlebury that same afternoon, having acquired a nice little skewbald mare and a side-saddle for me, while Ryder had a brown cob and Brockley a well-built chestnut gelding with a pillion for Dale, who much preferred this arrangement, since it meant that she didn't have to control the horse herself.

Like the journey from Carlisle to Tyesdale, it was a silent ride, although the reasons were different. I was thinking. The feeling that there was something I ought to remember, something relevant, still gnawed at me. Sooner or later it would reveal itself, and I knew that it would probably do so when I was thinking of something else. The problem was to make myself think of something else, when all the time my mind niggled at the puzzle just as one's tongue niggles at a broken tooth.

The track was muddy but no worse than that, and though

the skies were overcast, it didn't actually rain. We covered the seven or eight miles to Nettlebury by dinner time. In the village, a pleasant community of grey stone cottages, we found an inn and a small church. 'I think we'll have to try the parish vicar again,' I said. 'I hope it's the real one this time.'

Ryder suggested that we first of all went to the inn for some dinner. 'If the place is decent, we can arrange to spend the night here. We might be wise to stay overnight. The dark still falls early.'

'Most of the houses seem to be just small cottages,' I said. 'There are only a few that would need a household of servants. If the vicar can't help, we could call at all the likely ones, one at a time.'

'We could ask the innkeeper, too,' Dale offered. 'Likely enough he knows most of the people hereabouts.'

Master Medland, the landlord of the Unicorn, was a heavily built fellow with a face which was as near to a genuine rectangle as a human face can be: square of chin, straight of hairline, flat of cheekbone. Small broken veins in his nose and the whites of his stone-coloured eyes suggested that he made free with his own wares. He was, however, a competent man, able to provide rooms, dinner and information with equal ease. Dale had been right.

'Susannah Lamb?' he said, when we enquired. 'Oh, *her*!' He snorted. He sounded remarkably like Mistress Freeman.

'You recognize the name, then,' I said. 'Was something wrong with her? Who was it she worked for?'

'Me,' said Master Medland. 'And bloody nearly wrecked my reputation, she did. Folk stopping here kept missing this and that, and I couldn't find out who was doing it, at first. I was damn near accused of stealing, myself! It could have ended my good name and my trade or worse! And I was doing well. I can do without light-fingered Susannah Lamb driving my customers away.'

'What happened to her?' asked Brockley.

'She's bloody gone, that's what! She was here nigh on a year, and then I caught her thieving from my wife's purse and after that it was plain enough to me where folks' knick-knacks were going to!'

The women in the Windsor kitchens who said there had been whispers that Mistress Lamb was dishonest had probably been right. 'Where is she now?' I asked.

Medland snorted again. 'She should have been hanged. She would have been, except that I locked her in an empty room upstairs and left her there while I went for the constable. I couldn't find him – the fellow we had as constable that year was a lazy bugger and didn't want to be found oftener than he could help, if you ask me. I came home again, knowing I'd customers to see to and my wife would need to go marketing. All this happened early in the morning, before the day got going. When I got back I found that our dear Susannah had used a bench that was in the room to smash her way out of it and she'd gone and all her things with her. There was no one here capable of stopping her. She was a big hefty lump with a short temper and a bigger fist than mine is.

'The maidservants were scared of her, and the tapster lives out and wasn't on duty yet. I let her go. We never put out a hue and cry. I'm a bit funny that way. I didn't mind locking her up and going for the constable, but I never like the notion of hunting a fellow creature like a stag, not unless it's murder or something of that sort. She was gone, and good riddance. If you want to talk to her, you're about four years too late.'

'But where did she go?' asked Brockley. 'Have you no idea?'

'My wife reckoned she'd go to her brother in Oxford.'

'Master Hayward?' I asked, and he nodded.

'That 'ud be right, yes. He came here to see her a couple of times. He was a widower, but he got married again, and I recall he brought his new wife here so as Susannah could meet her. I did hear Susannah had been seen in Abingdon haggling with a boatman, the same day that she ran off from here, so likely enough she took a hired boat upstream to Oxford. As I said, I didn't bother about her any more. She's no loss. Nothing worse than a light-fingered servant; not in my line of business, anyhow.'

Light-fingered. The word brought Jonathan Bowman to

my mind. I could see him, sitting by his hearth, embroidering gloves while he talked to us. I remembered thinking that the back of the hand that held the needle must be uncomfortably near the fire. I remembered his complaints about his maidservants. *Lazy, Saucy, Lightfingers, that's what I called them.*

The women who worked with her had said that Susannah had probably lost her previous post through dishonesty . . .

And it was then that the fugitive idea that had been hiding in the depths of my mind suddenly chose to surface.

We would need dinner, and by the time we had eaten it, the short hours of daylight would be already passing. I hired rooms for us all at the Unicorn, and over our meal I said: 'I have remembered something. It's to do with left-handedness . . .'

We spent the night at the inn and set out for Oxford the next morning, early, reaching it well before noon.

'Well, here we are,' said Brockley as we came ashore at a landing stage and surveyed the crowded city before us. 'This is Oxford.'

Dale said dismally: 'It's much bigger than Abingdon and so . . . so thick with buildings. Ma'am, it's going to be like looking for a black cat in a cellar at midnight.'

'And if we do find Mistress Lamb,' John Ryder added, 'I hope she doesn't refuse to talk!'

'I think,' I said grimly, 'that we now know of a way round that.'

Dale had been needlessly pessimistic. Sometimes, when you're searching out something that is hidden and difficult to find, you may feel as though you've been seeking in vain for a century – and then there comes a moment of breakthrough. Suddenly, the skein unravels.

Once again, we used the system of enquiring at vicarages. The third vicar we tried was able to direct us. Yes, he knew of Master Hayward, tailor; in fact, he had married him to his second wife. The couple, along with Hayward's four children from his first marriage, were living in a rented house only two streets away.

We were there ten minutes later. The Haywards' home

proved to be a thatched cottage of fair size, prosperous-looking in an unpretentious way. We knocked upon the door, and it was opened promptly.

By Susannah.

TWENTY-THREE

Obnoxious Company

I knew who she was at once. The various things that people such as Sterry and Mistress Freeman and Medland, the innkeeper at Nettlebury, had said to us about her had created a picture in my mind, and this woman matched it exactly. She was about fifty, massively built, with thick red arms protruding from black stuff sleeves, a slabby face and an expression both suspicious and truculent. Hands on ample hips, she surveyed us, and then something about us – probably the sight of Ryder and Brockley, once more shoulder to shoulder – seemed to disconcert her. When she said: 'Yes?' the tone was wary.

'Mistress Lamb?' I said.

'I . . . Yes. But—'

'Mistress Susannah Lamb?' said Brockley.

'Yes, but I'm not the lady of the house. That's my brother's second wife. I housekeep for her. Pretty lass, she is, but half his age and no hand at running a house,' said Susannah. I thought she was attempting an air of good-humoured tolerance, but it came over as catty. Mistress Lamb was not an attractive personality. 'She's out,' she said. 'She's gone off with her maid, buying fripperies. The master's in his workshop, at the back here. It opens on the street behind this.' She jerked her head to indicate the rear of the house. 'He's a tailor. There's a customer with him now.'

'It's you we want to see,' I told her. 'Do you remember a man called Peter Hoxton, who was murdered in Windsor Castle something over twenty years ago? You identified a man called Gervase Easton as the killer. The death of Hoxton is being enquired into again. We want you to repeat your testimony and also to answer one or two other questions.'

She stared at us, out of large brown eyes, like the eyes of an ox. 'Peter Hoxton? What does anyone want to start that up again for, after all these years?' Her chin rose. 'And who might you be, anyway?'

But the indignation was forced. There was fear in those bovine eyes, and before she clasped her hands to still them, I saw them quiver.

'This is Mistress Ursula Stannard, one of her majesty's ladies-in-waiting. Her majesty knows of the enquiries Mistress Stannard is making,' said Dale boldly.

I gave her an appreciative glance. I loved that shrewd streak in her, which so often appeared at unexpected moments. She had just implied, without actually saying so, that I was here at Elizabeth's behest.

Susannah looked as if she would like to close the door in our faces, but Brockley and Ryder had moved unobtrusively forward, and Brockley, as if by accident, had put a foot in the doorway. 'May we come in?' he said. 'We may have to talk for some time.'

Most unwillingly, Susannah stood aside and let us enter.

She took us into a parlour. A fire burnt in the hearth, and she went to it to warm her hands. Brockley and Ryder stationed themselves between her and the door. With formality, I introduced my companions and then said that we had taken much trouble to find her, because there were things we wished to learn which only she could tell us.

'So what do you want to know?' Susannah asked sullenly.

'You identified a man you saw putting an extra dish on Hoxton's tray,' said Brockley.

'I saw a man putting a pie on *a* tray. Yes, I remember that much. Had to tell a whole lot of people that came asking questions. So I'm not likely to forget.'

'You said it was Gervase Easton.'

'What if it was? He worked in the Spicery. I knew him well enough by sight. That's what I said at the time, and that's what I say now. What else is there to say?'

'It was the truth?' I asked her.

'Of course it was the truth! What would I go pointing a finger at the wrong man for?'

'You hadn't been working at the castle all that long, though, had you?' said Ryder, stepping in with assurance. I had had plenty of time since leaving Windsor to make sure that Ryder fully understood the details of this enquiry, and I had not only done so with thoroughness, but I had also repeated most of it when I shared my thoughts with my companions in the Unicorn at Nettlebury.

'Not that long, but I knew Easton right enough. What *is* all this?'

'There was a second witness,' I said, 'a girl called Madge. She couldn't name the man she saw, but she could describe him. We've spoken to her, and she says he was left-handed. We have established that Gervase Easton was almost certainly right-handed. That seems strange.'

'I wouldn't know anything about that. I never noticed anything of that sort at the time. I was questioned, and I told what I'd seen.'

'But your honesty has been questioned as well, hasn't it?' said Ryder. 'Come, Mistress Lamb. You know you're no saint. We know why you left your post with the Medlands in Nettlebury, and we've heard that you came to work in the Spicery at the castle because you'd been caught out misbehaving in your previous place. You don't mind stealing, it seems. Do you mind lying?'

He was using his fatherly tone. It had never before occurred to me that to be fatherly can also suggest that one is uncomfortably all-knowing. Speaking in that mild voice, Ryder sounded positively sinister.

It worked better than any of us could have expected. Mistress Lamb's face went pale, and I saw the tremor begin again in the thick hands she had stretched out to the warmth.

'What . . . what are you talking about?'

'By the sound of it,' said Ryder, 'we've wakened your sense of guilt, but I'm wondering what you feel guilty about. Before you came to the castle, were you dishonest with your previous employers in Windsor? Who were they, by the way?'

Susannah's face now turned to the colour of goat's cheese. While we were still gazing at her in astonishment, Dale said: 'Careful, she's going to faint,' and taking Susannah's arm, steered her on to a nearby settle. She put a hand on the back of Susannah's head and thrust it down between her knees.

'The arrow's hit the target, I fancy,' said Brockley.

Susannah sat up again, the moment of faintness over though her face was still a bad colour. 'You had better answer our questions,' I said. 'The trouble you got into at Nettlebury wasn't so long ago. We are prepared to forget it, just as Master Medland has, but only if you cooperate with us. Otherwise, you could still find yourself before the magistrate. Most unpleasant things can happen to convicted thieves. Anything from the whip to the rope.'

Brockley suddenly grinned. 'So that's what you meant, madam, when you said that if Mistress Lamb proved difficult, you thought you could find a way round it.'

'B–but . . .' said Susannah.

Despite the chill of the room, her brow was sweating. She wiped it with her palm. Her breathing had become a wheeze. 'I'm sorry. I'm not well. I . . .'

'Where's the kitchen?' said Brockley. 'There must be servants there. I'll get them to bring a restorative for her.'

'Nonsense,' said Ryder. 'She doesn't need restoring; she needs to do some talking. Susannah! We mean you no harm. We are not here to bring you to justice for petty theft. But we are here to find out the truth about Hoxton's death. We aren't accusing you of causing it, but we strongly suspect that you know who did. And that it wasn't Gervase Easton.'

'Listen, Mistress Lamb,' I said. 'Is the name of whoever employed you before you came to the Spicery somehow part of this miserable story? We need answers to our questions. So come along!'

'But I . . . I . . . Madge saw the man who did it – she saw him, same as I did.'

'She saw a left-handed man. Who therefore probably wasn't Gervase. Why do you insist it was Gervase that you saw? Did you lie to protect someone?'

Once more the shaft struck the target squarely in the centre. Susannah's mouth went slack with terror. When she finally answered us, she stammered.

'I w–worked for Bowman b–before I came to the Spicery. Jonathan Bowman, him that married Judith Easton later on. He said I'd tried to steal from him. I didn't! It wasn't true! I was just curious, and looking through some things on a table, but there was money there in a little bag and he said I was trying to steal it. I was only looking! That's all! But he . . . he . . .'

This time, she really did faint.

She came round after a few moments, and we helped her back on to the settle. This time Ryder agreed that a restorative was needed, and Dale fetched some ale from the kitchen. Thus fortified, Mistress Lamb was capable of answering further questions, and did so, though not willingly. We got it out of her by fits and starts. She baulked at intervals, like a horse confronted by fences it doesn't want to jump. She still obstinately maintained that she had not been thieving when Bowman caught her looking at a bag of coins, but we were not interested in her guilt or innocence there, only in the outcome.

Perhaps Bowman himself hadn't been sure, for he had done no worse at the time than dismiss her and – as she now told us – had helped her to find the post in the Windsor Castle Spicery, using the castle contacts he had acquired through his glover's business.

When he went to the castle, though, it was to see customers there, and he would attend them in their quarters. Susannah, hurrying through the kitchens on some errand or other, had been surprised to find him in that part of the building and more surprised still to notice that he was apparently augmenting the dishes on a tray. He had been just as startled to see her. And he had ordered her to visit him in his home, above his shop in the town that evening – or risk having information laid against her as a thief.

By the time she went to the shop, the word had gone round that Peter Hoxton, though still alive, had been stricken by some new sickness and was probably going to die – and had very likely been poisoned. And, it transpired, she had been fairly sure that the tray on which the extra pie had been placed was for Hoxton.

'I knew about him being ill and needing trays sent up, and all about his tray being put out to be collected, see. I knew *where* it was put. And I'd seen Master Bowman d–doing something to a tray that was very likely Hoxton's, and he'd seen me, too! I was that s–scared when I went to see M–Master Bowman. I thought: this is something to do with Hoxton being poisoned, like people were saying. I thought: he's going to . . . going to k–kill me too! I told one of the other women where I was going, in case I didn't come back!'

'Why didn't you tell somebody what you'd seen?' I asked her. 'Before you went to see him that day, I mean.'

'Because I weren't sure enough! I weren't sure the tray he'd been messing about with was Hoxton's; I just *thought* it was. I only knew that if I upset Master Bowman, he'd tell on me, and then what would happen?'

'All right. Go on,' said Ryder, using his most paternal (and authoritative) voice.

Susannah took several more sips of ale and said: 'If I say aught about him, he might still tell on me!'

'We'll do our best to stop his mouth,' I said. 'Please continue.'

She looked about her in a hunted way, but finally, under the gaze of our accusing eyes, she consented to go on a little further.

'He offered me – Master Bowman I mean – offered me something to drink, and I wouldn't, and he laughed and said he wasn't going to harm me – I was precious in his eyes. I didn't know what he meant! He scared me more than ever, talking like that. Then he said that I'd seen him put an extra pie on a tray, hadn't I, and it was something he didn't want mentioned to anyone else. He cooked the pie himself, he said. He was as good a cook as any woman when he felt like it. It looked a bit like bilberries in the pie, but it was something more bitter than that, though that didn't matter because he'd put honey in it and . . .'

'And . . .?' I said as Susannah, her eyes frightened, hesitated.

She swallowed. 'He said it was clear enough, from the way I wouldn't say yes to a drink, that I'd got an idea that what was in that pie wasn't healthy. I said I'd heard that Master Hoxton, one of the Comptrollers, was like to die, and I knew he'd been having food sent up to him because he'd been ill, and I thought . . . I thought Master Bowman's pie had been sent up to him. And he said yes, Master Hoxton's illness meant he couldn't taste his food much. He said he'd been making gloves for Master Hoxton's manservant, Edwards, lately, and he'd heard from him all about Master Hoxton's feverish cold and the arrangements for getting his meals to him. It gave him an idea, he said. Gave him a chance!'

With that, she came to another stop, and Brockley said in a puzzled tone: 'But why? A chance to harm Hoxton? Why would Bowman want to do that? Didn't he say?'

Susannah had turned sullen again. 'No, he didn't say. I didn't ask.'

It was as though she felt that as long as she kept something back, she would somehow still be protected from Bowman, which was hardly reasonable, but Susannah didn't seem to be a very intelligent woman.

'Look, Mistress Lamb,' I said. 'I have visited Bowman, in the cottage where he lives now. Where you presumably worked for him for a while. He talked about maidservants. *I used to have maidservants when I could afford them, but they were more trouble than they were worth, mostly. I had three altogether and nicknames for all them – Lazy, Saucy, Lightfingers, that's what I called them.* That's what he said, and it seems to me that Lightfingers is now in front of us. You might bear that in mind. Let me remind you. We know of your – misdemeanours. You'd do well to obey us. Lately, I have remembered something else. During that visit I had a seat by the fire, and it was on my right-hand side. Bowman was opposite to me, embroidering. I kept thinking that the hand he held the needle in must be getting scorched, it was so near the fire. But if the fire was on my right, and he was opposite, then it must have been on his left. He's left-handed, even if Gervase Easton wasn't.'

'Which means you've very likely told the truth so far,' said Ryder. 'It presumably *was* Bowman who put that pie on the tray. But if we're to be believed when we take this news back, we need to know why.'

'Did he really never tell you why?' I asked, since Susannah remained dumb. 'By the sound of it he'd talked to you very freely. Thought you'd never dare to betray him, in case you ended up hanged for theft. Come on, Susannah. Tell us the rest.'

She stared at me like a bullock confronted by a butcher. I half expected her to moo.

John Ryder said to her: 'Do as you're bid, woman. You've said so much already that you might as well! You've already said enough to hang Bowman, so why hide the rest?'

And then the rest came out, with a rush. 'He said that Hoxton had been annoying Mistress Judith Easton and upsetting her and her husband. He said the world would be better off without Peter Hoxton in it, and if Easton were to be accused of killing him, then they'd both be out of the way, and then, well, he had hopes of Mistress Easton himself. Most beautiful thing he'd ever seen, he told me. She didn't dislike him, he said, and she'd need another man. He'd move in quick, before anyone else had a chance. He'd been going to say he'd missed his way in the castle and chanced to find himself in the kitchens and that he'd seen Master Easton do something to the tray. But it would be better if someone else said that, not himself, someone not linked to the Eastons or Peter Hoxton.'

'He meant you?' I asked.

'Yes. Questions would be asked, he said.' The story was tumbling out now, as if she were glad to be rid of it. 'Everyone in the kitchens would have to answer questions. When it came to me, I could say what I'd seen – only . . .'

For a moment she almost baulked again, but it came out eventually. 'Only, I'd got to say it was Easton I saw, not Bowman. It wouldn't be hard, he said. It scarcely meant lying, even, because he and Easton didn't look that different from each other. They were both short and dark with parroty noses.'

'Parroty noses?' I was puzzled.

'Master Bowman's got a nose like a popinjay's beak,' said Susannah. 'Only, those eyeglass things he wears hide it a bit.'

'I never noticed it,' I said blankly.

'All I'd have to say that wasn't true was the name. Easton instead of Bowman,' Susannah said. 'And if I didn't, he'd see that I was . . . that I was . . .'

'Arrested for theft,' said Dale. 'You know, you've no sense. I can't abide people with no sense. You're as scared of being caught as a child is scared of ghosts, yet you go on stealing. From Bowman—'

'I was only looking!'

'Phooey!' said Dale rudely. 'From Bowman, from the Medlands and I'd wager there were others.'

'You don't know!' said Susannah, suddenly angry. 'Look at you, settled with a husband! You're married to him, aren't you?' She jerked her head at Brockley. I had introduced Dale as Brockley's wife. 'If you were out in the world on your own, never paid enough, always ordered about and pushed here and there and overworked, maybe you'd take chances when they came your way.'

'In my employment,' I said, 'Dale has had to take long exhausting journeys, which she hates; and she and her husband have both been put in danger of their lives. You don't know what you're talking about.'

'It all hangs together now,' Brockley said. Susannah blenched at the word *hangs*.

I nodded. 'Yes, it confirms what I've slowly been coming to suspect, though the idea didn't take firm shape until just lately. All of a sudden, I realized that Bowman was there, in the cast of the masque, as it were. He was the man who eventually married Judith Easton. He'd already admitted that he thought her beautiful, even before her husband died. Maybe his feelings were stronger than that – much stronger. And then I remembered that he did his embroidery left-handed.'

'So he terrified you into pointing the finger at Gervase Easton,' said Brockley to Susannah, getting back to the point. 'And once you'd done that, you were a party to his crime and he knew you wouldn't dare to talk – until now, when we've left you precious little choice. Well, well.' He turned to me. 'What now, madam?'

I explained to Susannah how Gervase Easton's name needed to be cleared to give his son the chance to marry as he wished. 'We don't particularly wish to bring Bowman to justice,' I said. Brockley looked at me in surprise. 'It was twenty-three years ago,' I said, as much to him as to anyone. 'Bowman's an old man now. It's Mark and Jane who matter. Susannah, we'll protect you from prosecution too, if we can. But you must come with us to confront Bowman with your testimony. We will require him to give us a signed confession for Master Easton to use as proof of his father's innocence.'

'He'll never do that!' Susannah rocked back and forth in misery.

'In that case,' I said in a hard voice, 'we will take our information to the authorities, all of it, including the thefts while you were with the Medlands. You and Bowman will have to take your chance.'

Susannah set up a wail, and I raised my voice to be heard above her. 'Given that we get the confession,' I told her, 'we can put it together with other signed and sworn statements which I hope we can obtain from other people – one is Madge, who can swear that the man she saw tampering with Hoxton's tray was left-handed, and another is an artist who will, I think, testify that Gervase Easton was not. Then, perhaps, Gervase's son will have evidence enough to smooth his path to marriage. That's all we want.'

It was far too much for Susannah, who became hysterical, but I told her relentlessly that if she refused, we would insist that Medland bring a charge of theft against her. ('How did you propose to make him, madam?' Brockley asked me afterwards. 'I probably couldn't,' I said, 'but Susannah wasn't to know that.')

In the end, we prevailed.

A vague message was given to the bewildered servants in the kitchen, to the effect that Mistress Lamb had been called away on urgent business but would no doubt be back in a few days, and then we bundled her out, hired a boat – luckily, we found one quickly – and were on our way downstream towards Windsor within the hour.

It was a chilly, windy journey, and Susannah cried all the way, which disturbed me. I had thought, once, that I was going to see Gladys hang. It had been a near thing. She had come to the very foot of the gallows, and I had seen her terror. I didn't want to do that to Susannah. She was repulsive, but her fear and her misery only made her more pitiable.

But she was still obnoxious company, and I still hated her.

TWENTY-FOUR

Face to Face

We reached Windsor as dusk was falling, having stopped once on the way to change the crew and take refreshment at a riverside inn.

'Straight to Bowman's,' I said, 'let's get it over,' and we set off along the riverside path, until we reached the end of the lane that led up past Bowman's cottage. Halfway up, Susannah became crimson in the face and started to gasp. We had to let her rest before we went on. Part of it was obviously fear, but the breathlessness was real enough.

We had started off again, pushing her up the last few yards of path, when to our surprise we were accosted – indeed, almost ambushed – as a wizened figure in a brown cloak appeared on top of the bank to our left and waved at us.

'Gladys!' I said. 'Gladys? What are you doing here?'

Gladys gave us one of her fanged grins. 'Saw you coming along the river in that boat, I did. Saw you'd got *her* with you; at least, I supposed it was her. Couldn't think who else it would be.'

'Who's this?' gasped Susannah.

'This is Gladys Morgan. She helps in Mistress Stannard's household. She sews and makes medicines,' said Brockley repressively.

'She's your servant?' Susannah said to me, staring at Gladys with dislike. 'Doesn't she even say *ma'am* when she speaks to you?' Susannah, however light-fingered, evidently kept to a few conventions.

'Not often. Gladys doesn't go in for terms of respect,' I said. 'Did you come to meet us, Gladys? How did you know we wouldn't go straight up to the castle?'

'Didn't know. Saw you take this path, that's all. I was out and about, looking for a few plants I wanted. There're some you can gather at any time of year. Looks like you're going to Bowman's. Are you?'

'Yes. What makes you so sure?' Ryder said.

'I've good reason. I've something to tell you.' Gladys grinned. 'I reckoned that a bit of snooping was wanted. There was you, working yourself to death, trying to get at the heart of it all. I kept thinking: how can I help? What can I do that might come in useful?' Her dark eyes, still bright despite her years, suddenly lost their usual malicious gleam and looked into mine with such a naked gratitude that it took me aback.

'Dead I'd be, long since, but for you and him.' She pointed at Brockley. 'I were nearly done for, as a witch, twice back at Vetch Castle, and then again, in London. Every time, you or him stepped in and rescued me. You think I don't care? I wanted to help, and I got a notion.'

It was more than gratitude. It was an emotion so deep that there were tears in her eyes. I laid a hand on her shoulder. 'Gladys, we were glad to have saved you. Go on. Tell us what you've been doing.'

'You remember that Catherine Mildmay that you went to see?'

'Catherine Mildmay? Yes, of course!' Dale, listening to all this, was startled. 'But if ever there was a decent, honest woman—'

Gladys, her usual nature reasserting itself, made an impolite noise. 'Told us all about her, you did, after seeing her,' she said to me, 'and I didn't believe a word of it. Sounded as if she'd got a halo and wings – bah! I don't trust folk like that. I bin wondering about her ever since. You said she lived in Moor Street. So I asked Master Stannard for some money, and he said what for, and I said to help me find out who killed Hoxton. He give it me, but said to be careful. And I was. I dragged my old bones down your bloody stairs again and out through the town, and I found my way to the Mildmay woman and I told her such a tarradiddle. I'm an ignorant old woman, I am. Don't know nothing about herbs and things—'

'Gladys, what on earth are you talking about?' I said. Susannah looked from one of us to the other in confusion.

The others, knowing Gladys better, were silent, waiting for her to get to the point.

'Told her I'd got a nursling,' said Gladys with a leer. 'A dear sweet wench that I'd cared for since she was a little baby. But now she's a grown lass and she's in trouble. No, no, it's all right, Mistress Stannard, I didn't name any names. If you're thinking I said it was Meg, well, I didn't.'

'I should hope not!' I exploded.

Gladys merely chuckled. 'I just begged and pleaded with Mistress Mildmay to help. I said someone like her, with so much knowledge of herbs and whatnot, would surely know what to do. I couldn't believe she *couldn't* help. If only she would . . .'

'And?' said Ryder sharply.

'*She* wouldn't help. Oh no. *Her* hands have to stay clean. *Her* garden's as pure as Eden afore the serpent got into it. But she gave me a name. He might advise, she said. Only, getting the name would cost me. Three gold angels, that's what it would cost, and never, never, was I to tell anyone she'd told me. If I did, and the law got her, she'd see it got me too. Just asking where to get medicine to destroy an unborn child was a crime. So I swore to keep the secret, and I paid – said my young mistress had given me the money. And guess what was the name she gave me!'

'Bowman?' said Brockley.

'Aye. Bowman. Well, well, I said, I know *him*, though he never let on that he was in the potions business. So I come here to see Bowman and told my tale again, and said the Mildmay woman had sent me – and here it is. Another four gold angels it cost me.'

She put a hand into her skirts and, from a pocket, pulled out a phial. 'This'll be what that girl that died at Christmas used, I'd reckon. As for seeing what plants he's got in his garden, you can see better from his parlour window than the path. I'd never been inside his cottage before. Talked to him, I have, a good few times, but always in the garden, not indoors. But I was indoors this time, and while he fetched this –' she waved the phial – 'I stared out at the garden, and from the parlour I could see it plain enough. Not much wrong with my eyes, old as they are. He's got nightshade there all right, *and* yew. Got hemlock, too – what's called poison parsley. Wouldn't like to think what he's growing all those for.'

'He's growing them?' Ryder asked. 'They're not just weeds?'

'No, they're not. Growing them a'purpose is what he's been doing. Neat and tidy in tended beds, in a quiet corner, they are. Well, what if he were growing them behind his shop when he had his business in the town? Straightaway, I thought: well, here's someone in Windsor knows their poisons and was here at the time, *and* he married the woman Hoxton wanted, didn't he? And got rid of her husband too, I reckoned. I was sure, the second I saw them nice tidy poison plants, that it was him did for Hoxton.'

'Gladys, you're a marvel,' I told her.

She gave me another of her unlovely grins. 'You told us all what Madge said about the man who put the pie on the tray being left-handed, too. Well, Bowman's left-handed. I've noticed. Watched him pruning some bush or other with a sickle in his left hand. Got me thinking straightaway, Madge's tale did.'

I looked at Brockley, and he at me. Gladys, it seemed, had been a step ahead of us all.

'I hardly needed to go after that portrait,' I said. 'I should have left it all to you, Gladys! Except that I had to go north anyway on the queen's business.' Beside me, I felt the check in Brockley's mind, and though he did not speak, I knew that he was remembering Trelawny, who would still have been alive had we never gone to Ramsfold. I looked towards the cottage. 'There's smoke coming from Bowman's chimney. He must be at home. Come along.'

We made our way all together through the gate of the cottage. Gladys pointed to something in a corner of the garden, and I went to look. Coming back, I said: 'There's a plant there with a few black berries still on it. The leaves are kite-shaped. Is that nightshade?'

'Aye. Birds don't go for the berries; they've got more sense. Rabbits eat nightshade, though. Don't know whether it doesn't do anything to them or they like the wild visions. Wonder what rabbits have visions about?' said Gladys, with a lascivious leer.

Ryder laughed, but Susannah was snivelling and dragging her feet as we approached the cottage. Ryder gave her a sharp push forward.

The door opened as we reached it, and Bowman appeared in the entrance, a lamp in his hand. He said nothing, but moved back in a silent invitation for us to enter. We trooped inside, also in silence, and with an abrupt gesture he signalled us into his parlour.

It was as untidy as I remembered, though the fire was better this time and there was candlelight. Bowman was much the same, though: lined, wire-haired and – yes, now that I looked at him carefully – possessed of a nose like a parrot's beak. It was hardly Gervase's aristocratic eagle nose, but yes, it was curved. Bowman seemed to have aged suddenly. His skin was papery and pale, except for a flush over his cheekbones. He was the first to speak. He did so in one syllable. 'Well?'

'We're here,' I said, 'once more, to talk about the death of Peter Hoxton.'

'Are you, now?'

'You've got all the necessary in your garden,' said Gladys, never one to approach a subject with anything like finesse. 'Mistress Stannard here looked for herself just now. Pretty little bed of trouble you've got there, Master Bowman. Nightshade, yew, poison parsley. Everything you want for a witch's brew. How long've you been growing things of that kind, and what for?'

Bowman cast a glance of loathing at her but didn't deign to reply. Instead, he said to me: 'I wondered. I saw you coming from an upstairs window. I remembered what you were after when you came here first, and I recognized *her*.' His eyes flashed angrily at Susannah. 'And her.' He jerked his head at Gladys. 'The dear old soul who sometimes passed the time of day with me at my gate, and then came wanting help for her sweet nursling. How is the poor girl, may I ask?'

''Fraid she don't exist,' said Gladys with her most eldritch cackle. 'She was an excuse, that's all.'

'I see. Yes, I do see. A pretty tale you spun, to me and to

Mistress Mildmay. Let's not play the fool. You think I did for Hoxton, don't you?'

'We know you did,' said Ryder.

'Sure of yourself, aren't you? Well, since you've been talking to Susannah, yes, I suppose you do know. I hope you'll leave Catherine Mildmay alone, at least. If she helps me to help a few desperate girls, well, there's more than one way to look at that, and we don't all roll our eyes piously to heaven when we hear of a lass falling in love and being let down and not wanting her life wrecked because of it. We don't all say: ooh, how shocking, and bleat clichés about making beds and lying in them. And there's other things you can use nightshade for, besides killing. Easing pain, that's one. And lotions to brighten lasses' eyes. Belladonna, that's its other name. It means Pretty Woman. Oh, sit down, all of you, now you're here.'

We did so. Bowman glared at us. 'Hoxton!' His voice was full of scorn. 'It's twenty-three years next autumn,' he said. 'Pity that after being dead that long, he can't lie quiet in his grave.'

Bowman himself had taken the same settle as before: near the fire and beside the shelf of flagons and the elegant salt which had been part of his first wife's dowry. The flush on his face was explained now, for a half-full glass of dark red wine was on the floor by his stool. He picked it up and took a long swig. It occurred to me that without the flush, he would be very pale indeed. We were looking at a man who was both old and ill.

'So,' he said, 'what are you here for, *exactly*? Come to seize me and march me to the constable? Why didn't you bring the constable with you?'

'Let Master Bowman be quite clear about how much we know,' said Ryder. 'Susannah, repeat now, before us all, what you told us in Oxford. Beginning from where you were caught examining a bag of his money.'

Susannah glowered. She had taken a window seat. It was draughty, and she was sitting with her cloak drawn tightly round her. Her heavy, tear-stained face had acquired an obstinate expression. 'He said I was going to steal some money, but it wasn't true.' Her voice was monotonous, probably because she was repeating her denial for what no doubt felt like the thousandth time. 'I was just *looking*.'

'All right,' I said. 'You were just looking, and you were misunderstood.'

'No, she wasn't,' said Bowman. 'I'd missed money before. *Lightfingers*, that's the nickname I gave her, privately, so to speak.'

'That's rude,' said Susannah, attempting to be haughty and wiping away a few more tears.

'And true,' said Bowman.

'Never mind all that,' said Ryder, annoyed. 'Susannah, go on with the story. You know what will happen if you refuse.'

Reluctantly, between scowls and sniffs, Susannah repeated the dismal tale of how Bowman had suborned her to bear false witness against Gervase Easton.

Bowman listened in silence, sipping his wine as he did so. When his glass was empty, he took a flagon from the shelf beside him, poured himself a refill and added ground cinnamon from one of the trays in the salt. 'So,' he said, when the story was over. He dusted a little cinnamon off his fingers. 'What if I say that this woman is lying?'

I said: 'We know the man that Madge Goodman saw wasn't likely to have been Gervase Easton. Because we have established that Easton was almost certainly right-handed and she saw a left-handed man.'

'And I am left-handed and I was already in love with Judith. Ah, well. No, Susannah isn't lying. I made a mistake in not getting rid of dear Lightfingers, instead of making her my accomplice.' Susannah let out a faint shriek. 'At the time,' said Bowman, 'it seemed a good revenge for her thefts, getting her to name Gervase – making an accomplice of her. I wanted Judith Easton so much.'

He paused, looking not at us, but into the depths of his wine, as though he were seeing memories alive again in the glass.

'How can I make you understand? I was younger then,' he said. 'Later in life, a man learns more sense, but twenty-three years ago . . . Even then, I didn't know till it happened what it was like to be in love like that. I'd loved before, though not in that fashion. But I was only someone who made gloves for her, and she was wedded and never had eyes for any man but Gervase. He was a fool to worry about Hoxton. While Gervase was there, she couldn't even *see* Hoxton; I'm sure of it. I remember that soft glow in her eyes whenever she looked at Gervase or spoke his name. She could hardly see me, either, except as a glover. I paid her a compliment now and then, tried to let her know with a look, or a light remark, how I felt, but she never noticed. She never would, while Gervase lived.

'It was like a madness. It *was* a madness. Like being bewitched. She was the kind that can cast an enchantment just by breathing. I saw her image before the eyes of my soul, all day long. I acted out scenes inside my head, like a strolling player: inventing conversations, making love, with Judith. At night, I'd dream of her. I considered getting rid of Gervase, but then I'd think: there's Hoxton. Mostly, he tires of women quickly, but he's gone on and on hunting Judith. Maybe she's put a spell on him too, and women do fall for him. With Gervase gone, maybe then she *will* notice him, and where will that leave me?

'I wanted rid of Hoxton and Gervase alike, but how to do it? Besides, I was afraid that if I struck at Gervase Easton, someone would work out the link, or they would once I started courting Judith. Then I thought of striking at Hoxton and somehow putting it on to Gervase . . . Oh well. It's always a fool's business, letting women get mixed up in anything. The trouble was rooted in women, after all. I knew Mistress Mildmay in those days, to speak to – nothing more – but it was from her that I learned to recognize nightshade and heard what it could do. If I hadn't known that . . . It was her fault partly, though mostly Judith's.'

'How could it be Judith's fault?' I said indignantly.

'Too beautiful for her own good, and no use at standing up for herself,' said Bowman harshly. 'Marriage to her showed me that. Nothing like marriage for breaking an enchantment.' He took a long drink of his spiced wine. 'Poor, enchanting, foolish Judith. She couldn't deal with Hoxton; she couldn't even deal with Gervase. Well, she couldn't stop him from fighting Hoxton and half-killing him. It wasn't true, by the way, that I once heard Gervase make threats against Hoxton when he was drunk. I made that up. But the fight was real enough. It was all beyond Judith. I suppose you could say she couldn't deal with me either. I made a push to get her as soon as she was free, and she couldn't hold out against me. She was the kind that can't make their way through life without a man to lean on. They're faithful, but they're not strong in other ways. We got wed, but when she knew me better, she got to be afraid of me. Then I didn't want her any more. Who wants to love a mouse? I wanted to love a woman.'

'She had the resolution to run away with Gervase,' I said, nettled. 'They married against his father's wishes.'

'He ran away with her,' corrected Bowman dispassionately. 'Not the other way round, I'd wager. She put a spell on him, without realizing it, same as she did with me, and he offered her a life with a man to look after her and just swept her off her feet. That's how I'd read it. Well.' His pale blue eyes stared round at us. 'What do you want of me?'

Brockley said: 'We have made these enquiries on behalf of Judith's son Mark. As you know, Mark wishes to marry and the girl's family won't consent until his father's name is cleared. What we want of you is a written and signed account of the truth which we can show them. We don't intend to show it to the authorities.'

'You could forge that for yourselves,' said Bowman and swallowed another gulp of wine.

'Thank you, Bowman. Unlike you, we are not criminals,' said Ryder coldly. 'Forgery is a crime. We want your own confession because it will be more impressive than merely repeating Susannah's testimony, though it is true that we could do that, and swear to it, if necessary.'

'There will be other sworn statements to back up yours,' I said to Bowman. 'Testifying that Gervase was not left-handed, for instance.'

'I won't swear anything!' said Susannah, in a panicky voice.

'If you refuse to provide the confession,' said Ryder, ignoring her, 'then we *will* go to the constable with Susannah's testimony. You will probably hang. Susannah probably will, too. A confession, though, made privately to us, could save both your necks.'

Susannah set up a blood-curdling howl at this point, and Dale, kindly enough, went to put an arm round her.

Bowman, ignoring her, turned to the rest of us. 'All right. If that's what you want. If you reckon this girl's people are that persuadable. Why should I hinder a young man in love? I know what it's like. Where are my writing things? Get off that window seat, Mistress Lightfingers. You're sitting on them.'

Dale coaxed Susannah off the seat, and Bowman lifted it up. From the storage chest beneath, he took paper and a writing set. He carried them to the table and sat down. In silence, we watched while he sharpened a quill, opened a phial of ink and, holding the pen in his left hand, began to write.

He didn't write for long. After a very few minutes, he blotted the sheet and looked round. 'Who do I give this to?'

'What if *they* take it to the law?' wailed Susannah. 'These folk you'll be showing it to?'

'We hope we can persuade them not to,' said Brockley.

Susannah, clearly unconvinced, burst into fresh howling.

'Give what you've written to me,' I said to Bowman.

I took it from him and read it:

> *I, Jonathan Bowman, Glover, of Windsor, declare that in September fifteen forty-seven I poisoned Peter Hoxton. The witness who said she had seen Gervase Easton adding an item to Master Hoxton's dinner tray was in error. The man she saw was myself. There was a likeness between Easton and me. Easton had nothing to do with it. His wife Judith was the most beautiful woman I had ever seen and I wanted her for myself. Hoxton was in love with her, too. I feared that even if her husband should die, Hoxton might become my rival. By destroying him and making sure that her husband was accused, I could clear them both out of my way.*
>
> *I declare before God that what I have written here is true. Written and signed this 9th day of February, 1570.*
>
> *Jonathan Bowman.*

He had signed it with panache, in an ornate Italian hand.

I handed it to Brockley. He and Ryder read it together. Ryder looked up, straight at Bowman, who was sitting half-turned on his stool, watching us, the quill pen still in his fingers.

'I've been married myself, and widowed,' Ryder said. 'I know about love. But this love you've been telling us about . . . I can't imagine it. It's not . . . not *healthy*.'

Brockley and I said nothing, but it was the silence of agreement. I wondered what the love Bowman had described really felt like. I found it hard to believe in it, and looking at him, it seemed incredible that such a huge and murderous passion could ever have existed within this little, hook-nosed, ordinary glover of Windsor.

He was still holding the quill, but even as I gazed at him, he dropped it. He looked down at his left hand. 'It's gone limp,' he said and gasped, as though he found it hard to breathe. 'I'm losing strength. And I think . . .'

It wasn't until he retched, and suddenly we were all staring at him intently, that we realized, even by candlelight, that apart from the flush on his cheekbones, his face had changed from pale, to a sickly greyish-green.

'What is it? What have you taken!' Ryder sprang at him and grabbed his shoulders, but Bowman merely laughed, and then retched again.

Gladys scrambled for the salt and took out the spice trays, sniffing at them. 'Nutmeg . . . This one's cinnamon . . . Nothing wrong there . . . This looks like cinnamon again . . . Ah!' She put her nose closer. 'This one smells funny,' she said. 'Garlicky. That 'ud be hemlock, like as not. Mixed in with the cinnamon, I'd say. Reckon he put this in his wine.'

The story goes that the philosopher Socrates was executed with hemlock and died a gentle death. I doubt it, somehow. We lit more candles, so that we could see what we were doing, and tried to help him, but he thrust us away, refusing the warm salt water and even knocking away the basins we brought for the sickness and the dreadful liquid motions.

Ryder rushed out in search of a physician and brought one back eventually, but it was far too late by then for any treatment to work, even if the doctor had been able to recommend one.

Before he sank into his last coma, Bowman talked a little more, though jerkily, between gasps.

'Always knew, one day, someone would find out. I think that manservant, Edwards, had his suspicions, but I dealt with him. Watched out for him in the Antelope inn with something ready in my pouch and spiked his drink for him. That settled him. But then you started – sent your man, Roger Brockley here – to ask questions. Soon as I saw you bringing . . . Susannah Lamb . . . that very moment . . . knew the day was here. But I'd made my plans. Grew the hemlock, had it handy, mixed with cinnamon. I'm good with potions. I sell a lot, quietly – drops to brighten a girl's eyes, like I told you, tinctures to ease pain and give sleep, ointments for chapped hands. I make wine, too, and sell that now and again. It all helps. Keeps me solvent!'

'You work with Catherine Mildmay?' I said.

'She sends me customers. We keep it quiet. Catherine gets asked . . . often . . . she's respectable, scared for her good name . . . but she don't mind passing 'em on to me. Girls wanting love philtres . . . then things to get rid of the results of love. Started working with Catherine after I buried Judith. I still lived in the town then but . . . I had . . . a garden. I tell my customers I can curse 'em if they talk out of turn.' He even laughed, then, until another burst of vomiting came.

An hour after that, he died.

TWENTY-FIVE

Go Hunting No More

The physician didn't come until Bowman was unconscious and did not hear any of his last words. Nor did we repeat them to him. We told him, indeed, nothing of our purpose in visiting Bowman; only that we had chanced to call on him and found him very ill. At the inquest two days later, another physician testified that Bowman had had a disease, a growth in his abdomen, which must soon have killed him. The verdict was that because of this he had killed himself. With that, it was over.

Brockley found an inn for Susannah Lamb and a passage on a barge returning to Oxford the next day. Meanwhile, I had quietly folded the confession away in my hidden pouch. Hugh and I would obtain the other statements from Madge and Arbuckle and get them sworn. We would see that everything was sent to Mark, with a letter explaining how it was obtained and a plea that the matter should end there, without involving Susannah any further. Bowman, the prime mover in the crime, was dead, after all. Susannah, by comparison, was nothing.

I would also write separately to Pen in Tyesdale and to Ann and George Mason in Lockhill and tell them what we had learned, though without mentioning Susannah's name. I had done my best and could only hope that it would be enough.

'*Why* didn't we see from the start that Bowman was a likely candidate?' I said to Hugh. 'Looking back now, it seems so obvious.'

'I think I did see,' Hugh said. 'From the first moment I set eyes on him, I disliked him. I even noticed that parrot nose of his and remembered you telling me what Madge had said – that the man she saw had a beaky nose. Only, I saw him look at you, and he did that straight away, whether you realized it or not, and I thought my suspicions were just my jealousy. Though even then . . . I wouldn't admit it to myself, but I think something else was at work in me when I made Brockley burn the gift. Gloves can be soaked in poison, you know.'

'You really feared . . .?'

'Not openly. I told myself it was simple jealousy. I know that I don't think as clearly as I used to do, Ursula. I imperilled Hawkswood through muddled thinking, and we still don't know for sure whether Mark will pay. The statements have only just gone off to him.'

'I wonder how long it will be before they reach him?' I said restlessly.

But as far as that was concerned, we need not have worried. We sent our package with a royal courier who was travelling north and would be able to change horses frequently. He made excellent time. He found Mark in Carlisle, just back from an unproductive sortie over the Scottish border, where the fugitive insurgents had hidden themselves very successfully. This was annoying, Cecil said, but at least Anne of Northumberland and her adherents were now among them, fugitives instead of active conspirators. My brief and eventful stay at Ramsfold had, it seemed, most effectively ruined Lady Northumberland's scheming. She had had to flee from English soil, and the latest news was that her remaining supporters in the north of England had lost heart and nerve and were unlikely to regain them. Elizabeth was pleased with me.

For my part, I was pleased with Mark, whose response was immediate. In the letter that he sent back with the courier, he said he would be riding to Tyesdale at the earliest possible moment, but whatever the outcome, Hugh and I had done all that he could possibly ask of us – and here, with his love and gratitude, was the purse we had more than earned. The letter went on to say that he had successfully concluded the sale of his Devonshire property and was happy to tell us that he had done better out of it than he expected.

We counted the contents. Mark had actually paid more than he had promised. 'Hugh!' I said. 'Hawkswood is safe! It's safe!'

'Yes, it's safe. Thank God. And thank *you*, Ursula. Thank *you*!'

I looked at him. He was smiling, and I swear that even as I scanned his face, in that moment, the lines of pain and illness softened and grew fainter. The shadows in the sockets of his eyes lightened. Between one moment and the next, he had shed years.

'Shall we go back to Hawkswood soon?' I asked.

'As fast as we can. Meg said to me yesterday that she wanted to go home. We've never told her in so many words that Hawkswood was in danger, but she can hardly be unaware that we've been anxious and that Mark's commission was important. She may have overheard things, too. I might tell her the story, now that it's all over, and I really think she'll be glad to leave the court. Ursula, about Meg . . .'

'Yes?'

'We know now that Hawkswood will remain ours, so I don't think we need fear that young Hillman will change his mind about us, not that I ever really thought he would. If he and Meg get on well, next time they meet, should we get her married at sixteen and not send her to court as a maid of honour? We spoke of this once before, but I feel perhaps it's time we actually made a decision.'

'I think it would be an excellent idea,' I said. 'I suggest we invite young Hillman to stay as soon as possible.'

'I'd like to take her father's part at her wedding, I must say. She'll go away to Buckinghamshire, of course, but we can visit her. Even I could get there by coach in good weather, and later on, let us hope there will be grandchildren for you. I know that life isn't so very exciting at Hawkswood – or Withysham – but it could be very pleasant.'

'Exciting? I've had excitement enough for several lifetimes. What made you say that, Hugh?'

'Even now,' he said, 'after all your reassurances, I still sometimes think to myself – what about Matthew de la Roche, in France?'

'No! No, Hugh. I have told you before. I meant it then, and I mean it now. I shall remain dead to Matthew. He has a new wife, and a child, and besides . . .'

'Yes? And besides?'

'I have said this before, as well. I don't want to turn time back, and I don't want to live in France with one of Elizabeth's most implacable enemies. I want England. I want you.'

'I'm glad to know it. I'm so much older than you . . . You know, if anything should happen to me, I would like to think of you marrying again, and the best kind of husband for you would be someone like . . . Well, like Brockley. He's a good man, a good pattern, as it were. In fact, if he'd been free, I sometimes wonder if you wouldn't have preferred him to me.'

I shook my head. 'I don't think of Brockley like that. It's true that we're friends. But – it is only friendship.'

I spoke the truth and spoke it with certainty. Once, long ago, it had very nearly been more than friendship, but the moment had passed and, in the end, so had the desire. To be replaced . . .

To be replaced by that extraordinary, crazy and hilarious psychic union in the hall of Ramsfold House, which still echoed in my mind. Brockley and I would remain friends, close friends, until one of us died; I knew that now. We would never be less. Nor would we ever be more.

It is a rare situation between a woman and a man, but it can happen. Elizabeth was capable of it. I believe she had such links with both Robert Dudley of Leicester and Sir William Cecil. Even her father (and mine), the terrifying Henry the Eighth, who had two wives executed, possessed some of it, for in my days at court, I had been told that he had always remained on friendly, brother and sister, terms with Anne of Cleves after their marriage was annulled. He was better as a brother than a lover.

Mary Stuart, the Queen of the Scots, though, never achieved it. She used her sex too much and her mind not enough, and perhaps that was why she ended her days without a crown and, eventually, without even a head on which to put one.

Much of this – even, I think, some faint premonition of Mary's ultimate fate – flickered through my head as we sat there. 'Even if . . . I found myself once more without a husband, I would have no wish to marry again,' I said. 'Three times should be enough for anyone! I don't want to imitate my father.'

That made him laugh. 'I want to go home,' he said. 'Now. Immediately! Perhaps Brockley could go to Hawkswood and ask for my coach to be sent. Then we can start out at once.'

'So – Jane and Mark are married. I wish I could have been there,' I said, folding up the letter from Mark, which Brockley had brought to me. 'Pen and Clem didn't take too long to arrange it.'

'I fancy they're relieved to hear that Mark's family have been cleared, madam,' Brockley said. 'That wench Jane has an air of being good and biddable, but in my opinion she has a backbone of good strong steel. I remember how she said that if she couldn't marry Mark, she wouldn't marry anyone. Perhaps they were afraid she meant it and would stay at Tyesdale for ever, the spinster relative.'

'I can imagine,' Hugh said, from where he was engaged in tying up a rose stem which had been threatening to topple over on to the sundial which was the centrepiece of the rose garden at Hawkswood. 'And all the neighbours would be clacking their tongues and saying that they'd probably spent Jane's dowry and were keeping her at home as an unpaid servant.'

It was early May, a soft day, cloudy but warm, and we were spending the afternoon in the garden at Hugh's much loved Hawkswood, now safely his for as long as he lived. I was able to watch him as he moved among his roses, examining this one and that, tut-tutting over greenfly, exclaiming in pleasure over a new plant which had taken well and was already developing its first buds, grumbling about the speed at which weeds grew at this time of year and, as now, tying up stems in need of support. The peace in his face as he worked was a reward more precious to me than rubies. It had been worth all the long frustrating struggle to find the truth of Hoxton's death.

Above us, from an open window, came the sound of Meg practising the spinet and Sybil's voice encouraging her, and from where I stood I could see through the window below it into a parlour and glimpse the portrait of Meg which Jocelyn

Arbuckle had painted. And the letter in my hand held good news. I could recall few afternoons as happy as this one.

Brockley, remarking that he must make sure the courier had been given refreshments and that his horse was being cared for, took himself off.

'I hope,' I said, 'that Mark and Jane will be as content together as we are.'

Hugh finished securing the rose plant, used his small belt-knife to cut the twine he was using and stepped back. 'I love to hear you say you're content. Have I ever told you how moved, how touched, I was, those times when you said to me that even though Matthew de la Roche is still alive, you wanted to stay with me and the way of life we've built together?'

'Were you? But I only said what I felt.'

'You have paid me a great compliment, my Little Bear. Do you really not miss court life?'

'No. I never want to return to court. I never want to set foot in a palace again. That's why I don't want Meg to go to court, either. It's not the happiest of lives, being a courtier, male or female.'

'It may not always be up to you. It's possible, you know, that the queen and Cecil may have uses for you – uses that may send you into danger.'

I shook my head. 'The answer, from now on, will be no.'

'Yet you enjoyed some of the work you did for them in the past. You often say you didn't, but I know you very well.'

'I did it for money at first,' I said. 'I came to enjoy a good deal of it after that – not all, but quite a lot. I was younger then and more adventurous. But as time went on . . .'

I fell silent, because it was hard to find words for the distaste which had gradually come upon me, beginning the first time I grasped the fact that to be an agent for a queen as beset as Elizabeth could mean causing deaths.

It had occurred to me before that there was a resemblance between poor Judith Easton, the woman who bewitched men without meaning to, but hadn't the strength of mind to control her victims, and Mary Stuart, who bewitched men intentionally, but also lacked the strength to use with wisdom the power she had been given. It was a dangerous state of affairs.

Lately, observing the antics of Mary of Scotland, the queen who no longer had a crown but greatly desired one, and who would settle, it seemed, as easily for Elizabeth's as for the crown of Scotland, I had begun to fear that one day I might have to carry out an investigation with Mary's demise at the end of it. She was a menace, and I ought not to mind, but I had seen the terror of those who are about to die. I had seen Gladys like that. I did mind.

I said: 'The work I do – did – for Elizabeth and Cecil always seems to end in someone's death.'

'If someone doesn't do it for them, the deaths could be theirs. Cecil is your friend. And Elizabeth is both your queen and your sister.'

'I know. But I have done enough. Others can take the work on now.'

'That Papal Bull hasn't been issued yet,' said Hugh thoughtfully. 'Do you think it will be?'

'Yes. I had a letter from Cecil yesterday. He has eyes and ears in Rome, as he seems to have everywhere. It will be issued at any moment. It will certainly cause trouble,' I said grimly.

I stood looking at Mark's letter but no longer seeing it. The air was warm, the garden lush, but the thought of what might happen when Pope Pius the Fifth issued the decree – which would present hundreds of respectable people with the choice between treason and damnation – sent a chill through my veins.

'I am not going to become entangled with the business, this time, though,' I said. 'Nor ever again. I have served my turn, Hugh. I'll go hunting no more. My days as a huntress are over.'

'You are sure?'

'I am sure.' Then I said: 'I am happy to settle for a quiet life. Let us finish our walk round the garden. And then, shall we sit on the terrace and have a game of chess?'